I0699565

THE TIME KEEPER'S TALE

CHARLEMAYNE REEVES

The Chronicles of Caelium Series:

The Timekeeper's Tale

Coming Soon:

The Silver Strand

CAELIUM
GROVE OF EIKS
NORTH FOREST
WEST MOUNTAINS
TIMEKEEPER'S COURT
WALL OF MIST
COURT OF MOUNTAIN FAIRIES
SELKIE ISLES
COURT OF MERROWS

THE CHASM
HAIMA MOUNTAINS
TRAVELLER'S PASS
E PLAIN
COURT OF WARRIORS
MEALITA
OUTHERN SEA

Have courage in the darkness.
For in the end, there is always light.

PROLOGUE

The foul, black creature stalked her, circling the forest clearing. The light was fuzzy, falling diffusely through the trees to the forest floor. It blurred the edges of her vision, and she blinked, focusing. The air was freezing. Her teeth chattered, and her breath came out in a cloud before her face. Soft snow fell in thick flakes, already blanketing the forest floor. It clung to her lashes and the hood of her cloak. She shivered and pulled her bowstring tighter against her cheek, aiming the arrow at the black creature's chest.

Somewhere behind her, something tugged the hem of her cloak, drawing her backward. She frowned as the pull intensified and a gentle hum curled over her ears. It floated inside her head, tingling against the surface of her mind. Her feet moved as if they had their own will. Slowly, she stepped back toward the sound.

All at once, the creature lunged, his black fangs snapping at her neck. Panic gripped her chest as his jaws closed in, and she released her grip on her bowstring. She let the arrow fly as she was sucked backward.

And then she was falling,

falling,

falling in darkness.

She gasped, opening her eyes. Her heart hammered in her ears, and she sat up in bed, swallowing convulsively. She ran a shaky hand through her hair as she blinked out the kitchen window into the forest clearing. It had been a dream…an awful one.

Chapter 1

Evangeline Vasily stood at the washbasin in the corner of her bedroom and splashed cool, clear water onto her face. Remus lounged in the windowsill to her left, quietly grooming his scruffy orange paw. He looked up at her and meowed.

"Good morning to you, too."

She giggled as he narrowed his eyes, wiping her hands on the basin towel before she gave his head a pat. He pushed up against her hand with his pink nose and flipped onto his back, exposing his peach-colored belly for her to scratch. She wriggled her fingers into his fur, giggling as he playfully swiped at them. Suddenly losing interest, he plopped himself back onto the sill, peering at her with lazy, green eyes. Lifting his front paw, he resumed his morning bath.

She chuckled. "Silly little wolf."

Evangeline didn't know when she'd first started calling him that. But whatever the reason, the nickname seemed to fit.

She turned back to the cracked basin mirror and smoothed the wayward wisps of golden hair behind her ears. Picking up the brush, she worked its stiff bristles through her long locks. She braided her hair, then secured it into a loose knot at the nape of her neck. Immediately, some small curls escaped their bonds. They tickled her neck and ears, and she tried in vain to smooth them back again. She sighed, watching as they sprang back out of place. It would just have to do.

She placed the brush back on the table and smoothed her slender fingers over the gilded compact beside it. It was all she had left of her mother—a precious ornament decorating an otherwise rustic and practical home. She never went anywhere without it. Silently, she dropped the compact into the pocket of her day dress and smoothed the worn muslin over her waist. The tattered dress was her best one, and she only wore it for special occasions. Jacques had once said it brought out the blue-green color of her eyes.

She turned and faced the room. Her cottage in the forest clearing, although small and solitary, was cozy and warm. It was made of sturdy, large logs and had a wood-planked floor and a large, stone hearth. It had been her home with her mother for as long as she could remember. Until it wasn't. She had been eight when she had returned home from the woods to find the house empty and her mother lost.

Jacques, the village clock smith, had made most of her furniture. He was a master with the lathe. The full bed with its blue coverlet stood against the left wall nearest the door, and a small, well-worn burgundy rug lay at its foot. A rocking chair sat in the corner beside her bed, and her books were neatly stacked in a basket beside it. A small wooden table and two sitting chairs stood in front of the stone hearth, and beyond it, her tiny kitchen stood at the far end of the house. Above the countertop, a large window overlooked the forest clearing. A collection of dried herbs hung on string above the windowsill. Various scrawny root vegetables, nuts, and dried berries sat in bowls on the counter, while her paring knife, several chipped cups, dishes, and a wooden spoon were stacked neatly on rough shelving to the window's right.

Great oaks and elms circled her cottage, their long arms reaching quietly toward the soft earth. A mossy stone path led out from her front door to a wooden bridge that spanned a winding stream. Cool, clear water ran over the colorful stones at its base. It had once been a waterway teeming with life, but now, it was stripped bare. Any small fish or crustaceans had long been eaten, and those left had slowly died out. Small, thin ferns sprouted at the base of the tall trees, and bare rhododendron bushes gathered beneath the branches. Lina moved to the front door. Gazing out at the thin undergrowth, she pursed her lips. She couldn't remember seeing the rhododendron bloom in the spring, and hadn't the ferns been twice the size last year?

The summer season had hardly begun before the crisp air of autumn arrived. The wildflowers in the clearing barely held their blooms, and the lush, lingering green of summer she had known in childhood passed more swiftly each year. The sun that had often sparkled through the high leaves now hung low. She peered up at it. Its light was rather diffused for midday. Already the trees had begun to let loose their leaves. They trickled past Lina's window on the soft breeze. Some branches were completely bare, awaiting the stark cold of winter. Evangeline narrowed her eyes and pressed her full lips together. Surely autumn had not already begun.

She sat down on the bed and tugged on her worn leather boots. Turning out her foot, she examined the sole. Two of the numerous spots in the leather would soon be worn through. At the rate the seasons were passing, it would be winter before she knew it. She would need new boots before then. She would have to haggle at the cobbler's shop for a new pair. These had seen well over their allotted number of patches. As a matter of fact, they were nearly all patches. She sucked her teeth and licked her thumb, rubbing at a scuff on the toe. It wouldn't budge. Sighing, she pulled the leather laces tight and wound the ends around the tops of her boots.

She straightened, smoothed her dress, and lifted her cloak off the peg by the door. It had nearly as many patches as her boots, but at least it kept out the wind and cold. Draping it over her shoulders, she spun, searching the cottage. Where had she left her bow and quiver? It wasn't at its usual place on the wall near the door. She searched the small room, looking beneath her coverlet, by the hearth, and under the table, but it was nowhere to be found. At last, she turned to the narrow, wooden staircase at the right of the kitchen and took the steps two at a time. At the top, she tugged open the door and searched about her.

The loft had been her room until her mother had gone missing. A tiny twin bed and nightstand stood against the right wall, and a faded, yellow rug lay at the end of it. In the alcove at the room's end, a small, circular window overlooked the clearing. Now she preferred to sleep downstairs near the front door. The bed was bigger. Anyway, there was more chance to stop an intruder if she slept by the door.

Sometimes when the loneliness of her mother's absence overwhelmed, she would climb the stairs and sleep in her old bed. Her chest would ache with her solitude, its wound sucking inward and threatening to rip her in two. She would tuck her arms over the spot, imagining her mother singing and moving about in the great room below. Last night had been one of those nights. Inevitably, Remus had wound his way up the narrow staircase and perched himself luxuriously at her feet. His purring lulled her to sleep as tears escaped onto her pillow. She smiled. She could always count on Remus to be by her side. Remus: her shadow and friend.

Evangeline peeked behind the loft door, grinning. Her weapon was in the corner. She had left it there last night. She swiped it and slung it across her back, then jogged down the stairs to the kitchen. She tucked some nuts and berries into her pocket from the kitchen counter and stowed some small root vegetables into her pack, then she paused before the basin, taking one last look in the mirror.

She had taken extra care with her appearance. Now she wondered if she had done too much. She tugged at her dress, doubting herself. Turning her face left and right, she examined her fine features, smoothing her fingers over her creamy skin. She pressed her full lips together and blew out a breath. Her collarbone peeked out from beneath the fabric of her dress, and she brought her hand to it self-consciously, tightening her cloak about her neck. Her heart fluttered in anticipation, and she realized she was nervous. But there was no reason to be. After all, she saw Jacques nearly every day. Sighing, she straightened and turned toward the door.

Remus was perched on her coverlet. She patted his head as she passed and opened the door swiftly, attempting to prevent his escape. The little cat was determined to go with her everywhere, even into town. However, with food scarce and animals slim, the market was no safe place, even for a mangy, orange cat. Too slowly, she shut the door, and Remus's thin frame leaped nimbly through the opening as she did. She chuckled and turned, grabbing this morning's kill from a hook by the door.

Remus meowed, winding around her ankles. No doubt he smelled the dressed rabbit and wanted his share. Rabbit was a special treat indeed. Even though it was on the thin side, she was thrilled to have gotten it. She couldn't remember the last time she and Jacques had dined on rabbit. The only meat she had been able to get in months was from a few small birds and thin squirrels, often with Remus's help.

She swung her arms happily, enjoying the soft sunlight on her back as she walked the dirt path toward the village of Jalda. Remus trotted beside her, his tail raised into a curled S-shape. Her stomach grumbled, and she reached her hand into her pocket, searching for some dried berries. Her fingers brushed the compact, and she smiled fondly. She lingered there for a moment, resting the compact in her palm as memories of her mother flooded her mind. Then she lifted the fruit into her mouth. As she walked, she hummed absently a quiet tune with a lifting melody. It was a song her mother used to sing. The tune was soothing and sweet. It helped to pass the time on the dirt path. Before she knew it, their walk was almost over, and they had crossed the bridge into the village.

Jalda had once been a quiet and safe country village, but its streets grew more dangerous each passing day. Mysterious disappearances had plagued the town for several years, casting a dark pall over the entire place. The lovely stone storefronts with red doors and peaked wooden roofs were shrouded in darkness.

The jolly hanging lamps that had so long lit their storefronts had long since burned out. There was just not enough oil to light the darkness that increasingly encroached on the shortening days.

Due to the loss of daylight and reduced shopping hours, many shops had been forced to close. The shopkeepers had taken to setting up a large tent market that now dominated the streets. The market had done nothing for the safety of the village. Thieves often ransacked the market in the cover of darkness, and shopkeepers often slept in their market tents to guard their goods during the night. More than one of these had disappeared, their wares taken.

Trading was the source of exchange in the marketplace. Evangeline had purchased most of her goods and clothing in trades. She could obtain most of what she needed with the skill of her bow and arrow, but with shortening days, her prey was growing scarce. Of late, the nights stretched the landscape into increasingly long shadows and the darkness bent the people and nature to its will. The lack of sunlight meant the animals had less food. Many of them had died in the past few years with no young to replace them. She grew what root vegetables she could in her forest clearing and foraged for the rest, but often her stomach grumbled in protest as she lay in her bed at night.

Jacques' shop was the first shop on the left once she crossed the bridge. She bent to wipe the dust from her boots on the stone paver outside of it, then she straightened her dress and reached to check her hair. More pieces had escaped their bonds on her walk. They now hung in loose ringlets to frame her face. Remus meowled to her left, looking up at her with squinting eyes. It was as if he was telling her to hurry up. She gazed down at him and grinned.

"Okay, I'm going, I'm going," she said, chuckling. Straightening her shoulders, she cleared her throat and tapped the rapper gently on the red wooden door.

Jacques appeared almost instantly. His tall frame dwarfed her as he wrapped her into a bear hug, lifting her feet off the stone. "Happy birthday, Lina!" he boomed. "Eighteen years old. I can't believe it!" He swung her around in a circle then set her gently back on the stone. She chuckled and pulled away, her delicate cheeks pinking at the close contact. Jacques's brown eyes crinkled at the corners, and a giant smile covered his face. As usual, his wayward brown hair was standing up in all directions. A thick swath of it had flopped down over his forehead. Lina eyed it, grinning, and when he caught her looking, he swiped it back with his palm. For a moment, it stayed in place. Then it sprang forward again, flopping over his eyes. He shrugged, and Lina giggled, covering her mouth with her hand.

"Well, come in," he said. "Not like you have to knock anyway. I mean it was your home once, too." He gestured to the crowded shop floor, grabbing the dressed rabbit from her hand and eyeing it with appreciation. "Rabbit! Wow! Where did you find it?" "Past the valley in the far wood. I almost couldn't believe my eyes. I haven't seen a rabbit in ages."

Remus wound his orange body around the doorframe and helped himself to the hearth seat, where he promptly curled into a C-shape and closed his eyes. "Make yourself at home, little wolf!" Jacques chuckled. Lina stepped into the clock shop, and Jacques shut the red door soundly behind her. He bolted it as he peered warily out the round shop window into the street beyond.

The shop was fuller than she'd ever seen it. Lina spun, looking about her in amazement. Jacques's workspace near the hearth was full of half-finished timepieces, bits of metal, strips of sanded wood, gears, clock faces, and hands. His well-used lathe stood to the left of the work bench. Wood shavings curled beneath it and spilled out into the front floor. Pots of paint, brushes, stains, and metal working tools littered the countertop. Clocks of every shape, size, and color in various stages of repair covered the room from floor to ceiling.

Beside Lina's left ear, a wooden, yellow cuckoo suddenly popped out of its door, calling *cuckoo* loudly, marking the hour. Lina's heart leapt into her throat at the sound. She started, turning to look at the wooden bird springing out from its house. It bounced wildly on the end of its small spring. Jacques grinned, covering his mouth with the back of his hand. Sighing, Lina rolled her eyes, swatting the house's hanging pine cones as she laughed at herself. "Stupid bird," she said, giggling.

He followed her gaze about the room. "Sorry about the mess." He grinned. "I'm overrun. The people in the village bring more clocks every day. I'm doing all I can, but I can't keep up with the demand. They run so fast that their gears jam, and the balances are so off-center that I can't seem to set them right." He shrugged in frustration, running his large fingers through his hair. "I don't understand it."

He placed his hands on his hips. His shirt collar was loose, and the tail was untucked. Paint and stain splattered his neck and sleeves under his leather work apron. His faded brown work pants were worn down at the knees, and his brown leather boots looked no better than Lina's. Patches replaced both toes, and the front of the right sole was loose. Lina snickered at his disheveled appearance, covering her grin with her hand.

Gazing at her sidelong, he smiled broadly, swiftly tucking his shirt tail in. He chuckled as he took off his apron, moving to hang it on a hook by the door. His arm brushed her shoulder with his reach, and she blushed, stepping back. Folding her arms behind her waist, she stared intently at the floor, focusing on her patched boot making circles in the sawdust.

"Come see what I got you!" he said suddenly, turning for the back room.

Jacques slept in the upstairs apartment, and he kept the space behind the central hearth as a sitting room and kitchen. She smiled at his back, tucking a lock of loose hair behind her ear and following softly behind him. He laid the rabbit on the kitchen counter and turned back toward the hearth. He stoked the fire and checked the pot that simmered over it, soon to be rabbit stew.

Lina lifted the scrawny root vegetables from her pack. She sat them onto the countertop and hung her cloak and weapon on a peg on the back wall. Then, she took her seat by the fire. She sat close to Jacques's back, and when he turned, he started at her unexpected appearance. He sucked his teeth and chuckled lightly, running a hand through his hair. "You're so quiet you move like a ghost!" he exclaimed as he laughed. Lina grinned. "So I've been told."

He turned back and reached into the woodpile at the right of the hearth, lifting extra logs into the fireplace. The muscles beneath his white work shirt flexed with the effort, and Lina lowered her lashes, trying not to notice. He stoked the fire once more and placed the iron poker in its stand on the hearth. Then he stood, searching about the room. Frowning, he patted his pants pockets and reached into the pocket of his shirt. "Where did I," he muttered. He spun, searching in corners, under papers, and behind chairs. Lina watched him, giggling quietly. Jacques had never been the most organized. "Aha!" he shouted, reaching toward the windowsill above the kitchen counter. "Found it!"

There, on the sill, sat a small parchment. The delicate white paper was lined with silver swirls and tied with a red ribbon. With a wide smile, he held it out to her on his palm. She received the parchment in awe, carefully fingering the ribbon and tracing the silver swirls with her fingers. The paper alone must have cost a fortune. She had never seen such fine paper in all her life. "That's just the wrapping, you know," he teased. Grinning, he braced his hands on his knees and sat down in the chair across from her. She smiled softly, pink tinging her cheeks. "I know," she said quietly.

She pulled the red ribbon slowly free and gently unwrapped the beautiful paper, doing all she could to keep from tearing it. Inside sat a single piece of cake. Lina's full mouth formed a small *o*, and her slim brows lifted in surprise. Light, pink icing sat atop airy sponge cake, and pearled toppings graced the treat's top. It was a true delight, and a very expensive one.

She had only had something sweet one other time in her life. She had been so young. The memory was hazy, but she still remembered most of it. She remembered being very ill and lying under her mother's coverlet. She had shivered, and sweat had beaded on her brow. Her eyes had been so heavy that she could hardly keep them open. Her chest burned, and it was hard to pull in breath. Everything hurt, and she had lain as still as a stone. Her mother's beautiful face had been drawn and streaked with tears, and Lina remembered wondering why she was so sad. Softly, her mother had murmured a sweet song into Lina's ear.

Then she disappeared. She was gone for what seemed like a long while. But time passes in odd patterns when one is sick. Days can feel like weeks, and sometimes, mere moments can seem like an eternity. When she had returned, her mother had placed small morsels of a crisp wafer topped with delicate cream into Lina's mouth. It was sweet and light as air. Later that night, her fever had broken, and the next morning, she had sat up and asked for water.

She smiled in appreciation of Jacques's cake and glanced up at him under her lashes. "I traded for it," he explained. "I fixed the baker's clock this week. He says he can't bake properly without a working clock." He shook his head, blowing out a breath. "I never thought I'd get it fixed, but I did and…well, you're welcome." It was Jacques's turn to blush now. He lowered his eyes, bobbing his knee under his large hand.

Lina smiled softly. "Thank you, Jacques," she said quietly. "It's wonderful. We can share it for dessert."

She sat the cake reverently back on the sill and turned to the kitchen counter to chop the vegetables. Jacques stood and scratched the back of his neck. "You're welcome," he said through a smile. He took his place beside Lina, grabbing his knife and carefully chopping the meat into chunks for the stew. They had stood like this often, shoulder to shoulder in the small kitchen at the back of the clock shop. It was comforting to Lina. Familiar. She always hummed to herself while Jacques quietly worked.

Ten years her senior, Jacques had taken her in when her mother had disappeared. He had given her the living space above the workshop, while he slept on a pallet in front of the hearth. He had provided for her and fed her little cat, Remus, who appeared with her in the street in front of his shop when he was eighteen. After an extraordinarily long life, his father had died that winter, and he was left alone in the shop most of his days. Loneliness had weighed heavily on his heart and mind back then. But that was before he found Lina and Remus.

He had taken pity on the poor little girl he saw out in the street, attempting to steal bread from the baker's cart. Jacques had marveled at her ability to pocket the rolls as the cart hobbled down the cobblestone streets. She was swift and moved in silence. No one had seen her appear from the alley and slide her small hand under the cart's flap, jamming two rolls into the pockets of her stained dress. She had lifted onto her small toes to reach the baked goods, her bare feet silent as she fled on the pavers.

He had waited until she was safe in the alley before he opened his door and beckoned her to him. She had peered at him around the corner with her large blue-green eyes, hiding behind a long, golden mass of curls. Remus had wound himself about her feet, casting squinted eyes in Jacques's direction. When he had opened his door wider, Remus had leaped inside. Lina had come to stand in the street, craning her neck to see where her little cat had gone. Jacques had stepped back from the door, and she had snuck inside on her small, quiet feet.

In the years that followed, Lina had grown into a beautiful young woman. It had not escaped Jacques's notice. The quiet little girl he had taken in from the village street had transformed into a lovely young woman with fierce independence. Despite Jacques's fear for her safety, she had insisted on moving back to the cottage in the forest clearing when she turned fifteen. It had terrified him.

In the years she had lived at the shop, the cottage had been ransacked by thieves. They had emptied it of all the furniture on the first floor. Still, Lina insisted on returning. They had gotten into a huge fight over it. She had refused to speak to him for several days. It had been the longest they had ever gone without talking to one another. Of course, Lina had won their fight in the end. Mostly because Jacques couldn't bear to tell her no. So, she had moved back into the cottage despite Jacques wishes. She slept in the loft, and he had slowly built her new furniture over time.

He made sure she could defend herself too. Using strips of wood and bits of metal from the old clock he kept covered in the back corner of the shop, he fashioned her a beautiful quiver of arrows and a bow. He had inherited the clock from his father, who had tinkered with it almost every day. It had never run properly, at least, it hadn't in many years. Over the years, Jacques had tried to repair it, but he had never been successful. The hands moved so quickly over its face that the gears stuck, and he had long since given up his repair efforts. It had sat in the corner of the shop, covered with a linen sheet for years now.

He gazed at Lina sidelong, being careful not to chop his large fingers with the knife. In the beginning, she had been nothing more than an orphan girl in need of a home, and later, she had become his close friend. But now, he could feel himself regarding her as something more.

He watched her as she hummed to herself, chopping vegetables and tossing them into the simmering pot. Her long, golden hair shimmered in the firelight, and tiny curls escaped their bonds, swirling above her ears and at the nape of her slim neck. She swiped at them with the back of her hand. Light brown lashes curled over her wide, almond eyes, flicking up at him as she raised her gaze. He had never seen eyes as lovely. They were aquamarine. A striking color. He had tried to mix his paints to match it, but he could never get the shade quite right. She grinned at him, raising her delicate brow, then turned back to her work.

Jacques watched as her full lips parted and she sucked in a small breath, pressing them together in a hum. He followed the pattern of tiny freckles that marched across her delicate nose to high cheekbones above her ear. The color there was dusted pink, and it was most becoming. Her slim face curved down over a smooth jaw, trailing to a point at her small chin. He pressed his lips together, wishing he could follow the line with his fingers. She was lovely, so lovely.

He was so lost in his examination that the knife slipped, slicing his finger. "Ah!"

Dropping the blade, he quickly brought the wound to his lips, sucking through his teeth. Lina gasped and spun to grab his hand. "Let me see," she said, pulling it up to her face. She grabbed a clean kitchen rag and pressed the corner of it to the wound. Picking up the edge of the cloth, she peered at his skin through her long brown lashes. "It's a shallow wound," she said. "It should heal quickly." She tore the worn kitchen rag nimbly in her slender fingers, breaking it into thin strips with her teeth. Winding the strips around his finger, she secured it tightly and patted the top of his large hand. "There. All done."

She was so absorbed in tending his wound that she didn't notice his nearness. As she finished with the bandage, Jacques stepped toward her, bracing his free hand on the countertop. His upper arm grazed her shoulder, and she dropped his hand, stepping back against the counter. He didn't step away but instead reached toward her, lifting her chin with his bandaged hand. He studied her features, wrapping his free arm around her back and tugging her closer to him. Lina's heart thrummed in her ears. She watched him hover above her, eyes smoldering. He craned his neck, filling the space between them, and Lina's heart tripped over itself. Wordlessly, she tipped her face upward, winding her hands over his upper arms.

At that moment, a screeching howl came from the shop room hearth. Remus shot through the kitchen in a scruffy orange blur. He leapt behind the woodpile, hiding beneath the logs. Lina quickly unwound herself from Jacques's arms. She moved to crouch at the woodpile, peering in at him. He squinted his green eyes at her, licking his tail in desperation. "Oh, Remus, I'm sorry," she said, crooning. She smoothed her dress and stood, looking toward the hearth where Remus had been sleeping. A glowing ember had popped from the hearth, landing on the poor cat's tail. She walked over to it and picked it up with the hem of her dress, tossing it back into the fireplace.

The cuckoo clock chimed again, and she jumped, bringing her hand to her chest. She laughed at herself, tucking her hair behind her ear. Jacques' deep chuckle rumbled to her ears from the kitchen. Shyly she raised her eyes to him. He was leaning against the kitchen countertop, staring at her sheepishly. He shifted his weight and stood, running a hand through his hair.

They had almost shared something in the kitchen. It had made things awkward. She pulled a face at him, trying to lighten the mood, and Jacques chuckled again. Lina looked away as she turned to read the cuckoo clock. Her eyes widened. Time had flown.

She raced to the window. The sun was already touching the horizon. She turned her head quickly to Jacques, who now stood behind her on the shop room floor. Disappointment colored his face. "We'd better get a move on," he said quietly. She nodded, and they went to work on the rabbit stew, finishing it in short order. As she ladled the soup into bowls, Remus reappeared from his hiding place in the woodpile, meowling at her feet. She spooned chunks of rabbit into a smaller bowl and set it down for him in front of the fireplace. He meowed appreciatively, curling his tail into an *S* as he dipped his head into it.

She and Jacques ate their stew quickly. They shared the piece of cake that Lina savored and ate in small bites. She focused on the sweet taste, trying to ignore the longing glances Jacques sent in her direction. Finally, she sighed and pushed back her chair. It was growing late, and she needed to get off the road and into the cabin before darkness fell. Remus roused and stretched his back, sticking his paws out onto the hearth and sinking onto his haunches. He hopped onto the floor and padded lightly to the front door of the shop, looking back at her lazily with squinty green eyes.

She gathered her weapon and cloak, draping it over her slim shoulders. Jacques placed his hands on his knees and stood, gazing at her forlorn. "Can't you stay a bit longer?" he asked, running a hand through his hair. She looked toward the window's waning light and back at him. "I'd better go. I want to be off the road before dark." Sighing, he smiled, crinkling his brown eyes at the corners. "Of course. I know. I just wish…" She raised her brows expectantly, and he shook his head. "Never mind."

He led the way out of the kitchen, reaching his hand to touch the linen cloth covering the tall timepiece in the corner of the front room. The large, ornate clock was unlike anything Lina had ever seen. As a child, she had snuck to stand beneath the cloth, admiring it. It towered over her head, its large glass face staring ominously down at her. She had wanted to run her hands along the strange carvings in its wood frame, but something deep within her had kept her curious hands from touching it.

Great beasts and winged creatures, like those from fairy tales, adorned the wooden clock from top to foot. Curved glass covered its gilded face that held strange numerals and symbols. Some of them she knew, and some even Jacques did not. He had inherited the clock from his father, who had spent the remarkably long years of his life trying to repair it. He had died unable to do so. Often, she had seen Jacques with his ear pressed tightly against it, listening intently with his eyes closed. He had told her many times that he could feel the *tick* of the clock in his own chest. Although he had been able to repair a great many clocks brought into his shop, just like his father, he had never been able to mend this one.

Indeed, the *tick* of the large clock had become so faint that he could barely hear it. The hands of the clock spun around and around, much faster than the appointed hour, causing the metal gears to stick and the balances to shift out of place. He was so frustrated by the timepiece that he had long given up his repair efforts. Instead, he kept the great thing covered and pushed to the corner of the shop.

He let go of the linen cover and swiped a hand through his wayward hair. At the front of the shop, he peered out the window and down the street, scanning the street market carefully before opening the door. By now, the shopkeepers were rolling down their tent doors, shutting their market shops for the night. He turned back to face her, his feet shifting uncomfortably. "Happy birthday, Lina. Be careful on the road," he said gruffly.

Lina knew he wanted to walk her home, but she wouldn't let him risk leaving the shop unattended. Besides, it was too risky for him to walk alone in the dark back to the village. She knew he didn't agree. He would've gladly allowed himself to be jumped on the dark road to know she was safe behind her doors. Still, she knew he would let her go alone. She studied his knitted brows, grinning. As much as it troubled him, Jacques allowed her to have her independence. It was one of the reasons she loved him.

He swept her into a swift hug, crushing her to his chest. He held her longer and tighter than he normally did. Lina grinned against his shoulder. She returned his embrace and then slowly, she stepped back, clutching her cloak at her neck. She slung her weapon onto her shoulder and smiled. "I'll see you soon," she said.

Jacques eyes were full of meaning. The look in them made her chest flush under her cloak.

"Soon then," he said, grinning. "Off you go, Lina, Remus." He nodded once to the small cat.

Remus squinted up at him and purred, swirling his orange body around the doorframe. Lina stepped onto the pavers, lifting her cloak to cover her head against the biting air. It was much colder outside than it had been on her earlier walk to the village. She shivered, tucking her arms across her middle as she hurried across the bridge. She didn't see the snowflake fall onto her hood as she and Remus started the long walk back to the cottage.

CHAPTER 2

Lina moved her feet swiftly on the path, watching the setting sun with wary eyes. She shivered, clutching her cloak tightly about her. It was early in the year, yet already, the air bore the heavy weight of coming winter. Fallen leaves crunched under her boots, and bare tree limbs cast long shadows on the ground, reaching their limbs toward her like twisted fingers. She cast guarded eyes to them, imagining the scratching branches grasping at her waist. Fear bit at her neck, and she looked away from them, forcing her feet to go faster.

A loon soared above her head, his legs trailing behind him. She lifted her face to watch him soar. He was already wearing his gray-and-white winter plumes. As she watched his flight, something cold and soft landed on her nose. She blinked her eyes in surprise, tucking her chin into her neck. Lifting her finger to the spot, she blotted her nose and examined her finger. An intricate six-pointed snowflake lay softly on its tip. She squinted at it in disbelief, watching it melt into a dot of water on her skin. Time was flying. It was too soon—much too soon for the first snowfall.

She crossed the stream to her cottage in her forest clearing just as the last of the diffuse golden rays of the sun shone sideways through the trees. Quickly, she tucked herself behind the door. Her body was trembling with the cold as she hurried to hang her cloak and weapon on the peg by the door. As quickly as she could, she moved to the hearth, stoking the embers. She wiggled her fingertips above the flames, loosening the stiffness in her fingers. Remus took his post on the hearth and curled into his familiar C-shape, his eyes becoming slits. He purred softly, swiping his tail against the stones. Lina smiled down at him as she moved to the sitting chair facing the kitchen, propping her feet on the hearth. It felt good to sit by the fire after the long walk from the village. She let herself relax, allowing her head to lie back against the seat.

Her mind drifted to the cake and rabbit stew. For the first time in months, her belly was full. She smiled as she braced her hands across it, allowing Remus' purr and the warmth of the fire to make her eyes heavy. She had almost closed them when it happened.

Out of the kitchen window, a quick, shimmering movement at the edge of the clearing caught her eye. Lina lifted her head, peering at the spot. The wood was still, and she blinked, searching the tree line. She was certain she had seen something. She focused on the spot where the shimmering motion had been. The movement had been momentary, and when she looked directly at it, the disturbance was gone.

Warning bells trilled in the back of her mind as her sharp eyes scanned the clearing for danger, but she couldn't see anything amiss. Again, the brief ripple moved the air to the left of her gaze. *There.* She sat up straighter now, bracing her arms on the sides of the seat. There it was. Just beyond the clearing, to the left of a large ash tree, a strange, wavering movement smudged the landscape. She stood, moving swiftly to the kitchen window to get a better look.

Remus lifted his body and stretched, circling her feet. The twilight was waning, and it was hard for her to see beneath the shade of the large tree. She squinted through the window, watching as the ripple smudged the air. There was definitely movement, but she couldn't see what had caused it. She needed a closer look. Silently, she lifted her cloak and weapon from the wall, slinging them over her shoulder as she secreted out the front door. Remus trailed her, jumping through the crack before she closed it without a sound.

The air was charged outside the cabin, and a sense of dread tickled the back of Lina's neck. The tips of her hair stood on end, and heart thumped hard in her chest with some unknown fear. As they moved from the front stones and slipped around the side of the cottage, Remus's tail began to stand on end. When they reached the back corner, he puffed out his fur and lifted his orange back, then lowered his head and crouched into a hunting position. Panic built in Lina's throat at the sight, and she watched him warily, lifting her bow in defense. She scanned the tree line for the wavering movement, catching it again from the left corner of her gaze. She frowned, watching the strange ripple disturb the air. Something strange was happening.

She pushed her back flat against the house, sucking in deep breaths to calm her hammering heart. When her body relaxed, she slowly rolled to face the rippling shape. She pulled her bow taut against her cheek as she and Remus silently stalked the clearing. The woods were eerily still, and the air was heavy with silence. It was as if the clearing was holding its breath, waiting for something to happen.

The shimmering disturbance by the ash tree was constant now. Lina frowned, eyeing it nervously. She had never seen anything like it. The wavering section of air curved from the ground into a large oval shape, much like a gate. Its surface looked like rippling water, and it shimmered against the forest air in the failing light. The edges of the gate wisped outward, fluttering in the twilight before disappearing into the trees. Something about the strange gate was foreboding. There was an air of darkness creeping about its edges. In fact, the light around the gate itself was muted, like the woods had dissolved into nothingness. Lina moved toward it cautiously, with Remus close on her heels.

Curiosity pulled her forward as she approached, and she lowered her bow in amazement, taking cautious steps toward the rippling shape. The closer she came, the more pull the gate exerted on her body. It tugged at her cloak, pulling the hem softly outward, and she was drawn forward until she was merely inches from the surface. As she closed in, a faint humming sound curled about her ears, and her hair stood on end. A tingling sensation ran down her spine, and her skin prickled. Thrill mixed with terror swirled in her belly, jostling for position as she gazed at the mesmerizing disturbance, and her hand lifted of its own will, reaching to touch the rippling surface.

Just as her fingers hovered above it, a violent sound, like the tearing of metal, ripped from the shape. The air around the gate darkened, and Lina smelled heavy soot as a massive roar obliterated the soft hum of the gate. A scream built in her throat, but it didn't have time to escape before the largest black wolf she had ever seen leaped through the surface, knocking her flat to the ground. His growling roar rang in her ears, and she shut her eyes, turning her face against his hot breath and snapping black fangs. His weight was crushing, and Lina lifted her hands to push against his massive jaws. They covered her palms with slick, wet slaver. The wolf snapped close to her ear, and panic threatened as she drove her knees upward into his abdomen. She whimpered as her foot made contact, wincing. His dark body was as hard as stone.

Just then, a violent howl screeched behind her, and she popped open her eyes. Remus was a scruffy orange blur as he leaped through the air above her, landing on the beast's back. He gripped the massive wolf with his claws and sank his sharp white teeth into a shoulder. The creature roared, lifting his weight off Lina. She scrambled from beneath the great wolf, swiping slaver from her hands on the front of her dress as she stood upright.

Lina watched as Remus held tightly to the massive wolf's shoulder with his teeth and claws. His orange tail stood straight on-end, and his ears were flattened to his head. The beast reached for him with large, clawed hands and shook his body violently, roaring in protest.

The black wolf stood up on his hind legs, glaring behind him with knowing, intelligent eyes. Although he had the head of a great wolf, his muscular torso was that of a large man, and his great hands were equipped with long black claws. His legs had a wolfish look, too, but they were larger than any wolf's legs Lina had ever seen. Giant paws with sharp black claws ripped up the earth as he tried to free himself of the little cat.

Lina was frozen in place as she stared in terror at the wolf-man. She couldn't believe what she was seeing, but she shook her head, fighting through her fear, and sprang into action. Reaching into her quiver, she loaded her bow and aimed it at the great wolf's chest. Her hands were still slick and her arms were shaking so badly she couldn't keep a steady aim. She sucked in a deep breath and furrowed her brow, steadying her weapon.

The wolf-man was moving in a jagged line, growling and swiping at Remus on his shoulder. Lina pulled the bowstring taut against her cheek, following his movements with her arm. She was having a hard time keeping her aim. Just then, Remus sank his back claws into the dark fur of the great wolf's back. The beast paused, howling, and she released her breath with the arrow's flight, exhaling a cloud of smoke.

In the same moment, the great wolf succeeded in extracting Remus from his shoulder. He held the little cat's orange body aloft, directly in the arrow's path. "No!" Lina screamed. She lunged toward them, but it was too late. Remus howled with the impact of the arrow that lodged beneath his right foreleg. Tears seared Lina's eyes, and her scream ripped through the clearing as she fell to her knees. "Remus!"

Remus peered at her before his body went limp and his head lolled forward. The great wolf snarled at her with glee and bared his teeth in a gruesome smile, casting the small orange cat aside. Remus landed in a small heap on the ground, the arrow protruding from his right chest. He was still and made no sound.

Lina fell onto her hands over Remus and sobbed great tears onto the ground. She braced his small body and removed the arrow's tip, staunching the flow of blood with the hem of her dress. It spread quickly across her skirts, staining a dark red splotch onto the fabric. "Please, Remus. You've got to wake up," she whispered shakily.

Remus opened his green eyes briefly at her voice. He peered up at her face, his gaze dim and distant. Then he closed them again.

Lina scratched her fingernails against the cold ground and glared up at the vile wolf-creature through watery eyes. Her breath came in short bursts and her brow knit together as she bared her teeth. A guttural sound of grief escaped her throat, and she swiped furiously at the traitorous tears streaking down her face. Her hair was escaping its plait and ran down her back in long golden rivulets. It stuck to her wet, dirt-stained cheeks.

A growl rumbled from the great wolf's throat, and he dropped onto all fours to face her. Lina was determined. She was going to kill him for what he had done. She fumbled her stiff fingers, quickly reloading the arrow and gathering herself to her feet. He stalked her quietly, weaving towards her like a predator stalking his prey. Lina focused on his movements, working to calm her hammering heart. The only other sounds in the clearing were the chuffs of the great wolf, which curled past his black teeth in tendrils of smoke, and the faint hum of the gate somewhere behind her.

The air was freezing, and it vaguely occurred to Lina that snowflakes had been falling for some time. The ground around her was spotted with patches of snow. The beast stalked her around the clearing in a crescent shape, until her back was facing the ash tree. He began to edge toward her, backing her farther toward the rippling gate. He snarled and snapped, baring his black fangs at her arrow's tip. The hum in her ears grew louder, and the gate pulled softly against her cloak, drawing her back toward its wavering surface.

The great wolf roared as he leaped. He lunged at her neck, toppling her backward as she let her arrow fly. She watched as the arrow hit its mark. The light in his knowing eyes dimmed, and his clawed hand fumbled weakly for the arrow protruding from his chest. Lina yanked it free, and black blood spewed from his wound. His eyes lolled backward, and he fell heavily to the snowy ground. On impact, his body began to disintegrate, melting to ash. The ashes floated upward, swirling in the air before blowing away in the breeze. Then he was gone. Lina tried to pull herself onto her feet, but the pull of the gate behind her made her stumble backwards. As she fell through, the soft humming of the gate was overcome by a great metallic rip as she passed through the surface.

She squeezed her eyes shut and brought her hands to cover her ears as the roaring sound of the gate enveloped her. Her body was being sucked backward and she was falling, falling in darkness. The pull was strong, and she was moving at an incredible speed. Her hair blew up over her head and her dress billowed as she tumbled, struggling to find which way was up. Soon, she would surely make impact. She reached her hands below to try to catch her fall, but there was nothing beneath her except open air.

Her speed suddenly increased, and a deafening scream pierced her ears, which she was surprised to realize was her own. The scream echoed, bouncing back to her from all directions. She sucked in a breath and opened her eyes. A kaleidoscope of colors swirled about her, twisting and turning as if she were in a long tunnel. As she fell further, the echoes of her scream fell away, replaced by a soft hum that gradually grew into a melodious song. Faces of creatures and people she did not recognize and colors she could not name spiraled around her.

The longer Lina fell, the more she gained speed. She realized that she would not survive an impact at this rate. Tucking into a tight ball, she braced her body, listening as the melody around her grew to an almost deafening sound. The colors and faces stretched and pulled into ever-longer shapes, winding above and below her in long, cylindrical rings.

The tunnel pulled against her limbs, and her body stretched into an impossibly thin line. The pressure on her head was enormous, and she felt as if it would burst under the weight. She held out her hands, examining their shape. The tips of her fingers were lengthening into long ribbons. As she watched, they became so thin that she could no longer see them. The flesh of her body flattened, blending out into the colorful patterns around her. She was being pressed to death, and she attempted to mount another scream but found that her chest could no longer pull in air. She tilted her head back to suck in breath, water squeezing out of the corners of her eyes, and opened her mouth in a silent *o*.

She coalesced into the cylindrical crescendo until she was one with the sounds and shades. She was nothing but a swirl of sound and light, and it occurred to her that she might never be her whole self again. It was a strange feeling, a terrifying thought.

Suddenly, without warning, she rebounded into her original shape. Her pace halted abruptly, but without any pull, any pressure, any pain. Here, there was only bright white light and silence. She floated gently in this relief, like a feather floating softly on top of the water. The cool white light saturated her, and she bathed in the silence. The light moved around and within her. Flowing. Free. She inhaled deeply, allowing herself to sink farther into it. A great knowing began to enter her being, and she felt a wholeness she had never known. She wanted to stay there, wanted to know more, but she somehow knew she wouldn't.

Too soon, the humming resumed, and she again felt the effects of her stretched shape. Straining in discomfort, she continued her plummeting fall. She couldn't breathe. Her chest was pressed impossibly flat. She wondered how her heart was still beating under the pressure. A moment more, and it would be too late. Just then, a metallic rip cut the air, and her body immediately collected into her original shape. Her chest was whole again, and she sucked in a deep breath as she exited the other end of the glimmering surface, just before her back hit water.

She plunged down, down into the depths, flipping and turning as she tumbled in the waves. Dark water pressed over her ears and sucked into her chest, choking her. She opened her eyes, blinking against the murky sea. Her heart began to hammer, and she frantically kicked and flailed her arms, fighting for the surface. The dark water was disorienting, and she couldn't be sure if she was going up or down. Her chest burned, and her mind screamed for relief. She fought against the billowing fabric of her dress and pumped her legs, reaching her arms in what she hoped was the right direction.

Just then, her face breached the surface, and she sucked in a breath, coughing and spluttering salty seawater. When her lungs were clear, she lay back in exhaustion and floated on top of the water, gently sweeping her arms to keep afloat. She closed her eyes, breathing slowly in and out and allowing her heart rate to slow.

Here, wherever here was, the sun was high in the sky. It warmed her skin, and she peered up at it, squinting. It sat higher in the sky than her own sun at home, and it was much brighter, too.

Absently, she touched her shoulder, checking for her bow. It was gone. Her heart leaped into her throat, and she sat up quickly, frantically chopping at the waves. "Where is it," she whispered to herself. She spied it floating in the water just ahead of her, next to her leather quiver, and she paddled over to reach it. Relief surged through her as she secured them across her back, and she kicked about in a circle, searching for the shore. It was a far distance away from her. Her body was exhausted from fighting the passage and the dark water. She wondered how she would make it there.

As she fought down her rising panic, she caught sight of a small wooden boat. It floated some distance away from her, paddled by a stooped man standing on its stern. She shielded her eyes and peered in its direction. The man rowed the small boat steadily with his single oar, his thin arms moving rhythmically back and forth. Despite its size, it cut through the waves at a surprisingly swift speed.

A gentle current was pulling backward at her skirts. It lifted the fabric of her cloak, and she frowned over her shoulder and raised her arms, paddling forward to escape it. At once, the current became stronger. She pulled harder as rivulets of seawater streamed over her hands and shoulders and pulled at her waist. Her feet lifted, and water tugged at her boots. Lina peered behind her in panic. She couldn't escape the current, and it was growing stronger every moment. She began to kick, paddling her arms in earnest.

Instead of moving forward, her body was being pulled backward. She laid her body flat and grunted, kicking mightily with her legs and pulling herself forward with her arms. As she struggled, she realized that she was being pulled in a massive circle. Her muscles burned, and she was quickly running out of strength. The swirling water pulled her faster and faster as more and more water streamed into the vortex. Panting, she peered across it, her eyes widening. The circle of whirling water was so wide that she couldn't see the far edge.

Suddenly, the center of circle dropped. It reached down, down into the depths, further than Lina could see. The water roared around her, and she swirled helplessly in the gigantic whirlpool. She eyed the base of the vortex with terror, swimming frantically, but there was no escape. The current was too strong, and despite her best efforts, she began to swirl downward.

Dread pushed at her chest as she fought the maelstrom. Rushing water roared in her ears, and her limbs burned heavily. As she sank, she lifted her eyes to the massive whirlpool's edge. There, the bow of the small wooden boat rowed perpendicular to the swirling water. The stooped captain held fast to his oar and peered over the edge at her. He braced the oar on his middle and lifted his hands, making wide cutting motions in the air with his arms. He gestured at her, making a half turn with his body and pointing at the open sea behind him. He continued to cut the air, nodding to her.

Lina stared up at him blankly, watching his tanned arms form arcs in the air. Then, all at once, she understood. She followed his commands and began to swim furiously in a transverse motion to the swirling water. She held her breath as she plunged through the whirlpool's wall and swam with all her might until she could no longer feel the tug of the vortex on her feet. The wall of the whirlpool was wide, and she almost didn't make it through without running out of air. She strained for the surface, pulling with her arms, until she burst upward near the boat's keel.

The man reached down and pulled her over the side, plopping her unceremoniously onto the deck. She shrugged the bow and quiver off before collapsing, exhausted.

Lina lay flat on her back and stared up at the sky, sucking deep breaths of waterless air into her lungs. Her arms and legs, heavy with exhaustion, lay limply on the floor of the wooden boat. Long, wet locks of hair spilled out above her, creating little rivers of water along the wood, and her dress clung to her slender frame. Her worn leather boots were heavy with water, and bits of seagrass and debris stuck to the bare skin of her neck, chest, and legs. Wordlessly, the captain took his place at the stern, rowing the boat slowly through the choppy waves. She peered up at him above her head.

Even though his back was bent with age, his gnarled hands moved the oar as if it was an extension of himself. He wore simple, homespun clothing in earthen tones. The top of his head was balding, speckled by the sun, and the ring of gray hair above his ears was tied back in a tail at the nape of his neck. His braided gray beard hung below his chin and was secured with a small strip of leather. He had a craggy face and a long, hooked nose, and piercing blue eyes peered out from under bushy gray eyebrows, squinting toward their destination.

Turning his head to the right, he exposed his ear. Lina raised her brows. It came to a point at its tip. From deep in his throat, he hummed a simple tune. Although the melody was rather flat, Lina was calmed by his simple, gruff tones. The sun warmed her damp skin, and the rocking of the boat soothed her jumbled nerves. She sighed and closed her eyes, feeling the deep pull of exhaustion. Soon her breathing evened, and she was lulled into a heavy sleep.

CHAPTER 3

Lina woke sometime later to the choppy rocking of the small boat. She peered down at her dress, which was now mostly dry. She smoothed it along her middle and pulled a deep breath into her chest, stopping short with the lingering burn of seawater in her lungs. Coughing wracked her body and she grimaced, rolling onto her side. She heaved heavily and vomited, spitting out the brine. Then she pushed her arms up to sit and brought a hand to her head. It throbbed, heavy with fatigue. She laced her fingers into the back of her hair, which was matted, tangled in large knots down her back. With a wince, she removed her plait, smoothing it as best she could.

In the distance was a rocky shoreline. The waves were larger and tumbling here, and she braced her arms to keep from falling over in the small wooden boat. Her captain was silent now, his throaty humming quiet. She turned her head to peer up at him. The breeze blew wisps of what was left of his gray hair across his face, and his tan linen shirt and brown pants billowed in the sea air. His balance never wavered, and he stood solidly on the stern against the choppy waves, not acknowledging her even as she studied him. His feet were bare and flat with spread toes, as if he had never worn any shoes. They were as brown as the wood of the boat. In fact, they looked as if they were a part of it. She studied them curiously a moment more before she turned back, shielding her eyes with her hand to gaze at the shore.

A menagerie of stones and sea glass in various colors dotted the beach. Lavender, aquamarine, coral pink, deep blue, and various muted brown and gray tones decorated the shore. The beach extended to the right as far as Lina could see. To the left, the shore disappeared into a shroud of mist in the far distance. Waves crashed heavily onto large boulders near the boat, spraying seafoam onto the slick rocks. Above the beach was a sheer, rocky cliff that rose high above the shoreline.

As they grew close, Lina saw a thin woman bent on the beach, gathering sea glass into a basket. The waves of the sea lapped at her feet, wetting the hem of her gray dress. She paused to peer up at them, tucking long, whipping strands of gray hair away from her eyes. Before Lina could get a good look, she lifted the hood of her cloak, shrouding her face. She quickly gathered her basket and skirts, dropping the pieces of glass she held in her hand as she spun on her heel.

Narrow stone steps hewn from the rocky cliff wound from the beach and climbed up the stone precipice to a ledge halfway up the face. The woman climbed the staircase rapidly, glancing back at them warily as she climbed. When she reached the top step, she squared her shoulders to the stone and placed her hand flat upon the rock. To Lina's surprise, an opening in the rock materialized under the woman's palm. She strode purposefully through the opening, disappearing from view. When her body was clear of the entrance, Lina watched as the opening returned to stone behind her.

Before Lina had time to consider what she had seen, the hull of the wooden boat slid onto the rocky shore, lurching her forward onto her palms. She brushed her tangled hair from her eyes and righted herself, turning to the silent captain. The old man squinted down at her from his post, lifting his chin in the direction of the staircase. When she hesitated, he grunted at her and balanced the oar at his waist, reaching one crooked finger toward the rock precipice. Lina looked to the narrow, winding stone steps and back up at him. The strangeness of the situation, the world around her, felt like a weight keeping her down. Impatience starting to show behind his blue eyes, the captain grunted at her again, gesturing for her to stand. Uncertainly, she reached for her bow and quiver and slung them across her back, grasping the side of the boat to steady herself as she stood. Her legs were still weak and sore from her miraculous whirlpool escape. The boat rocked as another wave nudged, and she held her arms out for balance. Staggering on quavering legs, she moved to the side of the boat and swung one leg over.

Just then, a large wave tossed the wooden boat, and she tumbled forward onto the beach. She rolled, wet pebbles and bits of sea glass clinging to her face and dress. Wiping herself, she stood and straightened her tattered dress, peering up toward the narrow stone staircase. She glanced backward, taking one last look at the captain, who appeared to have no intention of following her. He had resumed his throaty hum, and his weathered arms steered the boat left, heading down the shoreline.

She moved slowly, easing her feet over the smooth pebbles. The sway of the boat lingered, and she had trouble staying upright. She held out her hands to keep steady, but still, she stumbled over the uneven rocks. Just as she started to gain her balance, a slick of rock gave way, and she pitched forward. She hit the jagged edge of a rock as she fell, bloodying her knee. The spot burned with the sharp cut, and she hugged it to her, tears pricking her eyes. Grimacing, she wiped it with the hem of her dress, pressing the wound with the fabric to staunch the bleeding.

An oblong smudge of Remus's blood still stained her hem. As she stared at the dark spot, the tears spilled over, wetting her cheeks at the thought of her brave little cat protecting her from the ferocious wolf beast that had come through the shimmering gate. Remembering the terrifying creature, she crawled as quickly as she could over the uneven rocks. Standing unsteadily, she wiped her hands along the sides of her dress, scanning the beach for shadowy figures. She was alone, but the image of the great wolf lingered, making her wonder what other evils lurked on this side of the gate. Slowly, she approached the cliff face.

Gazing upward, she placed her unsteady feet on the narrow stone steps. The staircase was higher and narrower than she had first thought. She sucked in a breath and hugged her body to the rock wall, pressing her cheek to the cold stone face as she climbed. About halfway up, she stopped for a moment to catch her breath and made the mistake of looking down to the beach. The surf roared in her ears as her vision tunneled and her head began to spin. Her hurt knee gave way as she took another step, and she stumbled backward, catching herself at the last moment and hurling herself flat against the rock wall. She remained there for a moment, catching her breath. Closing her eyes, she breathed slowly in and out, then opened one eye, assessing the world's spin. She waited until it slowed, easing air into and out of her lungs. Carefully she shifted one foot off the stone and lifted it to the next one, ensuring her footing was solid before taking another step. She completed her ascent in this way, moving in small, measured increments, until she was standing on the stone outcropping at the top.

She turned toward the stone face and repeated the actions she had seen from the woman on the beach. Squaring her shoulders, she placed her right hand flat in front of her on the stone. She waited. Nothing happened. "Open, please," she requested meekly. She dropped her hand and gazed quizzically at the stone. Huffing, she redistributed her weight. She squared her shoulders and lifted her hand again, pressing hard and flat against the rock. "Please. Open. Now." Nothing. She dropped her hand and examined the stone door.

There were no cracks in the stone in which she could jam her fingers. In fact, there was no sign that there had ever been a door in the rock. She flicked her eyes around what she estimated was the outline of the opening, but she couldn't see anything of interest. Retracing her visual line, she paused at the stone high above her, frowning. Small figures were inscribed there on the rock. She pursed her lips, certain they hadn't been there moments ago. The words were written in a language she did not recognize. She stared hard at the unfamiliar letters, their possible meaning swirling in her mind, laying her hand flat on the stone once more.

Suddenly the inscription wavered, and the words became clear. She blinked in surprise. "May the Source Bless the Friend Who Enters," she whispered to herself. The stone face in front of her immediately dissolved, and she was left standing in front of a black opening in the rock. She chuckled and peered up once more at the strange inscription, but it had vanished.

Lina tentatively placed her hands on the entry walls, bracing herself and placing one foot gingerly inside the opening. She eyed the dark hole warily, stepping through. Immediately the stone face returned behind her, and she was left standing in utter darkness. Her breathing hitched and her heart began to race. Blinking her eyes rapidly, she tried to dispel the oppressive darkness. Panic rose in her throat, and sweat began to bead on her back despite the coolness of the cave. Images of the wolf-man swirled before. What if there was another one of those awful beasts inside? With trembling hands, she reached out and touched the cold rock walls to steady herself.

At her touch, a bluish-purple light began to glow on the rocks around her fingertips. It created a gentle light illuminating the path at her feet. She stepped softly forward, dragging her fingertips along the wall. The light followed her touch, gliding in a trail behind her. She paused, fascinated, and walked her hands up and down the wall, swirling her fingers softly on the cool rock. The light followed her touch, glowing wherever she placed her hand. She moved along warily, scanning for wolf beasts and creating trails of soft light along the walls as she went.

Lina continued along the narrow path, walking for what felt like ages. The trail had angled downward for long enough that she knew she must be deep beneath the surface of the ground. Gradually, the columns of rock around her narrowed, and she had to turn sideways to fit through. Ahead of her was a gap in the rock that was quite small, the sheer darkness continuing past it. She peered at it and grimaced, continuing the sloping descent. She refused to let herself imagine what lay on the other side.

At the end of the tunnel, she examined the opening more closely. It was scarcely big enough to fit her body through. She withdrew an arrow from her quiver, sticking it through the hole in search of the ground. She pushed down, scraping rock with the tip. Thankfully, it was a shallow drop. She placed her bow inside, bracing her hands on the opening's edge and pushing one leg through. Her toes found the ground and she flattened herself, readjusting her arms. She brought the other leg through and made her body as slim as possible, raising her arms over her head. Turning her face sideways, she slid her head through and brought her arms in last.

She stood upright inside the new room, dusting her hands on the front of her dress and replacing her weapon across her back. The darkness of the new space cloaked her as if it had weight, and the air was thin. She reached out her hand in the darkness and touched a rocky shape. Immediately the bluish-purple light appeared under her fingers. This time, it spread from her fingertips in slow winding pathways, covering the entire cavern in a soft glow. She gazed about her in wonder. The cavern extended high above her head. Columns of pointed rock as big as her body hung from the ceiling, and rock formations much taller than her head were situated in clusters about the large room.

In the center of the cavern was a small, round pool of crystal blue water. Its surface was as smooth as glass. It glowed invitingly, and Lina smiled as she made her way down to it. She hadn't had anything to drink since her birthday dinner at Jacques's shop, and she was thirsty. The rock floor at the pool's edge dropped off in a steep bank, and she had to lie flat on her stomach with her head over the water to reach its surface.

Extending her arm down toward the still pool, she cupped some of the glowing water in her palm and brought it to her lips. It was cool and sweet. Refreshing. She smiled and reached to get another palmful. As the back of her hand touched the water, the top of a beautiful woman's head surfaced just to the right. Lina startled, jerking her hand upward, but the woman grasped her forearm and tugged her flat, back onto her stomach. Her long, sharp nails cut into Lina's skin, and she yelped.

The woman lifted herself slightly out of the water, gazing quizzically at Lina's face. There was something wrong with the woman's eyes. They were milky white and almost translucent. Lina could not bear to look at them. The woman opened her full mouth and smiled, turning her head left and right and lifting her nose high to sniff at the air. Her teeth were pointed, white, and terrible. Lina yelped and jerked her arm as the woman tightened her grip, and blood oozed out of Lina's skin. She brought her face close to Lina and sniffed, ruffling the hairs over her ear.

"What have you brought me, young traveler?" she rasped. Lina shut her eyes. She wished she could shut her ears to the horrifying sound of the woman's voice. "You have disturbed my pool. I require payment for slaking your thirst," she hissed.

"P—payment? What payment? I have no coin."

"Coin would do, yesss. But if you have none, you could give me something precious."

Lina thought a moment. She only had one precious thing, something she desperately wanted to keep, but it wasn't as valuable as her life. Silently, she reached her hand into the deep pocket of her dress. Grasping her mother's mirrored compact, she held it out above her head.

"That will do, yes, now dearrr. Only…I do have one other request."

"And then you will let me go?" Lina squeaked.

"Of coursssse. Yesss," she crooned, laughing a hiss. Just look into my eyes so that I may see your lovely face. It has been so long since someone disturbed my pool. I grow weary of only seeing my own reflection."

Lina's eyes were still squeezed shut and her face averted from the awful woman's milky, translucent gaze. She slowly turned her head and was just about to open her eyes when she heard a loud screech behind her and felt something hard knock her to the left. The impact twisted her arm out of the woman's watery grasp and slung the mirrored compact to the cavern floor. "Don't dare look at her! She will drag you to your watery grave!" spoke a chittering female voice.

Lina hit the ground with a hard smack. She grunted, but quickly righted herself and spun to see who had spoken. The woman in the pool slunk backward, frowning as her head disappeared slowly beneath the watery surface. Tiny ripples followed in her wake. Then the pool was once more still and silent.

Lina swiped up her compact and dusted it with the hem of her dress, holding it up to examine for damage in the bluish-purple light. "Wicked Water Wraith," the woman muttered. "Stingy, goading beast. Wants it all for herself, doesn't she?" The face of the woman came into the light, her bulging eyes gazing up at the compact longingly. "Such a pretty treasure," she said warmly. "Would you mind if I…hold it a while?"

She peered out at Lina under a heavy cloak, her bulging eyes questioning under nearly nonexistent brows. She reminded Lina somewhat of a bird. Stiff gray hairs hung raggedly from beneath her hood. Her nose was thin and crooked, and she had very little teeth inside her thin, small lips. Her face was very thin, and her chin came to a small point above her wispy frame. She laced her bony fingers in front of her as she admired the compact, smiling a nearly toothless grin.

Lina held the compact close to her chest. "I…I think I'll just keep it safe in my pocket for now," she said. She dropped it inside the waist of her dress and closed her hand protectively over the fabric. The woman drew her bony fingers back into her cloak and cast her bulging eyes to Lina's hand. She smiled a flat line and returned her gaze to Lina's face. "Let's be off then," the bird-woman chirped. She spun on her heel and hopped off in the opposite direction. Lina followed her, turning a small corner and easing her way through a thin opening in the wall. They were climbing, and there was light up ahead.

As they walked, the bird-woman continuously searched about her feet. She kicked over small stones and bent to inspect objects and coins that had been lost on the path, muttering to herself as she went. She lifted many small, shiny objects and held them to the light, turning them over and over in her bony fingers. Some she pocketed inside her cloak and others she cast aside. By the time they neared the daylight, her pockets were full, jangling with her treasure.

At the end of the passage, three roughhewn steps led up to a small wrought iron gate. The bird-woman climbed the steps nimbly and pushed the gate with her thin hand. It swung outward, creaking on its hinges. She clutched her cloak about her neck and peered her bulging eyes warily outside. Quickly she stepped her spindly legs up onto a cobblestone street. She held the gate open silently and peered back at Lina, jerking her head past the opening. Lina followed her, squinting as she adjusted her eyes from the darkness of the cave to the late afternoon sunlight.

She closed the gate silently behind her. They had come up in the narrow alley, near a bustling village street. The gate was tucked at the end of the alley, behind the corner of a tall, tan, stone building. Lina waited silently behind the bird-woman as she tucked her face farther under her hood of her cloak and tiptoed to the street corner, scanning left and right with eyes that were too large. Lina trailed her feet, holding right to her heels, watching as crowds flowed past their alley, footsteps and indistinct voices filling the air. The woman turned toward her and startled, not expecting Lina to be standing so close. She jerked her head to the right for Lina to follow. Turning, she whipped around the corner of the building, hugging it tightly with her thin frame. She trained her eyes upon the street in front of her, her small body unobtrusive in the busyness of the lane.

Lina had no idea where they were going, but still, she followed her. She had no other choice. She had nearly met her death twice since coming to this side of the gate from her forest clearing, and she certainly didn't want to risk herself a third time. Silently, she stared at the back of the bird-woman's cloak. She hoped she could be trusted. This strange, little woman had saved her from the Water Wraith, after all, so she had no reason to believe otherwise.

CHAPTER 4

Lina could not keep her eyes trained on the bird-woman. This village was much, much different than the one at home. Tan stone buildings rose high above her. Their roofs were steeply slanted, made of metal that had taken on a slate blue hue. Iron doorways large and small dotted the street, and large iron lamps hung above them, lit against the dimming light of evening. Picture windows lined the storefronts, and many swung outward, open to the street. Creatures of all sorts hawked their wares from the open windows and market stands along the lane.

Lina passed a large open window and peered inside. Above it, a sign read "Meallta Meat Market." Inside, a massive, bald, brutish creature with hands as big as her torso was wielding a large axe. He had enormous muscles and wore a bloodstained butcher's apron.

He brought the axe down with a clang and chopped a severed leg on his butcher's block. It appeared to have, at one time, belonged to a large horse. Lina squeezed her eyes shut and averted her gaze, her stomach turning.

A towering baker's cart rolled down the center of the street, stacked high with fragrant rolls and loafs of bread beneath a burlap cover. Its owner shouted his prices to shoppers as he pushed the cart. He was short and sprouted horns from the top of his balding head that curled about his ears. A scraggled beard hung low above his light linen shirt, and furry brown legs peeked out from under it. Little hooves made clacking sounds on the cobblestones as he hurried up the street. Lina gawked at him, and he frowned at her angrily as he passed.

To her left, a street vendor was selling seafood laid out on great chunks of ice. Some of the sea creatures still moved. Their tentacles squirmed and their mouths moved in silent *o*'s. A few of the selections appeared vaguely familiar, and others she could not even begin to recognize. A spiderlike creature with arms as long as Lina sat atop a bed of ice, massive pincers slowly clicking open and closed. A fish with black scales that sparkled in the sunlight peered vacantly at her with one large yellow eye, its mouth full of black fangs. Small, pinkish balls of long, spindly spikes squirmed and sparkled in a crate to the left of the ice stand. A milky white creature nearly as long as the vendor's cart lay on display near the back. Its tentacles curled softly at the ends, and it followed Lina with its large blue eye. Spiky, purplish dots appeared briefly in a line down its body, and then its eye was still, its body gone pale once more.

The vendor made eye contact with her, the cheerful smile on his lips matching the iridescent green eyes glittering behind long, dark lashes. His hair was long, and it was tied in a braid down his back. The hairline above his pointy ears was dotted faintly with pale-blue and green scales. His shirt collar came up high about his neck. He nodded and turned back to speak to a customer with broad, iridescent wings, exposing three small slits in the skin just behind his right ear. Reaching for a fish, he wrapped it in parchment while the customer dug out a copper coin.

The bird-woman had turned a corner up ahead. Lina hurried to catch her. She wove in and out of the thoroughfare, dodging throngs of women, men, and strange beasts great and small before turning to the right. This street was narrow and less busy, but it was darker, overshadowed by the sloping roofs overhead. The end of the street was blocked by stone walls. Lina looked above her at the second-story windows.

Ornate iron balconies protruded from the stone, and gauzy curtains billowed outward from the frames into the shadowed street. Beautiful women sat on the balconies, their long, shapely legs dangling between the bars. They were scantily dressed in clothing that cut high on their legs and low at their chests. The red-haired woman nearest to her was singing a sultry melody that drifted down to the street below. A man with pointed ears and shopping bags stood there, gazing up at her. She smiled seductively in his direction, swinging her feet.

The woman pulled her legs through the iron railings and stood on her toes, all the while continuing her song. The man dropped his shopping bags, in awe as he stared up at her with arms limp at his sides. She turned her back to the street and shuddered, unfurling four delicate, translucent wings. Looking over her shoulder, she smiled provocatively, lifting her toes off the balcony and floating down to the street on her iridescent, dragonfly wings.

She lifted him by his shirt collar, his feet leaving the ground. Planting a kiss on his lips, she whisked him up and into her window, the curtains billowing outward in the breeze. Lina watched as his clothing was tossed from the railing. Coins and keys from his pockets clattered onto the cobblestone street.

When the bird-woman heard the coins dropping onto the cobblestones, she turned back, her large eyes trained on the sound. She hurried to the spot on her spindly legs, stooping to gather the man's clothing and shopping bags in her arms. Swiping the ground, she placed his pocket items into her basket and stood. Eyeing Lina for a long moment, she jerked her head in the direction of the small door. Lina followed her there silently, being careful not to look up at the balconies as she passed. As she opened the small door, the man screamed in terror from the second-floor window.

Lina shut the door soundly, pressing her back against it and blowing out a breath. Her heart thrummed in her chest as the man's scream echoed in her ears. She wondered what had happened to him. Whatever it was, it wasn't good.

The bird-woman went to the kitchen table, lighting a lamp. The flame had barely had time to flicker before she dumped the unfortunate man's personal items onto the already crowded table. She held each item aloft, turning it over and over in her bony fingers. Muttering to herself, she examined them all closely in the firelight. She scooped the man's coins up in her hand and held them to her ear, jingling them softly and smiling a wide toothless grin. Then she laid all the items in a neat row on the table. One by one, she began sorting them into various areas about the room. She stuffed her new treasures inside vases, tucked them in shoes, and buried them between faded chair cushions. Some pieces she set lovingly on a small table by the overstuffed chair in the corner of the room, touching them softly and muttering with delight. Standing, she laced her bony fingers, admiring her treasures.

Lina scanned the room in amazement, spinning to take it all in. It was jammed floor to ceiling with every imaginable item. Large and small vases, wheels, vendor carts, men's and women's clothing, hats, shoes of all sizes, chipped dishes, plates, cups, cutlery, jewelry, paintings, and various broken and patched-up furniture items were stacked from floor to ceiling, tucked away in corners, and hung on pegs from the walls. Pots and pans, dried flowers, sparkling baubles, and fragments of sea glass hung in glittering rows from thin cords attached to the low ceiling.

Presently, the bird-woman seemed to remember her presence. She spun, fixing Lina under her large, bulging eyes. "Come, now, dear. You must be tired. Let's get you to the back room," she chirped. She eyed Lina's tattered dress and matted hair. "I've a washing tub. I'll lay out some blankets for a cot by the hearth and bring you some clean clothes."

"Thank you," said Lina, finally allowing her exhaustion to set in. The woman ushered her past a heavy, patched curtain that separated the front and back rooms. As the woman gathered water from a pump behind her house and heated it on the hearth, Lina sank onto the chair by the washing tub, placing her quiver and bow at her feet. She laid her head back on the chair and closed her eyes.

Suddenly, she was back in Jacques's workshop. They had just finished the rabbit stew, and the fire was warming her feet. He was laughing about something, his head thrown back and his smile wide. He brushed his fingers through his hair and sat up, gazing at her. The look of longing in his face gripped at her heart. She wanted to comfort him, to wrap him in her arms.

The image swirled, and she was back in the forest clearing. Her breath came out hard and fast, curling like smoke in the air. Remus lay limply at her knees, and she scraped her fingernails against the cold ground. A low growl threatened from in front of her, and she stood, watching as the wolf beast stalked her, turning her around and around in the clearing. His pointed teeth dripped thick black blood and his glittering eyes narrowed as he growled from deep in his chest. In her mind, his voice rasped, "You'll never escape," but it was the voice of the horrid Water Wraith. Her heart leapt into her throat as he lunged for her neck, and a moment before he struck, she jumped to one side, drawing an arrow back and letting it fly.

The arrow stuck squarely in his chest. The light left his eyes, and his snarling jaw went slack as she ripped out the arrow and his body fell. Soot singed her nostrils as his carcass disintegrated into ashes before her. She watched the ash blow up in the breeze, and she stuck out her fingers, touching a slip of it. She rubbed it to dust between her thumb and forefinger.

The image flipped, and she heard another growl, softer this time, a gentle rumble. When she lifted her eyes, a very large but ordinary gray wolf stood where the wolf beast had been. He was as tall as her chin. Her body stiffened, and she froze. She fumbled to reload her arrow, but the wolf bowed low to the ground, tucking his nose beneath his paws. He whined, and she furrowed her brow, lowering her arrow and bending to pat his head. He rolled in response, and she chuckled, scratching the pink skin on his furry stomach.

Clattering dishes woke her out of her sleep. She sat up quickly, rubbing her eyes. Her bath was drawn, and steam curled toward the ceiling from the surface of the water. Fresh clothing sat on the chair opposite her, and a gilded comb lay by a round bar of soap atop a fluffy towel. The bird-woman bustled about the room, gathering various dried herbs, a chipped blue cup, and a saucer.

She tossed several of the herbs into a bowl and ground them to a fine powder. They had a bitter smell that singed Lina's nose. She took the mixture to the pot above the hearth and poured it in. Muttering softly to herself, she stirred it with a large wooden spoon. The aroma from the mixture filled the room with an irresistible flavor. The bird-woman ladled some of it into the chipped blue china cup, then she moved into the back room, passing it to Lina.

Lina inhaled, savoring the sweet-smelling elixir. Her nose filled with its heady scent. She blew across the cup and tasted a small sip with the tip of her tongue. It was delicious, yet unlike anything she had ever tasted. She sipped more heavily, pulling gulps down into her empty stomach. When the strange concoction was gone, she was sorry and lifted her cup for more. The bird-woman smiled toothlessly, ladling another full cup from the iron pot above the fire and placing it into her hand. She drank it quickly, enjoying the full feeling in her belly. She raised her arms over her head, stretching, and sighed. Her limbs felt strangely heavy, yet she felt better than she had in a long while.

The woman disappeared behind the curtain, and Lina began to strip off her tattered dress. She laid it on the chair opposite her and reached into her pocket for the compact. She placed it gently on top of her dress. She bent, pulling off her patched boots, and lifted her leg into the bathtub.

The water felt heavenly. She held her breath and ducked her head under. Resurfacing, she sighed, wiping her eyes with her fingertips. Grabbing the soap, she rubbed it between her hands. It had a lovely lavender and lemon scent. She scrubbed her hair and body, slaking water over her head with her hands. When she felt clean, she lifted from the tub and wrapped herself in the cozy towel. As she stepped to the floor, she tripped over the edge of the chair and stumbled, bracing her hand against the washtub. Her head was beginning to feel dizzy, the exhaustion from the day catching up to her.

She laid the towel over the side of the tub and picked up the clean clothes. The bird-woman had left plain cream underclothes and a dress of dark green with sleeves that stopped just below her elbows and a hem that fell to her ankles. Warm, gray woolen socks and a new pair of brown leather boots sat on the floor beside them. She tugged the socks over her aching feet and set the boots aside.

She emerged from the back room to find the woman sitting in the overstuffed armchair. She was holding up coins and sparkling baubles to the firelight and muttering to herself. Chuckling quietly, she held a shiny silver pendant aloft. Lina watched her curiously then went to lie on the pallet in front of the hearth. Exhaustion was weighing heavily on her limbs, and her head had begun to swim. She had scarcely lain down under the warm blankets before sleep pulled her under and she was floating in a peaceful white light that bathed her in soft silence.

She awoke the next morning to the muttering bird-woman stirring the pot above the hearth. Lina's stomach grumbled, and she pushed herself upright, scratching the side of her head. The bird-woman smiled warmly with her toothless lips as she handed her the chipped blue cup, and Lina readily accepted the elixir. She drank deeply, savoring the heady scent and delicious flavor. When the cup was empty, she stood, looking about her uncertainly. Her surroundings were unfamiliar. She frowned, watching as the bird-woman bustled about the room, tucking coins and jewelry from one vase to another and rearranging her treasures in new piles. Lina narrowed her eyes. She had no idea who the woman was. She could not recall having seen her before. Her head throbbed, and she touched the spot, massaging the middle of her brow. Absently, she tapped the pocket of her green dress. She froze. She was missing something, but she couldn't remember what.

She stood, scanning the floor about her. The bird-woman lingered in the front corner of the room, rearranging the items on her small table by the overstuffed chair. Lina watched her bony fingers as she lifted her treasures from one pile to another. Just then, she held up a gilded, mirrored compact, muttering to herself.

Suddenly Lina remembered what she was missing. "Hey!" she shouted. "That belongs to me!" She marched over and snatched the compact from the woman's bony grasp, dropping it safely into her deep dress pocket. The woman spun quickly on her spindly legs, facing Lina. Her bulging eyes were furious. Her small frame began to tremble, and she brought her skinny fingers up to encircle Lina's throat. Lina jerked backward, falling through and ripping the curtain separating the front and back rooms. She landed on her bottom beside the tub, the bird-woman lunging over her. Lina snatched an arrow from the quiver beside the chair and swung it up at her, but the bird-woman was too fast. She ducked and brought her foot up to swat Lina's hand, knocking the arrow out of her grasp. Lina rolled to her feet, grabbing her bow and slinging the quiver over her back. She swiftly loaded and stretched the bow taut, aiming her weapon at the woman's bony throat. The angular bulge in her neck bobbed, and she raised her arms, panting through thin lips. Lina kept the arrow trained on her as she backed into the front room. The bird-woman blinked her bulging eyes and nodded once, dropping her arms. Then she turned and began to rearrange the treasures on her table, muttering again in singsong to herself. Lina lowered her bow, dropping the arrow into her quiver.

She sat down heavily onto the nearest chair. The room was beginning to spin, again. She bent forward, bracing her head in her palms. She couldn't remember why she had gotten into a fight with the bird-woman or even how she had come to be in this room in the first place. Her limbs were growing heavy, and her head ached for sleep. She laid it back onto the chair, closing her eyes.

She wasn't sure how long she had sat sleeping in the chair, but when she opened her eyes, it was twilight. She looked about her and furrowed her brow. She had no memory of this place. Brown leather boots sat at her feet. She rubbed her head and stared, reaching for the boots and lacing them up her ankles. She moved to the wall, where a chipped mirror sat above a small, ornate vanity. She combed her hair and plaited it in a knot at the base of her neck.

Just then, a birdlike woman appeared in the doorway of the small room. A hood was pulled low over her head, and she smiled toothlessly at Lina under her hooked nose, peering with bulging eyes. She extended a bony hand to Lina, and Lina took it, allowing her body to be lifted from the vanity seat. Her legs felt unsteady, and she stumbled behind the woman as they left the cramped house and made their way into the street.

It was eerily quiet as they wove their way through the towering stone buildings. Lina was tired, and it seemed to her that they had walked for a very long way. A variety of creatures, some with hooves or horns, some beautiful men and women with pointed ears, scales, and sometimes wings, walked silently in the same direction. Lina tried not to stare at them, but she had never seen such creatures before.

They turned one last corner and finally came to a large dead end where a makeshift platform had been erected with strips of wood. A pale man with dark hair and eyes stood in fine black clothing at the podium. He scanned the crowd with his shrewd gaze, but strangely, he never moved the rest of his body. Lina drew back when she saw the two creatures standing below him. Large beasts with wolfish heads and human torsos guarded the street in front of the podium. They bared their black fangs at the townspeople, and their glittering eyes scanned the crowd for disturbance. She felt like she had seen something like them before, but she couldn't remember where.

The bird-woman jerked Lina's arm and they wound through the crowd until they were standing near the front, at the left of the makeshift platform. Lina cowered from the wolf beasts, trying to hide among the townsfolk. She managed to wedge herself behind the tall back of a beautiful woman with long dark hair and the body of a large horse.

The speaker placed a roll of parchment on the podium as he began to speak. "The Court of Orm will now begin trial for this cycle's Second Quarter. Will the accused now stand?" His silken voice dripped with boredom, and his body stayed eerily still. Only his mouth and eyes moved, scanning the crowd.

Two great brutish men, with bald, bare bodies down to their waists, carried a kicking woman with delicate dragonfly wings to the stage. As they moved, their large, bare feet shook the platform under their heavy weight. They were giants. Huge. Terrifying. The woman yelled as she writhed and kicked in their grasp, tossing her red hair back from her pointed ears. Despite her thrashing, she couldn't shake the grip of their massive hands. Lina frowned. She had seen the red-haired woman with wings somewhere before.

The giants held her fast at the center of the platform, just to the right of the podium. The speaker never looked at her. He simply gazed down at the podium from his frozen face and read from the parchment. "The Court of Orm finds you guilty of the crime thus committed: theft. You are sentenced to pay the debt you owe. A life stolen requires a life in its place." His lips stopped moving, and he looked up from the parchment, his face a mask. "The court will hear the next accused," he said flatly.

"Nooo!" the winged woman screamed. She lifted her legs and kicked, pumping her arms and twisting to escape the giants' grasp. One of the giants reached his massive hand to her back, ripping the delicate wings from her frame. Blood spurted from the spot, and she screamed in agony. Her knees buckled as the giant tossed the severed wings onto the platform. Then they dragged her away, her feet scraping against the floor. Her head was thrown back, red hair draping her bloody wounds as tears streaked down her lovely face.

The bird-woman tugged on Lina's arm, guiding her out of the crowd and up onto the platform. Lina's head still felt fuzzy, and her vision was hazy around the edges. She stumbled along behind her. The bloody wings lay in a pool at her feet. Iron and copper tinged her nose, and she swallowed convulsively, averting her eyes from them. The speaker's voice was muffled as he read from his parchment. She blinked and shook her head, attempting to clear the haziness. The speaker was still droning, but she couldn't understand his words. The bird-woman held tightly to her arm, muttering and peering about with her too-large eyes. The crowd was beginning to spin, and Lina wished she could lie down. She didn't understand why the bird-woman was holding her arm. She wished she would let her at least sit. She was growing too tired to stand for much longer.

The speaker stopped talking and the bird-woman shuffled her forward. The speaker did not look at her and began droning on again. His voice echoed in her ears. Her legs felt heavy, and her vision tunneled. She stumbled forward, nearly falling into the pool of the winged woman's blood.

Just then, a disturbance broke out in the crowd to the right of the stage. A tall, dark-haired man with a large double-edged sword broke through the front of the throng and pointed his blade at the wolf-men. His heavy cloak was pulled low over his face. No one in the crowd moved to stop him. The wolf-men lunged at his neck, but he deftly stepped around them, slashing with his sword, neatly severing one's head. The other turned and leapt over the felled body, a mouthful of dark fangs open. Before the beast could find his mark, the man spun, bringing his blade down and through the shoulder of the beast. He roared and fell flat to the ground, one clawed hand slashing wildly at the air. The cloaked man lifted his sword, jamming it heavily into the creature's chest and rendering him limp and silent. He pulled out the blade, wiping the black blood, and replaced it at his waist.

Hopping lithely onto the platform, he swept Lina out of the bird-woman's grasp. The bird-woman screeched and clawed at him with her bony fingers, but he ignored her, shrugging her hands away. He hopped off the platform, curling Lina into his cloak and weaving his way quickly through the crowd below. The crowd parted for him to pass. Lina looked back at the platform over his shoulder. The screeching bird-woman was being escorted from the stage in the hands of the giants, her bony legs kicking the air.

As she passed the speaker, he spun rapidly, almost faster than Lina could see. He hinged his jaw wide open, placing his still, pale hands on the bird-woman's shoulders. Time seemed to slow as the bird-woman followed his slow movements, his unnaturally large jaws clamping around her scrawny neck. Her eyes rolled backward, and her body went limp as her face sank inward and the folds of her skin sagged against her bony frame. The speaker removed himself from her neck, returning to stand still at the podium. The giant threw the bird-woman over his shoulder, her thin gray head bouncing against his back. Teeth marks were at her throat, and crimson blood trickled from the wound.

Chapter 5

The tall, cloaked man carried her swiftly, his feet moving silently on the stones. He spun around the corner, pressing his back flat against a closed storefront. Night was closing in, and the windows were all shut tight. No street vendors remained, and everyone else was still at the platform. He jerked his chin, scanning the streets. Lina's head lolled against his chest as he took off to the right, turning two more corners before backing into a narrow alcove. There, waiting for him, was a large white horse.

The horse's back was three heads taller than Lina. The man slung her astride and came to sit behind her, bracing his forearm tightly across her abdomen. Lina lurched forward in her haze, her dress sliding past her knee. She swiftly brushed it down, thankful for the cover of the gathering darkness.

"Hold on," he commanded, his voice gruff. He gripped one fist in the horse's mane and clucked to him softly. The horse pricked his ears, lifting his neck. Lina looked about her for something to hold. There was no saddle or bridle. Instead, she knotted her fists into the horse's long gray mane. She tightened her thighs on his flank, hopeful she could stay upright in her addled state.

The takeoff was so swift that Lina lost her grip and was certain she would topple to the ground. She slid sideways on the horse's back, but the man held her fast about her middle, and she kept her seat. She grunted as he flung her back against him, her head spinning.

They raced down the cobblestone streets, and the wind pricked her eyes, forming tears at their edges. Strangely, the horse's hooves made no sound. Lina tucked her neck and pressed backward, her fingernails biting into her palms as she gripped the horse's mane. She had never gone so fast in her life. The man adjusted his grip and pulled her tighter against him, his warm breath tickling the top of her ear.

The man gripped the horse's mane lightly, and he didn't appear to be guiding him. Wherever they were headed, the animal knew the way. He galloped down the streets at an alarming speed, making hairpin curves around the corners of stone buildings with little effort. Lina was already disoriented, and all the turning only worsened matters. She peered past the horse's ears in confusion, unsure which direction they were going. She only hoped they were headed away from the horrifying speaker on the platform.

Suddenly they burst past the edges of the stone buildings. Before them, the road extended toward a wide stone arch in the city wall. Beneath the arch was an enormous wrought iron gate, its bars tightly shut. The horse galloped at blinding speed directly toward it. Panic bit at Lina's neck as she eyed the approaching gate. Sentries stood on both sides of it, but they stared straight ahead and did not move to open it.

They were only about five strides away from the gate now. There was no way they could clear it. The iron bars were narrow and too small for them to pass. Lina shut her eyes and turned her face into the man's shoulder, her breath coming in short bursts. She was sure they would make impact at any moment. This would be her fourth brush with death on this side of the gate. This time, she was sure she was going to meet it.

The man clucked softly to the horse as they galloped headlong, and Lina heard a faint rustling sound by her knees. Almost immediately, a warm rhythmic wind began fanning the side of her face. Instead of ramming into the gate, Lina felt herself lifting off the ground. She popped her eyes open and gasped. The massive horse had grown two large wings that sprouted just in front of her thighs. His dappled feathers pumped powerfully, carrying them easily up and over the high gate and into the landscape beyond.

He glided swiftly above the ground, high above the trees. Lina was terrified, much of her stupor cast off, as if caught by the wind. She dared a glance past her boots. She couldn't see much in the gathering darkness, but the abyss below her spoke of a great distance. Her vision tunneled, and she snapped her head upright, squeezing her eyes shut. She pushed the back of her head tightly against the man's chest, pressing against his cloak. He grunted, tightening his grip on her waist. Lina didn't know which death was worse: ramming at top speed into an iron gate or falling to the ground from a delirious height.

They soared through the twilight, until the bright moonglow bathed their backs in silver light. The horse's movements were smooth, and Lina began to relax, letting her head rest against the tall man's chest. Suddenly, without warning, the horse swooped toward the ground. Lina's heart jumped into her throat, and her breath stuck behind it. Her eyes widened, and she let out a little yelp as the horse tucked his wings and soared downward at a sickening angle. "Quiet," the man ordered. She obeyed and snapped her mouth closed, tightly squeezing the muscles in her belly and thighs.

With more grace than any creature that size seemed capable of, the great horse touched down, tucking his wings tightly against his body. Silently, he trotted through the tall grasses of a meadow. The only sound was the whispering of the grass against his sides as they passed. Slowing to a walk, he led his riders to the edge of the clearing and into the cover of trees.

The horse stopped and shook his mane then gazed back at his riders. The man dismounted first and then held his hands up to Lina. She glanced at the ground, judging the distance. It was too high, and her muscles still felt weak and heavy. Reluctantly, she braced her arms on the man's shoulders. She was at his mercy. He tucked his large hands around her narrow waist and lifted her easily, setting her softly on the ground at his feet. She gazed shyly up at him, and he peered down at her with hard, dark eyes. He was much taller than she had first thought. The top of her head barely reached his chest.

Flustered by the closeness and contact, Lina stepped backward, stumbling, and bumped into the horse's flank. He nickered and nudged her with his nose. "Sorry," Lina muttered. She looked after him weakly, watching as he walked a few paces ahead of her. He dipped his head for a drink in a small stream, and Lina crossed her arms over herself, eyeing him curiously. The horse's wings had vanished. If he hadn't been so large, he would've looked almost like any other white horse. He swished his gray tail, pawing for fallen nuts on the ground.

The man had already begun to set up a camp. His linen shirt was rolled to the elbows, and he had removed his cloak, hanging it on a tree branch behind him. He stooped, gathering several small sticks and dried underbrush, forming them into a pile. He faced the pile and stuck his palm toward it, then rolled his fingers in on themselves as he twisted his palm toward his face. To Lina's surprise, a small golden spark appeared in the center of the pile. The underbrush quickly caught, and soon, he stood before a crackling fire.

He brushed his hands on his thighs and reached to take off a leather pack from across his back. Crouching to the ground, he unwound the leather straps and began lifting items from it. Though the pack was quite small, he removed a large bedroll, a lantern, a cooking pot, a metal trivet, a wooden bowl and spoon, a metal cup, some dried herbs, coffee beans, nuts, berries, root vegetables, and strips of dried meat.

Lina stood watching him, mesmerized. She was certain there was nothing else inside. Reaching his hand deeply into the bottom of the pack, he pulled out a large piece of folded canvas and several wooden posts. Lina raised her brows in amazement.

He gathered the canvas and posts into his arms and stood, tossing them up into the air. The cloth swirled outward, making a large circular shape, and the posts took positions in the center and on the edge of it, forming a large circular shelter. The shelter floated softly to the ground as Lina looked on. Wordlessly, the man pulled back the door flap and tucked the bedroll and lantern inside. Then he let the flap fall and turned to the fire.

He dusted his hands and picked up the cooking pot, walking to the stream. He filled it with fresh water and hauled it back to the fire. He hung the pot over the flames, dropping in various herbs. Then he took a small blade from his side and set to work chopping vegetables. He added these to the pot and stirred. The simple stew smelled delicious. Lina's stomach grumbled, and she tucked her hand over it self-consciously. She hoped the man hadn't heard.

She hugged her shoulders, shivering. The night air was cool, and the green dress under her cloak was thin. Despite herself, she inched closer to the fire, inhaling. The food smelled heavenly. The man did not acknowledge her and continued to stir the pot. Without a word, he stood, walking to the far side of the camp and retrieving a small log. He carried it back to the fire and lowered it at Lina's feet, then crouched again over the fire, stirring the pot. Lina stepped around it gingerly. "Thank you," she said quietly. Her voice sounded strange in her own ears. Hollow and too high. She swallowed, clearing her throat nervously.

The man didn't answer her. Wordlessly, he ladled some of the soup into a bowl and handed it to her. She dipped the spoon and brought it to her lips hungrily. The root vegetables were soft and sweet, and the herbs gave the broth a light nutty flavor. She savored it, swallowing the last sip before passing her empty bowl back to him. He took it from her silently and filled it for himself, downing it quickly. He refilled the bowl once more and held it out to her, but she shook her head. He shrugged, craning his head back as he swallowed the last bite. Then he reclined on his side, staring into the firelight in silence.

From her perch on the log, Lina covertly examined his profile. His dark hair fell in waves to sharp cheekbones, which planed downward to his masculine jaw. It needed a shave. A shadow of a beard grew over it, like he had spent many days on the road. Thick, dark brows knit together on his forehead. They bore much worry and grief. Dark almond eyes pierced the firelight, turning up slightly at their edges. His straight nose perched over a full mouth, which was set in a hard line. Lina pressed her own lips flat, examining his neck. A healed scar ran from his right earlobe to his collarbone, and his ears were ever-so-slightly pointed at the tip.

He adjusted his weight and crossed his ankles, glancing up at her briefly. Her heart leapt into her throat. Quickly, she dropped her eyes, pretending to stare at a spot on her boot. When he looked away, she peeked up at him again under her long lashes. His frame looked much different than Jacques' broad, disheveled one. His light linen shirt fell open at the neck and was rolled crisply to the elbows. The lithe muscles of his chest and arms were strong and powerful beneath it. Light brown riding pants were belted at his slim waist, and he wore dark leather riding boots that laced up to his knee.

She cleared her throat quietly, shuffling her weight on the log. He glanced at her then flicked his eyes back to the fire. She sucked in a breath. "Where are we?" she croaked. She coughed, clearing her throat again. The delirium in her head and weakness in her muscles were beginning to dissipate, but she still felt disoriented and fatigued.

"Halfway to the West Mountains. Many lengths from the city of Meallta," he grunted. Lina nodded mutely. She pressed her lips, thinking.

"What if someone follows us?" she asked.

"They won't. The townspeople don't care to, and the others won't know where to look. Bayard knows all the best hiding places." He smirked, jerking his chin in the large horse's direction. The beast lifted his head, pricking his ears at his name. He chuffed then resumed munching at the ground. The man gazed back at her. "You're safe with me, for the moment."

It was the most she had heard him speak. She digested his words, curious. "What's your name?" she asked, studying the side of his face.

He paused, biting the inside of his lip as he studied his hands. "Arturo," he answered. He peered sideways at her. "What's yours?"

"Lina," she answered softly, looking at her feet.

He nodded mutely, and they returned their eyes to the firelight, sitting again in silence.

Arturo sat up onto his palms and gestured behind him to the tent. "You sleep there," he said gruffly. Without another word, he retrieved his cloak and lay down beside the fire. He rolled the leather pack up into a ball and placed it behind his head. Taking his sword from his waist, he laid it beside him, covering himself with his cloak. Then he stuck out one arm and laid his sword over his body, blade toward his feet. He sighed, closing his eyes.

Lina stood and made her way uncertainly to the flap of the tent, casting glances at Arturo's long frame. He never moved. In fact, his breathing was already even.

She lifted the canvas and gasped, stepping in and letting it fall behind her. The lantern now hung from the center of the room, bathing the shelter in soft light. It glowed against the ceiling, which was made of one large tapestry gathered in the middle. The tapestry was beautiful, and Lina craned her head to look at it. Stars made of silver satin were sewn into the deep blue fabric, and they twinkled and glowed in the firelight. Woven into the edges of the tapestry were images of great green trees and majestic mountains. Bronze winged beasts hovered in the sky above them.

The room was much larger than she had anticipated. A partition was rolled up in the center making the circular tent into one large room. Colorful, plush woven carpets lined the floor. Lina bent and unlaced her leather boots, setting them by the door. She took a few steps and wriggled her stockinged feet into the carpet, sighing with delight. She had never felt anything so soft. It felt much different than the threadbare rug at the end of her bed at home. She turned herself in a circle, smiling.

Everything in her stopped, even her breath and mind catching, when she saw a stone hearth roaring a warm fire on the west side of the room, and a large clawfoot bathing tub sitting before it. Lavender-scented water filled it almost to the brim, steam curling up toward the ceiling. A thick bath towel and scented soaps sat on a low stool beside it. Two armchairs upholstered in thick, deep green fabric sat to the right of the tub in the middle of the room. A small, reddish wooden table with rolled feet perched between them.

A large, four-post bed sat along one side of the tent. Gauzy curtains draped over it, and several overstuffed satin pillows were arranged at the head. The bedroll Arturo had pulled from the pack sat atop the thick mattress, but it was deep, plush, purple satin and much larger than it had looked before. A soft nightgown was laid carefully atop the bedroll. Its light blue threads sparkled in the firelight. Lina moved towards it. She gasped in delight as she examined the nightgown, grazing her fingers gently along the fabric. It was as soft as downy feathers and almost too fine to wear.

She sat on the plush mattress and peeled off her stockings then stood, untying the stays at the back of her dress. She let it fall to the floor and walked to the clawfoot tub, savoring the feel of the plush carpets between her toes. She eased herself into the water, laying her head back against the tub. She was exhausted. The roaring warmth of the fire, her full belly, and the delicious steaming water nearly lulled her to sleep, but the idea of wearing the blue nightgown and climbing into the cozy bed was too delicious to pass up, and she coaxed herself awake.

As she scrubbed her body clean with vanilla-scented soap, she reflected on the events she had experienced in Meallta. Her thoughts were becoming less hazy, and her memory was beginning to return. She was tired, but the heavy, weak feeling in her limbs was greatly improved. She frowned. It seemed that her confusion and weakness had occurred after she had drunk the bird-woman's elixir. It had tasted delicious and filled her empty stomach, but now that she considered it, her thoughts had become muddled after the drink, and her dreams had been jumbled and frightful.

Memory of the trial was coming back to her now. The raised platform. The speaker. The giants. The bloody wings. There had been a woman in the crowd with the lower body of a painted horse and long, straight, black hair, a thin rope of leather tied around her forehead. Her beautiful, bronzed face had been pulled in anguish as she stared at the platform, and her hands were balled into fists.

Lina remembered the bird-woman coaxing her to the platform. She had stumbled willingly, her mind and body too weak to resist. The crowd had made no sound as she mounted the stage, and the pale, still speaker kept his hard eyes trained on the parchment. His muffled voice echoed back to her now. *The court will hear the next accused.* She had been trying to keep her eyes off the red-haired woman's limp, bloody wings at her feet. The smell of her pooled blood was overpowering. It turned her stomach. *The citizen Havrah Alkonost accuses the young traveler of theft of her goods: one gilded, mirrored compact.* Lina remembered the bird-woman's bony fingers reaching into the pocket of her dress, attempting to pull out the compact as proof. She had gripped the woman's forearm weakly, wrestling the compact out of her grasp. Surely the woman had intended to keep the treasure for her own and rid herself of its owner.

The speaker had continued. *The Court of Orm thus finds the young traveler guilty as charged. The court will now hear the next accu…* She had been passed toward the giant, his massive hand reaching for her shoulder. There had been blood caked around his fingernails. Her legs had given way just as Arturo had pushed his way through the crowd. She had watched with blurring vision as the wolf beasts had lunged. Arturo had moved with impossible speed, slashing and spilling their dark blood onto the stones.

She shut her eyes as another memory surfaced. She was standing in the forest clearing, and the great wolf's hot breath spewed on her face. His glittering eyes glared at her as he lunged at her throat with his snapping black teeth. She had fired her arrow, hitting his chest, and then she had fallen through the gate. She frowned. It seemed so long ago. Unlike the lingering nights and shortened days of home, the days on this side of the gate moved slowly, and the sun hovered in the sky. Here, on this side of the gate, time seemed to stretch out.

She lifted herself from the tub, wrapping her clean skin in the fluffy towel. Padding to the bed, she lifted the light blue nightgown, slipping it over her head. She smoothed the front, savoring the feeling of her skin against the soft fabric. Toweling her hair, she searched about for some underclothes.

She spied a large trunk in the corner. Kneeling before it, she lifted the heavy wooden lid. Inside she found several day dresses, a spare nightgown and robe, a collection of shoes, and several pairs of delicate lace underthings. She grabbed one pair, slipping them on beneath her dress as her face flushed crimson. She hoped Arturo hadn't packed the contents of the trunk.

Standing, she went to a long, gilded mirror, which was situated next to a crystal washbasin. She picked up a brush and worked out the long tangles of her golden hair until it lay in a smooth stream down her back. She wound it into a tight plait and twisted this around her head, securing it with pins. Standing back, she examined herself in the long mirror, smoothing the sleeves of the blue nightgown. She touched the delicate fabric around her middle, gliding her hands over her hips. Her already slim body was slimmer than it had been a few days ago, and her face was somewhat gaunt. And no wonder. She had barely eaten since she had passed through the gate, and she had been fighting for her life since the first moment she arrived.

She ignored her reflection and pulled out her skirt, spinning. The gauzy fabric floated delicately above her ankles. She grinned down at it. She'd never worn anything so fine.

The spinning made her dizzy, and she grabbed the bedpost, leaning her forehead against it. Sweat beaded her upper lip. Not so recovered after all. She chuckled to herself and lifted her tired body onto the plush mattress. Lying back, she breathed in deeply, exhaling a heavy sigh. The bed felt wonderful, nothing like her thin mattress at home. This mattress was thick and cozy, and her body sank down into it. She snuggled under the purple coverlet, flexing her feet. The silky fabric felt delicious against her skin.

No sooner had she settled than her lids began to get heavy. Her mind was still and calm, despite her recent terrors. Briefly she felt sorry for Arturo, who slept outside by the fire. She listened for his movement, but she heard no sound and thought he must have long fallen asleep. Settling back onto the pillows, she relaxed, allowing the sweet ache of fatigue to pull her under.

Sometime in the night, she heard Bayard's soft nicker at the side of her tent. She sat up onto her elbows and listened. He whinnied nervously, chuffing air out his nostrils. Arturo shushed the animal, speaking to him in soft tones. His sword made a *chink* sound as it brushed the fabric of his cloak, and he drew it upright.

Suddenly the tent and its contents involuted, and she was left lying on the plain bedroll between Arturo and the fire. Her head spun, and a scream built in her throat, but Arturo brought his left hand over her mouth, tamping it shut before she could make a sound. She blinked up at his sharp eyes, hovering inches from her own. His dark hair hung about his face like a curtain, partially shading it from the firelight. "Be still, and make no sound," he commanded in a gruff whisper. "Close your mind to their words." Lina blinked twice, and he lifted his hand, holding his finger to his lips. He waved his palm flat over the fire, and it immediately quenched without a trace of smoke. Tossing his cloak over her, he covered her head and tucked her braid out of sight.

Lina lay under the cloak silently and as still as a stone. Arturo moved into a crouch beside her. His knees touched her back, pressing. His breathing was heavy, coming hard and fast. She could tell by the sound it made that he was turning his head, scanning the forest. He twisted his knees, gazing behind him, and she felt the cool metal hilt of the sword resting on her hip. Panic rose in her chest, but she tamped it down. Something was about to happen. Something bad.

Absolute silence cloaked the forest. Even the stream could not be heard. The air felt heavy and thick, and the tree branches folded inward, encasing them in palpable darkness. Lina held her breath. An intense fear gripped her chest, and her heart began to pound. Her breath came in short bursts, and her body began to tremble. She clamped her hand over her mouth, sure she would scream. Arturo placed his free hand on her upper arm, squeezing it slightly. She focused on his palm, breathing in through her nose and out through her mouth.

All at once, Lina heard them. Whispers in the dark. Long, low, weaving tones that buzzed her ears. Her skin prickled with the sound. She squeezed her eyes closed and concentrated on shutting the voices out of her mind, like Arturo had said. Arturo crouched beside her, tucking his face close to her ear. The whispers came from all directions, moving over, behind, and beside them. Swirling in circles. They hovered over the cloak, hissing low, winding words. She focused, careful to keep the doors of her mind tightly shut. Bayard chuffed, and the whispers turned, pausing a moment in his direction. Then they began speaking again, moving over Arturo and Lina in the darkness. One by one, the whispers drifted deeper into the forest. With their passing, the palpable darkness lifted, and the forest resumed its natural sounds.

At last, Arturo's hand relaxed on her shoulder. He sat back hard onto the ground, lighting the fire with his hand. "They're gone," he said as he sighed. Lina uncovered her head, sitting up furtively onto her palms. Bayard stood at attention near the stream, his gray tail swishing at his legs. He flicked his ears, then lowered his head to nibble at the ground.

"What were they?" she asked. He laced his fingers through his hair, brushing it back from his face.

"The Mumla," he answered. He brought his arms around, bracing his knees. "Whispers of the forest. Three foul female spirits who were once alive but now are long dead. The Histories say they were once beautiful, cunning women who pledged themselves to the Court of Orm in exchange for their Immortality. But he tricked them. Instead of keeping their beautiful physical forms, he encased them in darkness, where only their minds and voices remain. The three roam the forest at night, searching for willing travelers. If they sense an open mind, they will murmur lies into your ear, luring you to your death. Many travelers have stepped willingly from rocky cliffs and drowned themselves in forest streams, overcome by their deception. Usually, they travel deep within the North Forest, which is why we chose to avoid it. We thought this small grove of trees would be safe. Or Bayard did." He smirked in the horse's direction. Bayard nickered and flicked his ears but never lifted his head from the ground.

Arturo chuckled. "Obviously, he was wrong." He turned to Lina, his dark eyes still crinkled at the edges. "You can lie here the rest of the night. I'll move to the other side of the fire." He got to his feet and moved across the fire, readjusting his pack and placing the cloak and sword over his body.

Lina lay back onto the bedroll, folding it double over herself. Arturo's eyes were already closed, his breathing even. She sighed. There was no way she would be able to sleep now. Not after their encounter with the Mumla. She turned onto her side, studying his profile. The wrinkle between his dark brows had relaxed in his sleep, leaving his forehead smooth and calm. He rolled onto his side, and dark waves of his hair fell over one eye. His full mouth was slack, and small rhythmic snores escaped his lips. He mumbled in his sleep, and she pressed her lips. Lying there, he looked rather boyish. More like Jacques and quite unlike the tall, hard warrior who had rescued her from the platform. She studied his features, wondering about his age.

Flipping onto her back, she crossed her arms and stared up at the canopy of leaves. Soon, Arturo's snoring and the whisper of the breeze through the tree limbs calmed her racing mind.

Sometime later, sleep overtook her, and she drifted in a small wooden boat on a salty sea.

Chapter 6

Lina woke at dawn to Bayard ruffling the small hairs on her forehead with his soft muzzle. He chuffed, blowing the hair into her eyes. She wrinkled her nose and chuckled, reaching to touch his soft nose. He nibbled at her fingers, making small nickering noises. Opening one eye, she peered up at his large head. "Okay, okay, I'm up," she said. Satisfied, he stepped back and began snuffling the ground in search of his breakfast.

She pushed up onto her palms and yawned, stretching her arms up over her head. The early morning sunlight sparkled sideways through the trees, glittering on the stream. Birds chirped their morning songs, and the undergrowth was full of skittering animal sounds. She gazed across the fire. Arturo was already up, and a pot of coffee simmered over the flames. Inhaling its fragrance, she reached for a cup. She filled it with hot coffee and folded the bedroll around her, moving to sit on the log. Cupping her hands around the mug, she sipped, savoring its dark, nutty flavor.

Arturo was standing downstream, facing away from her. He had stripped to his waist. His pants were rolled to his knees, and he waded in the shallow water. She watched as he cupped his hands and splashed water over his head, running his fingers through his dark hair.

He turned toward her, and she quickly dropped her eyes, flushing from her chest to her hairline. She put her coffee cup up to her lips, hiding her violent blush behind it. Realizing she was still in the gauzy blue nightgown, she stood, folding the bedroll tighter across her body. She hadn't had time to take anything from the tent before it folded in on itself last night. She spun, unsure of where to look for her clothing. Helplessly, she sat down again on the log, careful to keep her eyes carefully trained on the fire and off Arturo in the water.

Arturo's boots appeared in her line of vision, and she bit her lip, letting her eyes drift up to his face. He was fully clothed, to her relief. He eyed the bedroll, pressing his lips together. Raising one dark brow, he grinned with one side of his mouth. Crouching down beside her, he held out a handful of nuts and fresh berries he had foraged that morning. She smiled, cupping her palms as he poured half the mixture into her hand. He seemed more open today. More relaxed than before.

Keeping one arm folded over the bedroll, she popped a fat black berry into her mouth. Her tongue exploded with the sweet, juicy flavor. She smiled, raising her brows. Her teeth were colored purple. Arturo chuckled, popping a berry into his mouth. They sat eating for a few moments, keeping their eyes on their breakfast as Bayard waited behind them in the meadow. He pricked his ears at them and nickered, gently pawing the ground. Arturo turned to look at him. "All right, all right, we're almost ready," he said, chuckling.

Wordlessly, he turned and picked up the canvas and wooden poles from the ground where they had landed last night. He cast them into the air, and the tent took shape above, before it settled once more at his feet. Then he turned, quenching the fire with a wave of his hand, and began stuffing items back into his small pack.

Lina dropped the bedroll, tucking her arms over the thin blue nightgown as she hurried to the tent. Arturo turned his head, watching her back as she scurried inside. He grinned to himself as she pulled the canvas flap open and let it fall behind her. His rumbling chuckle followed her past the door, and she dropped her arms, flushing. The nightgown was as good as a dress, but it was still embarrassing for Arturo to see her in night clothes. She shook her head, walking to the trunk and lifting the lid.

She shuffled through the stack of dresses until she settled on one. A dove-gray dress made of light, airy fabric. The neck grazed her throat, and the sleeves stopped just below her elbows. Delicate gray lace lined the loose hem that fell just above her ankles. It was a riding dress. Perfect. She laced the stays tightly across her slim waist and turned, smoothing the fabric against her hips as she examined herself in the long mirror.

Her blonde braid hung loosely to her midback, and wisps of curling hair were sticking up all over. She flattened them and sighed, unwinding her braid. Grabbing the hairbrush, she worked it through her tangled hair until it was smooth. She wove two thick braids over each other and around her head, securing them with pins. After splashing water on her face from the crystal basin, she tucked on some fresh stockings, then laced her boots. Turning about, she found her green dress right where she had left it on the floor by the bed. She picked it up, shoving her hand into its pocket and retrieving her mother's compact. She dropped it into the deep pocket of her gray dress, patting the fabric on top of it.

As soon as she exited the tent, Arturo lifted his palm upward from his waist and the tent involuted, landing in a neat pile at his feet. He picked it up and placed it in his pack, securing the leather straps. Bayard stood in the edge of the meadow, waiting impatiently. He chuffed at Arturo and gently stomped his right foot. Its impact shook the ground. Arturo chuckled and threw the pack over his back, striding toward him. "I'm coming!" he said loudly. Bayard nickered and nodded his head up and down. Lina grinned at their exchange. She slung her quiver and bow across her shoulders and followed.

Arturo stood waiting for her at Bayard's side. Without asking for permission, he placed his large hands around her waist and lifted her astride. Her ears pinked and she squealed, much to her embarrassment. She cleared her throat, patting Bayard's neck. "Thank you," she said quietly.

The large white horse turned, fixing his great brown eyes on hers. "Good morning," said a soft male voice. She turned to look at Arturo, who was adjusting the items in his pack. Feeling her eyes on him, he stopped to stare at her questioningly.

"Good morning," she said meekly, lowering her lashes.

Arturo knit his brows. "Uhm, good morning," he said.

Lina frowned to herself, confused. His wasn't the same voice that she had just heard. Bayard nickered, turning his eye to her again.

"Good morning, Lina," the male voice said.

Lina chuckled, tucking her chin and raising her brows in surprise. The *horse* had said her name.

Arturo lifted himself onto the horse behind her, his thigh brushing the back of her leg. "What's funny?" he grumbled.

"N—nothing, except I think Bayard just spoke?" Bayard lifted his head, jerking his muzzle up and down in rhythm. She laughed, stroking his neck. "Good morning, Bayard," she said in awe.

Arturo grunted, but he said nothing more, wordlessly wrapping his forearm tightly around Lina's waist. He waited for her to grasp the horse's mane and then he tied his free hand into Bayard's hair and clucked softly. Bayard snorted and took off, galloping through the waving grasses of the meadow. Lina's breath caught in her throat at his speed, and she gripped his flanks with her thighs to hold herself upright.

They were sailing through the tall grasses, and Lina's cheeks pinked as the breeze blew past them. Her skirt whipped at her legs and the grass pricked her skin as Bayard galloped even faster. Arturo tucked his forearm tighter about her abdomen and clucked once more to the horse. Lina braced herself, waiting for takeoff.

Her eyes had been closed the first time. She had missed it. She made sure to keep them open as a soft, sparkling, golden light appeared at the sides of the horse, just in front of her knees. It curled like smoke, rolling out in the air like a parchment. As the golden light unfurled, it took on the shape of a giant pair of transparent wings. Lina could still see the grasses whipping past them through the sparkling light. All at once, the wings became solid white feathers that faded to dove gray at the tips. Bayard shook them, testing their weight in the air. The feathers looked soft, and Lina had the sudden urge to reach out and touch them, but she knew better than to let go of Bayard's mane. Any moment, he would lift to the sky.

She peered ahead, tucking herself tightly against the horse's back. They were galloping toward the sea, a high rocky cliff standing above the beach before them. She tucked her chin, rounding her shoulders in suspense. At the last moment, Bayard lifted his wings and leaped into the air, soaring up over the cliff and above the beach. She let out a little yelp, despite herself, and Arturo tucked his knees closer to the backs of her legs. The salty sea breeze whipped Lina's hair into her eyes. She gazed to her left over the sparkling blue water. It was calm. Though she knew they had come a far distance since yesterday, there were no signs of the giant whirlpool that had almost pulled her to her death. She scanned the water near the shoreline. The small boat and the captain were nowhere to be seen, either.

They flew over the beach for a long while. Lina looked past her toes at it, testing herself. Smooth stones and colorful, rounded sea glass sparkled below in the morning sunlight. They tumbled in the shallow surf, creating a kaleidoscope of intricate patterns on the shore. She smiled to herself. There was no tunneled vision and no dizziness, this time. Enjoying the view, she patted Bayard's neck. She was growing to like flying high above the ground.

The sea breeze was cool, and she shivered, tiny bumps forming on her arms. Arturo let go of the horse's mane, sweeping his heavy cloak around her. She freed one hand and held it tightly about her shoulders. "Thank you," she murmured. But she wasn't sure he could hear her over the whipping air. Inside his cloak, she could feel the warmth of his close body, pressing against her back. She blushed and tried to scoot herself forward, and he loosened his arm, adjusting his position.

Up ahead, she could see a low cavernous opening in the rock face to their right. It was outlined by winding green vines and the twisting roots of a large tree that grew downward from the bank, encircling the opening like a frame. She wondered where it led. She focused her eyes, trying to peer inside as they passed it. The entrance was dark and somewhat obscured by the overhanging vines. She turned to ask Arturo about it, but his furrowed eyes were focused on the sea, and his hard expression made her hold her tongue.

Bayard flew on towards a wall of heavy mist. He pumped his wings, banking right over the overhanging rock face. They climbed, gliding over grassy hills and shallow valleys that rolled softly over one another in a soothing pattern. Groves of trees and small rocks dotted the landscape, and, to her surprise, Lina counted several small deer, rabbits, and birds. There were so many animals here. It was nothing like home. The sun streamed onto their backs, casting their shadow on the ground below. Lina peered ahead. She could see nothing past the mist that hung in the distance like a heavy curtain, obscuring the landscape beyond. It stretched as far as she could see to the left and right, and rolled out towards them on the ground and reached high into the sky, mixing with the soft, wispy clouds.

Bayard dove as they hit the mist, flying low and fast. Lina gripped his flank with her thighs and gritted her teeth, letting go of the cloak and grasping his mane with two hands. The mist pressed close, tucking over them like a heavy quilt and muffling all sound. The air inside was charged, and it tingled against the skin on the back of her neck. Lina blinked her eyes, trying to focus. She couldn't see past her hands in the horse's mane. She knew Bayard couldn't see either, and she worried they would smack into something at any moment.

Abruptly, they cleared the mist and burst back into the sunlight. Lina blinked in surprise. Sheer, towering gray mountains appeared before them, their snowcapped peaks encircled by feathery clouds. Bayard beat his powerful wings, carrying them swiftly past the jagged faces. They soared between two cliffs and banked left, swooping downward. A column of jagged rock rose high above them on both sides, and a wide, sparkling river flowed below their feet. Dark green moss grew on the stones at its banks, trailing up the cliffs. Giant oak and evergreen trees lined the passage and grew from jagged ledges high on the mountain sides. Their thick roots wove intricate patterns down the rock in search of the ground below. Willow trees shaded the riverbank and waved their long thin limbs out over the water. An eagle flew below them, gliding on outspread wings. He dove, swiping a fish from the river, and carried his prize high to a nest on top of a cliff.

They wove through the passage, following the wide river's flow. Bayard banked left, where the river dropped over the rocks. It spilled out below them over a high fall to a still, blue lake. He tucked his wings, diving over the fall and gliding low over the still water. Lina reached out her hand, letting her fingertips skim the cool surface. The water's surface was as smooth as a glistening mirror, and she peeked over the edge of Bayard's back, watching herself curiously as she glided over it in Arturo's arms.

A lush green valley spread out beyond the lake, surrounded on three sides by towering gray mountains. Small rocks and boulders had fallen from the rocky faces and now sat covered in mosses and twisted vines. Tucked in the east mountainside, in a grove of ancient evergreens and oaks, stood a sprawling stone estate. Lina ran her eyes over it with interest. It was the largest, most beautiful dwelling she had ever seen, and as the world turned with Bayard, they were headed towards it. Lina wondered anxiously what she would find behind its doors, but she had no choice other than to be whisked along with Arturo. She couldn't very well jump from Bayard's back, and if she did, where would she go?

Bayard seemed eager to reach the ground, and he pumped his great wings, flying directly past the front door. He touched down, tucking his wings and sticking out his front hooves. They plowed up mounds of dirt as he skidded along the ground, and Lina bumped her chin against Bayard's neck as they ground to a halt. Arturo grunted, holding her fast around the waist. His chest bumped her soundly against the back. "Ooph, you daft creature!" he growled.

Bayard stomped his foot, cracking the dirt beneath it, and jerked his head up and down. Angrily, Arturo slung his legs off his back and reached up for Lina. He grasped her waist roughly in his large hands and lifted her, setting her soundly on the earth.

Her heart pounded in her ears, and the heat from his hands lingered on her waist even as he stepped away. She brushed the spots with her hands, training her eyes on the ground as a stable boy came to lead Bayard to the barn. He reached for him, but the large horse whinnied and galloped away in the opposite direction, slipping out of the boy's grasp. "Fool horse," said Arturo, looking after him. Bayard nickered softly in the distance, and Lina chuckled to herself. Arturo glared and strode past her, heading for the front door. She covered her smile with her hand and turned to follow him.

The vast stone building was ancient. It looked as if it had been formed by the earth itself. The grounds and hillside were covered with lofty oak and evergreen trees whose great roots twisted and curled over the structure, crawling up and over the roof. She peered up at the heavy door. It was made of a cross-section from a single, ancient log, its stone facing high above her head and carved to an intricate scrolling point. Thick vines with slick green leaves wove their way across its frame, crawling out toward the glittering windows beyond.

Arturo lifted the heavy iron ring, ready to knock. At just that moment, the door burst open and a squatty woman with cheerful hazel eyes and a wide smile appeared before them. Her pointed ears stuck out from under a crisp white kerchief that tied back over her short gray hair. She grinned broadly and stepped through the door facing, circling Arturo's waist in a squeezing embrace.

"Arto, my dear! Welcome home at last. It has been too long."

He returned her embrace, stooping to wrap his long arms around her shoulders. "Hello, Ita," he said warmly.

Ita stepped back, keeping one arm looped around his back. She turned her sparkling eyes to Lina. "And who is this beautiful creature?" she asked. She appraised Lina curiously from head to foot, causing a pink flush to rise into her ears.

Arto angled his body toward Lina, smiling uncertainly with one side of his mouth. "This is Lina. We met in Meallta." He licked his lip, dropping his eyes to his feet and readjusting his weight.

Ita grinned and kept her sparkling eyes trained on Lina, taking two steps toward her. "Lina: a lovely name. Might it be short for something?" she asked expectantly.

Lina smiled. "Yes. Evangeline." Ita nodded encouragingly. "Vasily," Lina added.

Ita exchanged a glance with Arto, who flicked his eyes quickly back to the ground. "Ah yes," Ita nodded. "A lovely name for a lovely girl," she said, her eyes crinkling at the edges. She pursed her lips and brought her small hand to the side of Lina's face, patting her cheek and tucking golden strands of stray hair behind her left ear. She took her hand. "Come. Come in. You must be tired from your long journey." She shuffled them into the house, closing the great door behind them.

The entry hall was full of light. Curved, gray limestone walls rose in ornately carved columns to a massive glass dome above.

The dome had an iron lattice, patterned to look like large leaves. Magnificent picture windows rose from the marble floor to the vaulted ceiling down long, curved corridors to Lina's left and right. As Lina walked further inside, she saw a winding staircase. Its lofty steps wound up beyond the dome at least three stories. Beyond the staircase was a cozy drawing room. A chandelier made of shimmering sea glass hung over a glass top table. A large, upholstered settee and several high-backed chairs were clustered around it before a great roaring stone hearth. The hearth sat in the back wall, and it took Lina's breath away to see the circular estate out the two soaring back windows. A small flower garden sat just behind the house. Rosebushes, climbing honeysuckle vines, lilies, jasmine, gardenia, and many others grew around a small, domed pavilion. Lina spun, admiring the beauty of the view. She flicked her eyes to Arturo, who leaned against a stone column, watching her. "It's lovely," she grinned. "And it's your home?"

He smiled, staring up into the skylight. "Yes. For many cycles, now."

Ita squeezed his arm, bustling past them and up the marble staircase. She turned and motioned for them to follow. "Come now, my dears. Dinner will be ready, soon. I am sure you would like to rest a moment…maybe get a bath?" She eyed Arturo's weathered clothes dubiously. He smirked at her, and she smiled widely, crinkling the corners of her eyes. "Just a suggestion," she said brightly. She turned her heel, chuckling to herself, and continued up the steps. Lina followed closely behind Arto, craning her neck to follow the winding staircase up out of sight.

When they reached the second-story landing, Arto turned right, walking over thick green carpet to the end of the hall. Lina gazed after him, watching as he disappeared behind large wooden doors at the end. Ita was already at the left end of the hall, lifting the handle on an identical set of wooden doors. She paused, waiting for Lina inside. Lina turned, hurrying after her.

She followed Ita inside the room, looking around her in amazement. Ita began bustling about, gathering various ointments, combs, and brushes onto the vanity. After laying a soft robe on a chaise lounge, she went to a heavy wooden armoire and opened its doors. A beautiful oak tree was carved on the front of it. Reaching inside, she selected three formal gowns, and lace underthings, and laid them neatly across the bed.

The room was an octagon with eight stone walls separated by ornate wooden columns, and a large circular bed sat against the far wall. Its four posts wound like tree roots out of the wooden floor to a twisting canopy of leaves that laced across the vaulted ceiling. The thick duvet was midnight blue, and tiny flecks of silver thread were woven across it like a starry night. Two floor-to-ceiling dormer windows were set to the left and right of the great bed. Vines grew across the window frames, climbing up the wall to their high peaks. A window seat sat in the right dormer overlooking the courtyard. To the right of the room, a plush, amethyst rug lay under a deep emerald settee. A single stone quartz coffee table sat before it, and a carved wooden vanity with a mirror and crystal basin was situated next to the heavy armoire on her left. Lina went to it and peered at her reflection.

Her braids had come undone during their flight and wound over the front of her shoulders. Little wisps of curling hair had escaped them, trailing in front of her ears. Ita appeared behind her, placing her small hands on Lina's slender shoulders. She peered around Lina's shoulder at her reflection, smoothing her hair. "Just lovely," she said softly. "You have her hair and eyes, you know?"

Lina turned to face her, frowning slightly. "Whose hair and eyes?"

Ita crinkled her eyes at the corners, her cheeks picking up her smile. "Why, your mother's, my dearest," she said kindly.

Lina paused, her stomach dropping into her feet. Her mind reeled, confusion biting at its edges. "My mother? She was here?"

Ita paused, lacing her fingers. She glanced up at the ceiling, then down at her shoes. "Well, she was, and then she wasn't…And then she was once more," Ita said doubtfully.

Lina shook her head, her brow furrowing. Ita was speaking in circles. "I don't understand what you mean."

Ita placed her hand on Lina's cheek, peering at her with kind eyes. "Maybe you should ask Arto," she said softly. Sorrow tinged her gaze, and Lina searched her eyes for answers she wasn't willing to give. "It's not my place to say more." She patted Lina's cheek, her countenance brightening. "Dinner will be ready soon. Arto will meet you on the landing." She smiled softly at Lina, smoothing her hair once more. With that, she turned away, closing the heavy doors behind her.

Lina sat down heavily on a soft emerald chaise, staring after her. Slowly she lifted the compact from the pocket of her dress. She brushed its gilded case, wondering at Ita's words. What could she mean? Her mother was here, and then she wasn't… and then she was once more? It didn't make any sense. She put away her weapon and placed her mother's compact in a small satin box on the bedside table, then thoughtfully, she lay back on the mattress.

She lay her head back on the pillow, staring up at the ceiling as she puzzled over Ita's zigzag wording. Her mother had visited here? Or had lived here at some time?

Frowning, she thought back to their cottage in the forest clearing, where she had lived with her mother until the day she disappeared. Lina had relived the events of that day in her mind many times. She had come in from playing in the forest when she was eight, and her mother was gone. She searched the cottage and walked through the forest for hours, calling for her, tears streaking down her face. Briars scratched her arms, and she tripped over tree roots, scraping her hands and knees. But her mother was nowhere to be found. Finally, at dusk, in a haze of grief and exhaustion, she fell asleep at the foot of the ash oak.

Remus found her, curling his warm body against her middle. She had hugged his orange frame close, crying tears into his soft fur. The next morning, they walked to the village. The little cat wove his orange body between her bare feet as they walked the dirt path. She hoped she would find her mother among the villagers in the marketplace, but when she got there, she was nowhere to be found. Instead, she had found Jacques. Or rather, he found her.

She had been trying to steal bread from the baker's cart when he called to her from the clock shop door. He smiled at her with kind eyes, his broad face looking out from under his shock of disheveled hair. She had hidden around the corner, peering warily at his large frame. He held the door wide. The shop looked warm. Inviting. A fire was roaring in the hearth. She could smell stew cooking above it. Remus bounded inside, and she followed. For surely, Remus would never go where she wouldn't be safe.

Many times, she had snuck back to the cottage, in hopes her mother would materialize when she opened the door. She imagined her at the small kitchen counter chopping vegetables and humming a familiar song. But she had never been there. When Lina had been fifteen, she had returned to find that thieves had cleared the main floor of furniture and broken many of her mother's dishes. She had cried out in grief and fallen onto her knees, gathering the chipped china into her hands. The broken edges had cut her fingers. She had barely felt the wounds, gripping the pieces until blood mixed with her tears on the floor.

She had lain on the floor by the broken dishes until Jacques came to find her. He had carried her back to the shop, bandaging her hurt fingers. He had said she was crazy when she had asked to go back and live there. She had told him that the shop was too crowded, and she preferred to be alone. She needed space, is what she said. But deep down, she knew she just wanted to be near her mother's memory. Jacques had known it too. He had been worried. And angry. They had argued. Their first big fight. She had stormed out of the shop, crying on the road.

That's when he had given her the quiver and bow. He had shown up at the cottage the next morning with the gift hidden inside his cloak. The weapon was beautiful. Jacques had crafted it with fine slats of wood and spare metal from the clock he kept covered in the back of the shop. It was the one he could never fix. "That old clock is useless," he had said. "But at least now, it will be good for something."

Over the next few months, he had built her new furniture and supplied her with whatever extra supplies he could spare. Her eyes filled with tears. He was a man who had taken her in when she was all alone. The one who had accepted extra work in the shop so that he could trade for her clothing. He had saved her, had treated her like family.

She thought back to her birthday dinner. Jacques had given her such a beautiful gift: the cake wrapped in parchment. Jacques had always been more than her close friend. He was family really, but she had noticed his feelings had begun to shift lately. She thought of the way he had lifted her chin with his bandaged hand, of his lips hovering near her face. Her heart had raced. Lina pushed her lips together, sighing. The look of longing in his eyes had made her head spin. She sighed. She missed him. She wondered what he was doing now.

Smiling, she imagined him shuffling around haphazardly in his workshop, his untucked shirt tail, his stained apron. Familiar things. Comforting things.

He was probably bent with his head to the face of some broken clock, like she had seen him do so often. She bit her lip, and tears pricked her eyes. There was no way back to him, now that she had fallen through the gate. She hoped he was doing all right. By now, he had probably come to the cottage looking for her. She wondered what he would think when he found her gone.

Tucking her hands behind her head, she closed her eyes, thinking. She had to admit Jacques was kind and strong. Handsome even, in a boyish way.

Suddenly Arto's face popped into her mind, his dark eyes and full mouth. She thought of her back pressed against him as they rode Bayard. He had held her close, with his strong arm tucked around her waist. In her memory, his breath tickled the top of her ear. His gruff voice whispered, and she shot up off the bed, blinking. Where had that come from?

Swiftly, she peeled off her travel dress and donned the plush robe, moving to examine the gowns Ita had laid out for her. Her fingers touched the soft, gauzy fabric. They were so fine. Finer even than the nightgown. She chose a dark emerald one with capped sleeves. It wrapped across her body and tied with a golden ribbon at her side. The slim skirt had a gauze overlay that fluttered in gentle ruffles to her feet. Little golden flecks of thread were sewn into the bodice, fanning out under the fabric of the skirt. The flecks met at the hem, forming a delicate circular pattern just above her feet.

Several pairs of footwear sat at the end of the bed. She chose an emerald pair of flats made of soft satin that matched her dress. A single golden oak leaf was sewn into the toe. She slipped her feet into them, savoring the cool satin against her toes. She turned her toe left and right, grinning down at them. They were a fine alternative to her usual leather boots.

She brushed her long hair, smoothing a floral-smelling oil through it until it shone. Then she wound one thin braid about her crown and let the rest of her hair hang loose down her back. Smoothing her dress over her middle, she examined herself in the mirror. She smiled, pleased with her appearance. The emerald dress and golden threads went well with her hair and eyes. She walked to the doors, pulling the handle and stepping into the corridor.

Chapter 7

Arto leaned against the stone wall to her right, his arms folded, and one leg crossed at the knee. When she entered the hall, he stood, straightening his jacket, and clasped his hands behind his back. As she moved towards him, he flicked his eyes toward her feet and wove them slowly up to her face. His dark gaze paused at her lips, and she blushed, dropping her lashes to her toes.

He readjusted his weight, wiping his palms on his thighs. Clearing his throat, he brushed one hand through his dark hair, exposing the peak of his ear. It fell over his cheek as he dropped his eyes and turned, extending his arm for her. She stepped forward, winding her hand around his forearm. He flexed his hand, and his lean muscle rippled under the arm of his dark jacket.

Lina gazed at him sidelong, appraising his appearance. His face was shaved smooth, and his hair was oiled, its dark surface shining in the candlelight. A slim, midnight blue jacket hung open to his waist, revealing a crisp white shirt. The top button of the collar was open, exposing his long scar. Matching dark blue slacks fit his long legs. He stuck his free hand in their pocket, flicking his eyes to hers. Her chest flared under his dark eyes, and she cleared her throat, dropping her gaze to the carpet. Ita was right. He did look better after a bath.

Wordlessly, they descended the staircase toward a waiting Ita, who clasped her hands in front of her, beaming up at them. Her hazel eyes crinkled at the edges as she took in Lina's appearance. She grasped Lina's hands in hers, patting them softly as she met her on the floor. "Lovely, isn't she, Arto?" said Ita.

Lina smiled shyly, flicking her gaze in his direction.

He peered down at her beneath his dark brow, his straight lips twitching slightly. He cleared his throat. "She is," he said gruffly, dropping his gaze.

Ita grinned, placing Lina's hand back on Arto's forearm. "Right this way, Master," she said as she bowed.

They followed her dark skirts down the left corridor, her heels clacking on the marble. Lina peered out the soaring front windows. Moonlight had begun to peek over the mountaintops, casting dancing light on the waters of the lake. She gazed up at it thoughtfully. The moon on this side of the gate was larger than the one she knew. It was at least triple in size. She squinted, spotting a second, smaller moon sitting just off its center. A moon within a moon. Their light was casting milky, silver rays through the windowpanes and onto the pale marble floor.

Ita pulled open the dark double doors at the end of the long corridor. She bustled into the room ahead of them and moved to stand near an open doorframe in the back right corner, hands folded at her waist. Arturo guided Lina into the room, his hand hovering over the small of her back. She tried not to feel it, instead focusing on the room about her.

The floors, walls, and ceiling were made entirely of dark ancient wood. The vaulted beams of the ceiling curved upward into the open night air and met in the center at a peak. Stars twinkled down at her from the openings. Massive roots from the surrounding trees had woven themselves over the beams, twisting in a lattice that curled its way over the walls toward the floor.

A crystal chandelier hung from the center of the room. Its candles bounced shimmering light off the long table beneath it. The dark basalt tabletop sat on heavy, wooden legs that had been carved to resemble an eagle's talons at the foot. At least twenty highbacked wooden chairs sat around the table. Arto led her to the head of the table nearest them, pulling out the seat. She sat, and he silently pushed in the chair behind her. Then he walked to the far end of the table, pulling out the chair and seating himself. Lina gazed across the table at him nervously. It felt strange to be seated so far away from him. Nothing like her cramped dinners in Jacques' back room.

In the corner, Ita clapped her hands twice. At once, a trio of young men in serving attire entered the room, rolling a heavy wooden cart laden with food. Each of them had pointed ears. Lina recognized one of them as the stable boy who had tried to capture Bayard. He smiled shyly up at her, and she grinned back at him. They stopped the cart beside the table and stood, waiting with their hands clasped behind their backs. Ita clapped once more, and they began laying platters of meat, cheeses, roasted vegetables, fruit, and bread on the table.

Arto smiled at the closest young man, who was glancing furtively in his direction. "Benjamin, how go your studies?" he asked him.

The boy straightened, bracing his hand inside his vest. "Very well, Master. I particularly enjoyed The Histories of the Mountain Fairies."

Arturo grinned, clapping him on the shoulder. "I'm sure you did. Very well then. Keep up your good work."

The young man beamed, nodding once in Arturo's direction. Then he turned, assisting the others as they returned the cart to the back room.

Lina clasped her hands on her lap, surveying the beauty of the table. In the center of it, fresh flowers, likely from Ita's garden, sat in a glass vase. Fine silver utensils framed her bone china plate that was decorated in an oak-leaf pattern. Ita had folded her napkin elegantly on top of it, fastening it with a crystal holder. Her glass stemware had a bluish hue, its slender cup covered in a floral design. Vines wound down the stem, ending in wide leaves at the base. Ita brought a pitcher of tea, filling her glass. She sipped. It had a sweet tangy flavor tinged with citrus. She glanced over the rim at Arturo. He was already filling his plate, and she did the same. She sat down her glass, standing to skirt the table as she lifted every available item onto her plate.

Arto was standing at the table's other side. He didn't look at her as he spooned a heap of potatoes on his already full plate's edge. Wordlessly, he passed the spoon to her, and she took it, glancing shyly over at him. His steely eyes were stormy and dark, and she flicked her eyes away, wondering at his change in mood. He had been so cheerful earlier, but maybe something had changed. Silently, he moved back towards his seat. Lina stared after him, then she turned, moving back to her own.

The rich food was unlike anything she had ever eaten, and she enjoyed every bite. The crisp vegetables and fresh berries exploded with flavor, and the meat practically melted in her mouth. And the bread…It was soft, warm, and fresh from the oven. She grabbed a second piece from the basket near her chair, topping it with a thick layer of butter. Delicious. She would have eaten more, but her stomach protested against the fabric of her green bodice. She sat back and sighed, placing her hands over her middle.

The young men appeared at the doorway, returning to clear the table. Ita followed them, carrying a covered crystal platter. She smiled at Arturo. "Your favorite," she said as she uncovered the dish. Arturo smiled at her, but his grin quickly dropped when she turned away. Ita lowered the platter to Lina, and she frowned. Crisp wafers adorned the plate, stacked in a small tier. They were topped with delicate cream. "Have one," Ita said encouragingly. "You'll like it, I promise. It's made from the Tamarisk trees in my garden."

Lina smiled up at Ita's kind face, then she returned her eyes to the platter. Something about the small cakes was familiar. Hesitantly, she reached for one, biting into the edge. The flavor brought her back to the cottage long ago. She was lying on her sick bed, and her mother was feeding her small bites. Her face paled at the memory, and she swallowed her small bite with difficulty. Abruptly, she placed the wafer onto her plate and sat back, swiping up her drink.

She sipped a gulp of tea as Ita and Arto stared at her. "You don't like them, the Tamarisk Cakes?" asked Ita.

Lina sat down her glass, fingering the long stem. "No, no. It's not that. It's just…I remember them." She swallowed. "From long ago."

Ita glanced quickly at Arturo, whose elbows rested on the table, hands folded at his chest. He didn't look at her, but instead kept his dark eyes trained on Lina.

"My mother, she …" Lina's eyes filled with tears. She swallowed before continuing. "She brought one to our cottage when I was a child. I was very sick, quite near death. She fed it to me." She wet her lips. "And I got better…I …" She trailed off, her voice breaking. "It tasted sweet." She sat back heavily against the dining chair, biting hard at her lip.

Arturo's jaw flexed. He crossed his arms, flattening his mouth into a thin line. "Thank you, Ita. That will be all," he grunted. He pushed back his chair, scraping it hard against the floor. Lina watched as he threw his napkin onto his plate. Then, hurriedly, he strode out of the room.

Lina sat facing his empty seat, staring at her lap. Ita put her small hands to her rounded waist, casting her eyes to the ceiling. She blew out her breath, crossing her arms. "You must excuse him, dearest. The Master means no harm." She shook her head, staring past the door. "I expect he will be in the library then." She placed the lid back on the crystal platter, lifting it into her arms. "You'll find it at the end of the left corridor, behind the last set of doors." She lifted Lina's chin, looking at her with soft eyes. "Good night, Evangeline," she said quietly. "I hope you sleep well." Then she turned and disappeared into the doorway at the back of the room, her heels clacking on the hardwood.

Lina stared at the familiar confection on her plate. Everything was so confusing on this side of the gate. She didn't understand anything. She had so many questions about the Tamarisk Cakes, her mother's disappearance, Arto's taciturn behavior, and even her own identity. At least back home she had known who she was—

or she thought she did. Evangeline Vasily was just a common orphan girl, and that was that. She was no one. At least, no one that mattered.

She put her hands to her chin, resting her elbows on the table. Her mother had visited this strange place. Ita had told her so. Obviously, there was much about her own mother she didn't know. At the very least, she wasn't who Lina had thought. So, who did that make her? She pursed her lips. Ita seemed to know the answers to some of her questions, but she had said it wasn't her place to tell her anything. What did that mean?

More questions followed, one after the other as she puzzled over the last days. Why had she come to be in this strange place beyond the gate? And how would she get home? How had her mother come to have a Tamarisk Cake in their forest clearing? And why was Arturo so angry about it? Questions with no answers swirled in her mind. Lina sat back, crossing her arms. The problems of her other life seemed small. Searching for scarce food in the shortening days and juggling Jacques' increasingly longing looks seemed easy. Simple, considering all she had experienced since falling through the gate. She wished she was back there.

She sighed as she pushed back her chair and strode to the heavy doors, pulling them open and stepping into the moonlit corridor. Rows of doors lined the right of the hallway. She walked past them and into the entry hall, taking the left corridor all the way to its end. Pausing there, at the heavy doors, she pulled in a deep breath. She needed answers, and she wanted to go home.

The library was dimly lit. Sconces lined the bottom shelves, bathing the floor in dim golden light. She placed her back against the wooden door, letting her eyes adjust. Heavily stocked bookshelves covered the walls, rising several stories to the roof. A small spiral staircase curved its way up from her left. Its iron rails were tangled with green vines, and it wound past several platforms, the last of which almost reached the high ceiling, which she realized, was no ceiling at all. It was open to the air.

In the center of the room, an enormous oak tree grew out of the floor. Its roots spread from the thick trunk and wound out over the mossy carpet. The limbs spread above her, creating a crown of leaves for a ceiling. She padded across the soft moss, craning her neck to see it.

Distantly, she heard rushing water. Straining her ear, she followed the sound. She stepped gingerly over the tree roots until she came to stone pavers that had been set into the soft floor. She followed them past the bookshelves to the right.

Behind the bookshelves, the library spread out into a hidden alcove. Reading chairs and small tables faced the far wall, which was built directly into the mountainside. A small waterfall ran over the rocks, filling a shallow pool beneath it. A stream followed the pool, winding through the shelves in the library floor. It trickled between the stepping stones, disappearing below the floor under the roots of the great tree at the library's center.

Arturo sat with his back to her, facing the waterfall. She approached him silently. From her position, she could see him flex his hard jaw. His large hands gripped the arms of his seat with white knuckles. She cleared her throat, and he half turned then stood to face her with his arms crossed and his eyes on the floor. "What are you doing in here?" he growled darkly.

Lina ignored his behavior. She cleared her throat again and moved to sit in the chair beside him. Folding her hands in her lap and straightening her back, she peered confidently up at his stony face. Her voice shook slightly with her words, but still, she spoke them.

"Ita…Ita says I look just like her…My eyes and my hair?"

Arto shuffled his feet, staring at the waterfall. The muscle in his jaw feathered again. "Your mother…Yes," he said quietly.

Lina nodded. She pressed further. "You knew her? My mother? She was here?"

He adjusted his weight, crouching over the stream. "She was," he said, his voice almost a whisper. He reached his hand down, letting the water run over his palm. "But not any longer." He stood, putting his hand to the back of his neck.

Lina swallowed. "Wh…where is she now?" she asked.

"Gone," he spat.

"Where?" she asked quickly.

He turned to face her, his eyes blazing. "At the bottom of the sea," he growled. "*Why* must you ask so many questions?" He turned, sitting again in the chair. His head hung low, and he laced his fingers over the back of neck, staring at the floor with his dark, stormy eyes.

Lina stood, training her eyes furiously on his back. He was cruel to tell her that her mother was dead like this. Tears threatened at the edge of her vision at his words. She crossed her arms, leveling her voice. "I want to go home. I won't stay here with someone as cruel and heartless as you!" she seethed.

Arturo lifted his head, looking at her incredulously. He spun, striding toward her with his fists clenched. Lina stepped back, but he kept moving towards her. He brought his nose close to her face, bracing his arm on the bookcase behind her. His eyes were piercing, flashing anger under heavy brows. "That's not possible," he breathed, his warm breath tickling her chin. She swallowed, pressing her hands flat against the bookshelf. He glanced at her hands, gripping the bookshelf with white knuckles, and his eyes softened. Pausing, he stepped closer, studying her face. Her heart began to race as he lifted his other hand, penning her between his arms. For a moment, he held her there, fixed under his gaze. She stared up at him, amazed at his rapid changes in emotion. One moment he was furious, the next, he looked at her like…well, she wasn't sure what he was looking at her like. He moved his eyes slowly over her features, and she watched him curiously until he readjusted his weight, unintentionally grazing her leg with his knee. She stiffened, and he dropped one arm, stepping backward.

Her anger flared as his dark eyes returned, and she straightened, sticking out her chin and crossing her arms over her chest. "Why not?" she demanded. "Why isn't it possible?"

For a moment he stood there, and she glared at the side of his face, waiting. "It just isn't. Stop asking," he said defeatedly, not meeting her eyes. "The answer is *no.*" He brushed past her, bumping into her shoulder with his arm.

A few moments later, the slam of the library doors echoed through the alcove.

Lina dropped onto the floor against the bookshelf and crouched forward, placing her face in her hands. Tears squeezed from the corners of her eyes. Her mother was dead. At the bottom of the sea. She sobbed. She would never go home, and she would never again see Jacques or Remus or her cottage in the clearing. She was stuck, forever, on this side of the gate, with an impossible man who refused to give her any answers. He was cruel. Heartless. What kind of person told someone their mother was dead like that?

Lina sat by the bookshelf, letting herself cry for a good while. She cried for the loss of her mother, of Jacques, of Remus, and of her home. The cool night air was lifting from the water of the pool, and the skin on her arms chilled. Shivering, she wiped her face with the back of her hands. She stood, tucking her arms across her chest. Forlorn, she trudged back toward the doors. She closed them soundly behind her, wishing for all the world that she was at home. Her feet were heavy on the stairs, and she didn't bother to look toward Arto's room before she headed down the hall to her own. She didn't care if he was there, anyway.

Ita had already laid a soft black nightgown across her bed. An appropriate color, for her grief. She peeled off the emerald dress, shoving her arms through the holes of the gown. It fell softly to her ankles. She climbed into bed, tucking the covers up under her chin. Turning onto her side, she let tears slide from her eyes, wetting her pillow.

In her sleep, her mother drifted beneath the waves. Suspended. Silent. Her golden hair floated up over her head in long streams, and her white skirts billowed at her knees. Lina watched her from afar, treading water. The image shifted, and suddenly her mother's frame became her own. She inhaled, gulping seawater into her chest. It burned, and she fought the water, kicking and pulling for the surface. She couldn't breathe. The current was pulling at her skirts, dragging her down, down into darkness. Cold, dark water pushed on her chest, and the depths squeezed against her head. She kicked with all her might, but the glimmering light of the surface drifted away from her. Dark specks began to cloud the edges of her vision, and her mind screamed for air. She panicked, reflexively opening her mouth, her heart racing in her ears. And then she was drifting. Still. Silent.

She sat up, gulping air into her chest. Morning sunlight streamed softly through her windows. Sweat beaded on her upper lip, and her heart was thumping in her ears. She crossed her legs, pressing her hand to the center of her chest. It was just a dream. She forced air in and out of her lungs in slow, measured breaths as she anchored herself to her room. In…armoire…and out…bathing tub. In…and out.

Finally, her heart began to slow. She smoothed her hair behind her ears and swung her feet over the side of the mattress. Slipping into satin slippers, she padded to the vanity and gazed at her reflection. Her eyes were puffy, and dark circles cast deep, purple shadows beneath them. She sighed, splashing water onto her face and pressing them with her fingers. Grabbing the brush, she smoothed her hair, weaving it into a long braid down her back.

She went to the armoire and chose a pale-blue day dress, slipping it over her head. After fastening the stays at the back, she retrieved the compact from the satin box on top of the nightstand. Dropping it into her pocket, she sat on the window seat, pulling on her stockings and lacing her boots. She gazed out the window, tucking a knee to her chest and lacing her fingers across it. Sunlight streamed over the gray mountain faces and wove through the tall tree limbs onto the ground below her.

Arto was leading Bayard through the courtyard. She thought of their exchange in the library the night before. He had been angry, and he'd made her so. Then he had penned her inside his arms against the bookshelves. She swallowed convulsively. Her heart had hammered in her ears as his knee had brushed her leg.

Reddening, she sprang up in a huff, crossing her arms. Casting her eyes to the ceiling, she bit her lip, thinking.

It was true that he was taciturn and abrupt. Cruel, even. He had told her, with very little tact, that her mother was gone and that there was no possible way for her to return home. She sighed. But he *had* saved her from the trial in Meallta. He had also hidden her from the Mumla and brought her safely to this beautiful home. She tapped her foot. "I should apologize," she whispered. Maybe then he would answer more of her questions. Maybe she would like some of the other answers.

She peered down at him, squinting. He was wearing his cloak, and the leather pack was stashed across his back. He jumped, swinging his leg over the horse's back. She turned, hurrying down the steps and bursting into the garden just as he clucked to Bayard. The horse flicked his ears, lifting his tail and galloping across the courtyard with lightning speed. "Arto, wait!" she called. But Bayard had already unfurled his great wings, lifting them up over the sheer mountain. She stared after them, her hands on her hips. Turning, she made her way slowly back into the house.

Ita was waiting for her by the hearth. "Good morning, my dear," she smiled warmly. "Breakfast is laid in the morning room. Follow me." She bustled ahead of Lina, turning right under the great staircase. Her heels clacked on the marble, and she followed the curved corridor until it opened on the right into a high, bright room.

Lina stepped inside. The far wall was made entirely of glass and sunlight streamed softly from the panes onto the dark wood floors. In the center of the room, a small, pale-yellow settee and two matching sitting chairs were arranged around a glass breakfast table. Fresh flowers decorated the center of the table, and a plush, cerulean rug lay beneath them. The scent of gardenia, honeysuckle, and lilies floated to Lina's nose. "This is my favorite room in the house," said Ita proudly.

An enormous tapestry decorated the wall on her left. She moved to examine it as Ita placed pastries and fruit onto her plate and poured hot tea into the china teacup. Lina touched the tapestry lightly with her fingertips. It was a map. The word *Caelium* was stitched in large script at the top of it. Shades of blue thread had been woven at its base to create a rolling sea, while high, gray mountains shrouded in a wall of mist were woven to the west. At its southernmost border, a chain of two islands dotted the blue water in a crescent shape. To the north stood a large forest full of oak trees, and a reddish-brown desert with intricate rock formations was woven in the east. A village was situated above the sea. Lina recognized the tan buildings and sloping roofs as those of Meallta. In the northeast, beyond a central, grassy plain, a majestic castle rose out of sheer, gray mountain peaks. Beyond it, at the northernmost part of the tapestry, white, sparkling threads indicated a wintry scene of snow and ice.

Lina trailed her fingers from the center of the sea, where she estimated she had landed after she fell through the gate. Walking her fingers up and left, she followed the map out of the city gates and across the rolling landscape toward the woven mist that shrouded the mountain range. She lingered her fingers here. The mist swirled with silver and white threads, creating a shroud that hid the mountains from the rest of the map.

Ita appeared at her side, gazing up at Lina's fingers. She smiled. "Arto created it," she said quietly.

"The tapestry?" asked Lina, peering down at her.

"No, no, dearest, the Mist. A wall of protection from foul, prying eyes and dark hands." Ita touched the silvery threads lovingly with her small fingers. "Only the purest hearts can pass through."

Lina squinted at the tapestry, furrowing her brows at the Mist. "Protection from what exactly?" she asked.

Ita's face sobered, her eyes solemn. "From the Court of Orm and all his foul beasts. Arto fled from them, many cycles ago, and came here, to the Timekeepers Court. These West Mountains are the home of his ancestors. He sealed the mountains in the Wall of Mist, protecting this home and all who still live here. Though too late for so many, we who remain are grateful for it."

Lina turned to Ita, eyeing her solemn face curiously. "Arturo was part of the Court of Orm?" she asked. She remembered the eerie stillness of the speaker on the platform. He had mentioned the Court of Orm before the giants had carried the bird-woman away.

Ita smiled a sad smile. "Long ago, my dear, but no longer." She patted Lina's shoulder and turned, arranging the flowers in the vase.

Lina moved away from the tapestry, lowering into a seat. She dropped a sugar cube into her cup, stirring thoughtfully. "I saw him leave this morning. He and Bayard. They flew up over the mountains." She flicked her eyes to Ita, taking a sip of the tea. Then she sat down her cup. "Do you know where he's going?"

Ita sat her plump frame on the settee opposite her, pouring tea into her cup. "He is often away from home, but where he goes, I do not know." She smiled. "We are always glad to see his return. Especially now, with such a lovely guest." She grinned at Lina, lifting her cup and saucer into her lap.

"Do you know when he will return?" Lina asked.

Ita sipped, then placed her cup back onto the saucer, setting it gingerly on the table. "He is often gone for weeks, sometimes a full Quarter. Many times, he returns, and his eyes are all sorrow."

She stood, smiling down at Lina and smoothing her apron. "I must go. I've much to do. Please, stay here as long as you like. Enjoy your breakfast. After, you are welcome to explore the house and grounds. I will lay the dinner at twilight." With that, she turned and bustled out of the room, leaving Lina alone with her breakfast.

Lina popped a fat berry into her mouth and stood at the back window, gazing over the landscape. It was a lovely day. Maybe she would explore the grounds like Ita had suggested. She raised her arms, stretching. Despite her nightmares and fitful sleep, she felt clear-headed and strong, stronger than she had in a long while.

She pocketed a pastry and took the stairs to her rooms two at a time, retrieving her cloak and slinging her weapon across her back. Bounding down the stairs, she swung open the front door. Lina inhaled. The air was crisp and fresh, and a light breeze tickled the back of her neck. She would visit the stables. It was the perfect day for that. Sunlight streamed brightly on the lake, creating dancing patterns on the water. She headed left at the corner of the house, then she followed the rounded stone of the estate and turned right, into a flat piece of land encircled by trees and mountains.

The stables were made in much the same style as the house. Stone stalls were hewn from the mountainside and twisting tree limbs climbed over its roof, their tangled green leaves shading the sides. The stable boys were leading large beasts from the barn into a stable yard at the building's right. She recognized Benjamin from last night's dinner. He was holding a small rope tied to the neck of a large birdlike creature.

Lina eyed it as she approached the stable yard in wonder. The creature had the head of an eagle, and its legs and back were those of a lion. She had seen pictures of one in one of her books. Two great brown wings were folded at his sides, and his long tail had a tuft of brown feathers on the end. Benjamin led the large beast over to her, grinning. The creatures ruffled its wings, and she stepped back slightly, chuckling with a mix of fear and delight. Benjamin held the rein tightly, stroking the large creature's feathered neck.

She turned to the young man. "Hello, again," she said. "I'm Lina. You're Benjamin?"

"Yes, good morning," he said brightly.

"Good morning," she replied.

All at once, Ben bowed to her, placing his fist at his chest. She frowned down at him. *Strange.* He returned to stand by the creature, smiling. She grinned back at him, wondering at his odd behavior.

Tentatively, she reached out her hand. "Who is this magnificent creature?" she asked softly.

"This is Cyrus. He is our highest-flying griffin. And the fastest." Benjamin beamed up at the animal, patting his flank. It was obvious Ben adored him.

"Hello, Cyrus. Nice to meet you," Lina said.

Cyrus bowed his head low, placing his forehead onto her hand. She giggled, stroking his downy feathers. The griffin closed his eyes, making soft cooing noises in his throat.

Benjamin chuckled. "He likes you. Normally, he doesn't get on so well with others. He has been a *pain* to learn to ride."

Lina's eyes opened wide. "You *ride* these?" she asked, her face registering shock.

Benjamin chuckled at her expression. "Of course! They *are* the fastest form of travel in the West Mountains. Except for Bayard, of course, but nobody can catch him except for Master Arto." He laughed.

Lina studied Benjamin's face. He had kind eyes. She thought he must not be more than one or two years her junior. At least, that's the age he appeared. He looked sideways at her, grinning. "Would you like to ride him?" he asked. She eyed the animal dubiously, biting her lower lip. His long talons scraped at the dirt, and he lowered his head, pulling on the rope. "I…I'm not sure," she said uncertainly.

"Come on! I saw you ride in on Bayard. If you can stay on his back, you can certainly ride Cyrus, here." He patted Cyrus's furry back, and the griffin cooed appreciatively.

Lina grinned. "Okay." She tucked a blonde hair behind her ear, frowning. "But I need some lessons. I've never ridden a griffin before."

Benjamin smiled broadly. "*Excellent*. I'm just the man for the job."

He reached into a bucket by the stable doors and handed her a brush. She followed his motions, brushing Cyrus in long strokes from his head to his rump. The beast turned to her, nudging her with his large beak. She giggled, patting his feathery head.

Benjamin placed the brushes back in the bucket and fit a simple leather bridle over the griffin's head. He grabbed the reins in one hand, bracing himself on Cyrus's back as he jumped, swinging his leg astride. He patted Cyrus's flank twice, whistling through his teeth. The griffin took off, galloping across the yard. He lunged with his muscular legs onto a large rock and lifted his wings, taking smoothly to the air. Benjamin pulled the reins, leading them in a wide circle over the valley before landing smoothly at Lina's feet. He made it look easy. "Your turn," he said brightly, sliding off the griffin's back.

He handed her the reins, and she took them with one hand, standing at Cyrus's side. The griffin bowed his head sideways at her, making soft noises in his throat. She scratched his feathered neck with her free hand then placed both hands above her onto the short hair of his back. She jumped once, swinging her slender leg astride.

"Impressive." Benjamin grinned, nodding at her.

Atop the large creature, she was much higher off the ground than she would have expected. Soon, she would be even higher. Her heart leapt into her throat at what she was about to do, and she grabbed the leather reins tightly, squeezing his flanks with her thighs. "Great," said Benjamin, nodding. "Now put your left hand onto his flank and pat twice. Whistle through your teeth."

Lina pursed her lips and patted the griffin twice with her left hand. A sharp sound escaped her teeth, and the griffin was off, talons digging up dirt as he galloped across the yard.

Lina skidded backward onto his rump, losing hold of the reins. She lunged, gripping them tightly with both hands, and scooted her body forward, hugging his neck. She recovered her balance and sat upright, squeezing tightly with her legs. The griffin leaped, lifting his brown wings as they glided high into the air. She pulled the reins hard to circle, banking right just before her leg brushed against the sheer rock of the mountain face. The open air rushed over her face and hair. It felt wonderful, and she let out a *whoop* as Cyrus soared over the valley. The griffin fed off her excitement, and they flew three times over the yard before she pulled left and tugged upward on the reins. Instantly, the griffin tucked his wings and glided softly to the dirt in front of Benjamin.

Benjamin whistled low and clapped his hands. "Excellent! You're a natural." Lina slid from the animal's back, patting his soft fur. "Thanks," she said, grinning breathlessly. "Could I come again tomorrow?"

"Of course. Cyrus needs the exercise anyway. You'd be doing me a favor."

"Okay, see you then."

"Tomorrow, then," he agreed.

She smiled at Benjamin and waved, turning back toward the house. Riding Cyrus was the scariest, most exhilarating fun she had ever had. She couldn't wait to do it again tomorrow.

CHAPTER 8

Arto had been gone for days, but Lina still looked to the skies for him every morning from her window. To pass the time, she visited the stables, riding Cyrus higher and farther through the West Mountains as her confidence grew. She had formed a bond with the griffin, and she snuck him treats every day from her breakfast plate, stuffing food into her pockets when Ita wasn't looking. His favorite was berries. He had begun trotting to her side when she came to the stable yard, cooing and nudging her hand in anticipation.

Ita had hemmed a dark blue pair of Arto's riding pants for her. Lina had taken to wearing them under her skirts. At first, she had blushed at the thought of wearing his clothes, but the pants were practically a necessity for everyday riding, especially with the aerial acrobatics it took to ride Cyrus. She grinned, tugging them on beneath her dress. They slid snuggly over her hips, fitted perfectly to her slender shape. She turned in the mirror, lifting her skirts up past her knees. Maybe she would have Ita hem one of his shirts for her next. She giggled, imagining herself greeting him in the courtyard wearing his clothes. His expression of shock in her mind made her laugh out loud.

One evening, she returned to the house, pleasantly tired and happy from the day of sun and exercise. She had missed dinner. The scent of the meal wafted from the kitchens, but Lina was too tired to eat. Cyrus's acrobatics had worn her out, and besides, she had eaten two handfuls of wild berries just before they returned to the stables. She just wanted to get a bath and lie down. She was just about to take the stairs to her rooms, but she paused in the entry hall.

The windows by the hearth were flung open, and a soft melody drifted into the sitting room on the warm night air. Lina went to the window, quietly resting her head on the frame. Ita sat in the garden, facing away from her in the stone pavilion. She held a small stringed instrument on which her fingers played a familiar tune. Its melody folded about Lina's ears, pricking her memory. The words to the song trickled softly through her mind, and she thought of her mother, who had sung it to her so often as a child. The lyrics seemed a part of her very soul. Softly, she opened her mouth and began to sing.

The Source bids me sing
The return of the King.
Let darkness not shorten the Time.
Blessed are these feet.
All creation shall see.
King Ard-Mathan in mercy shall rise.

Ita turned to her, eyes glistening with unshed tears. Standing, she dabbed them with the hem of her apron. She walked to the window, peering up at Lina with kind eyes as she touched her cheek. "These words you sing are good news, Evangeline," she said softly. "It brings me new hope to hear you sing them." Lina smiled down at her as Ita tucked a curl of her hair behind her ear. Then, she carried her instrument down the corridor, humming the gentle tune as she went.

Lina watched her turn the corner then climbed the stairs wearily. She slid into a nightgown and lay back on the soft mattress, pulling the starry covers up under her chin. Flipping onto her side, she sighed, closing her eyes. Nighttime was when her homesickness was the worst. Thoughts of her mother plagued her, and she missed the familiarity of her home. Images of Jacques worried face at her absence filled her mind, and nothing would stop the pictures of Remus' limp frame lying in the patches of snow. It was sweet mercy that the nights were shortened on this side of the gate, and her pain did not linger long. Lying in the dark, the hollow place in her chest pulled at the edges. It ached and burned with physical pain. She crossed her arms, bracing herself against it. "Please…help me," she whispered.

Her mind drifted again to the cottage in the clearing. The image was distant, hazy about the edges. Her mother was there, humming the song Ita had played, but strangely, Lina's heart didn't ache at her absence. She frowned, testing the wound in her chest as she pulled Jacques's face up behind her eyes. She could see him working in the clock shop, but his features were a bit blurred. The hazy orange frame of Remus swirled about his feet. Try as she might, she couldn't see him lying in the snow any longer. She smiled. The memories from the other side of the gate felt lighter, somewhat detached. She flipped onto her back, relaxing her arms. The familiar ache in her chest was there, but it felt better.

Her mind drifted, and she thought about her new home on Caelium's side of the gate. There was beauty in the mountainside estate. She loved her room, the library, the courtyard garden, and the stables at the Timekeeper's Court. A warm feeling spread in her belly, and she smiled in the darkness. The stables had probably become her favorite place of all. Riding Cyrus had given her new purpose. Enjoyment even. It had also helped keep her mind off Arturo's absence. Her time with the griffin had become so routine that she couldn't imagine a life without him now. She imagined his large beak resting in her hand as she brushed his downy neck and grinned. Cyrus could never replace Remus as her companion, but still, she loved the griffin dearly. She sighed, snuggling under the covers.

Flipping onto her side, she tucked one hand under her head. She wondered what Arto was doing right now. She hoped he was safe. Frowning, she thought back to her rescue in Meallta. He had moved so neatly, cutting the wolf beasts down in silence. He had not been afraid of the horrid black wolf-men, and Lina was sure he would fight whatever other evils he might encounter with equal expertise.

Grinning, she remembered her first ride on Bayard's back. Though the effects of the bird-woman's elixir had muddled her mind, she still remembered the ride. Bayard had galloped through the village streets faster than any horse she had ever known, and he soared even faster. Surely, he could outrun or outfly whatever foul creature he and Arto might encounter. Wherever Arto was, she was certain he would be all right. And, she hoped, he would return home to the Timekeeper's Court soon.

She pursed her lips, thinking back on their fight in the library. She still had so many unanswered questions. And he was so angry with her. Lina frowned. She still didn't understand why. She would have to settle it when he returned. Apologize, like she had planned. Then, maybe he would tell her more. Sighing, she closed her eyes. She would do it as soon as he got back. Settled, she relaxed, finally letting sweet sleep pull her under.

In her dreams, she glided through the mountains on Bayard's back. Her fingers were knotted in his long grey mane, and the great white horse soared over the valley, flying high above the trees. The breeze blew past her cheeks, flowing long curls back behind her head. It felt exhilarating, and Lina let out a *whoop* as Bayard banked a sharp mountain side. He shook his white head happily, and she reached her hand to pat his neck, but he had transformed into a feathered griffin. The griffin soared over the still lake in front of the Timekeeper's Court. The water was as smooth as glass, and Lina leaned over the edge of Cyrus's back, staring down at her reflection in the water. Arto sat behind her, holding her close to his chest. His face was relaxed. He was smiling.

She woke the next morning ready to ride. The feeling of soaring through the valley with Arto's arm tight on her waist lingered, and she was anxious to be at the stables. Peering out the window, she glared at the gathering clouds. Not the best day for riding a high-flying griffin. Ben had warned her that it wasn't best to fly in foul weather. No matter. Her lessons with Benjamin had paid off. She was an excellent rider now. Ben had even said it was as if she had been riding her whole life. She smiled, turning away from the ominous sky. She would simply fly up and out of the cloud bank.

She hurried to dress, selecting a deep blue day dress and slipping Arto's hemmed riding breeches underneath. She laced her hair into a winding braid and secured it, encircling her head like a crown. Dropping the compact into her pocket, she slung on a fresh cloak, along with her quiver and bow. She bound down the steps, stopping briefly inside the kitchen at the right of the sitting room. Silently, she crept along the stone floor.

Ita stood facing away from her, chopping vegetables on a long wooden island. She hummed in time to the rhythmic slice of her knife. Lina knew Ita wouldn't want her to ride in such foul weather. She would have to be quick so she wouldn't ask her any questions.

On the countertop to her left, some dried berries and nuts sat in a small bowl. Keeping her eyes on Ita, Lina crept towards it. She swiped a handful of the mixture, folding herself silently back around the doorframe and dashing for the front door with Ita none the wiser. She closed it quietly behind her, stuffing a few of the nuts and berries into her mouth.

Thankfully, the stable yard was empty. She glanced upward at the ominous clouds. Ben and the others would not be exercising the griffins today. Ita probably had them busy inside with some task or another. With an estate as large as the Timekeeper's Court, there was always some chore for them to do. That was good. It would keep her from being seen.

She crept into the stables, silently checking each stall for Cyrus. The griffins cooed softly as she passed, sensing her presence. She had almost reached the last stall when she heard a familiar throaty caw at her back. She spun, startled by the noise. Cyrus hung his feathered neck out of the stall behind her, nuzzling her jaw with his beak. She giggled, patting his feathery head. "Hello, there," she whispered. Clucking to him, she grabbed a leather bridle as she swung his stall open wide. "We have to be quiet, okay?" Cyrus cooed a soft response as she slipped the bridle over his head and led him to the yard at the right of the stables.

Jumping once, she fluidly swung her leg across his back, grabbing the bridle in her right hand. Patting him twice on his flank, she let out a long, sharp whistle. The griffin's talons scraped the dirt as he galloped across the yard and lifted his wings. Tucking her legs tightly against his sides, Lina expertly balanced on his bare back as he climbed higher and higher into the air. She whistled, pulling down on the reins, coaxing him to go even higher. Lina's excitement only allowed her to see the dark sky as a challenge to face.

They were almost even with the mountain peaks, higher than they had ever flown. Heavy, dark clouds rolled dangerously close to Lina's head, and her feelings seemed to balance between fear and exhilaration. All at once, something sharp and wet landed on her cheek. Instinctively, she recoiled, touching the spot as more rain drops sprinkled her nose and forehead. The water seemed to bring her back to the moment, back to this world. A world that was not her own, but with storms not unlike what she was used to.

A downpour began in earnest. She pulled up the hood of her cloak, shielding against the sudden storm and patted Cyrus, clucking to him as he pumped his powerful wings up into the cloud bank. He chuffed nervously at the pouring rain, but Lina urged him on. "It's okay," she whispered, her urging dampened by the wind and rain.

Thick, gray storm clouds cloaked them on all sides, and rain pelted them in wet sheets. A flash of jagged purple lightening streaked the air to their left, then another lit the sky to their right. Cyrus screeched and pulled up from the bright flashes, nearly toppling Lina from his back. She gripped his neck and tucked her knees, her heart fluttering wildly as she fought for control. He pumped his wings nervously, but soon, he righted himself, steadying himself as he climbed.

Lina had not been ready for another streak of lighting to flash just in front of them, and its bright purple light caused her to squeeze her eyes shut. She yelped as Cyrus screeched loudly, and a burning smell tinged her nose. He pulled in his front paw, whimpering. He had been struck. His wings stuttered, and he lunged, flying erratically through the cloud bank. Lina hugged his neck tightly, burying her face in the soft feathers of his neck as he zigzagged through the clouds. Her stomach was doing somersaults, and she could barely keep her seat.

They were diving now, soaring hard and fast. Lina opened her eyes. The air around her was close and thick. She could not see past Cyrus's neck. Her heart dropped to her feet. They had entered Wall of Mist. She whipped her head to look behind her, just catching the outline of the mountain range before the Mist closed them in. Cyrus pumped his wings, and Lina held her breath, tucking herself tightly against his back. Fear cloaked her as Ita's words about the Mist flooded her mind. She had said the Mist was a wall of protection for those that called the West Mountains their home. *Only the purest hearts can pass through*. But what danger awaited them on the other side?

She gripped the reins and held fast as Cyrus took another steep dive. They burst from the Wall of Mist and found the ground approaching quickly. With a sharp yell, Lina pulled back, and Cyrus shrieked, skidding to a stop on the grass at the other side. She dismounted quickly and lifted his front paw, stroking his leg and speaking to him in soothing tones as she examined it. A small, jagged burn marked the end of his foot, and she hoped no serious damage was done. "You poor thing," she said quietly. Her heart squeezed that she'd been the cause of his injury. If only she hadn't flown so high, maybe he wouldn't have gotten hurt. "I'm so sorry," she whispered. She placed her hand over the spot, and he closed his great eyes, cooing softly in his throat.

Suddenly two large shadows passed over their heads. Lina shielded her eyes, peering up at them. Two enormous black crows circled above, their glossy black wings wet from the hard rain. They turned their heads, training their glittering black eyes on her face. One swooped downward, reaching for her with its sharp talons. Lina screamed as she leapt away, trying to take out her bow, but the crow picked her up by her cloak, pinning the weapon to her back. She thrashed against the crow's hold, and he pecked at her face, forcing her to shield her eyes. His beak bit into the corner of her forehead, and she hissed in pain as hot blood trickled down her cheek. Cyrus cawed frantically, galloping awkwardly on his hurt leg and flying up into the air after her.

He pushed up against the giant crow's breast with his feet, knocking Lina loose. She screamed as her heart lifted to her throat and she tumbled toward the earth. The rush of the fall pushed up on her stomach as Cyrus swooped, catching her on his back before she made impact. She landed with a grunt, clinging to his feathers as her feet dangled out over his rump. The other crow dove, landing his sharp feet on Cyrus's back beside her. The griffin screeched, pulling up as the crow's claws dug into his furry skin. The other crow descended, picking at her cloak with his feet, trying to lift her from Cyrus's back again. She raised one arm from Cyrus's neck, reaching back to pull an arrow and stab wildly at the crow. His claws scraped her fingers and he cawed menacingly, lowering his beak to peck deep punctures into the back of her neck. Lina gritted her teeth as pain seared from the wounds. Wet blood flowed from the marks, staining the back of her dress.

Just then, a deafening sound pierced the air to her right. The powerful neigh of the white horse was unmistakable. It was Bayard. She had no time to turn and look before Bayard was upon the great crows. He spun in the air, kicking at them with his powerful back legs, and Arto slashed at their dark wings with his sword. The great crows flapped their wings backward, cawing in sharp protest as they moved away in retreat. Lina pulled herself upright on Cyrus's back, wiping the blood from her forehead with her sleeve as she watched them fly away. She did not remove her eyes until they were two dark specks on the clouded horizon.

Arto turned to her, his face ashen. He held his sword aloft. Its blade was slick, still dripping with thick, black blood. "We must go," he said grimly. "He has seen us now. More of his foul beasts will be here any moment." He wiped his sword and stashed it at his waist as Bayard turned, flying toward the east.

Lina clucked to Cyrus, following closely behind them. She wondered what he meant. Who had seen them? And what other foul beasts did this mysterious *he* have at his disposal?

They flew hard across the rolling landscape, not stopping until the sun had dropped below the clouds on the horizon. It shimmered at the far edge of the land. The daylight had stretched long, longer than it seemed to have stretched even a few days ago, and Lina was exhausted. She hoped they would stop soon. Finally, Bayard dove and she followed, landing softly behind him in a clearing encircled by trees. Arto dismounted, striding toward her quickly. "What were you *doing* beyond the Wall of Mist?!" he bellowed. "I left Ita and Benjamin with special instructions to watch you closely. To keep you safe!" He half turned, running a hand through his hair, then faced her. He shook his head. "You don't understand what you've done. We're not ready. I haven't found them yet, and the others have not agreed." He turned back to her, putting his nose close to her face. "And now *he* knows you are here!"

She blinked at him in shock, and then her anger flared. She frowned up at him furiously. "It was an accident!" she yelled, pushing her chin toward him. "Ita and Benjamin had nothing to do with it. Benjamin has been teaching me to ride, and you've been gone for *days*! I…I snuck out. Cyrus and I flew too high. He was struck, and then, I lost track of where we were going. Ita doesn't even know I left the house." She tucked her arms around her chest, glaring at him as she huffed. "And what do you mean *he* knows I am here? Who is he?"

Arto sighed. He dropped his face defeatedly as he sat heavily on a flat stone. He tucked one knee, lacing his fingers across it as he looked up at her. "Orm. I'm talking about Orm and his court. The crows are his spies." He paused, looking in to the distance as a muscle feathered in his jaw. Lina waited patiently, not breaking her gaze as he looked back at her. "When Orm murdered King Ard-Mathan, the king struck him with blindness, thus ensuring he could not see the corruption he has created. The crows are his eyes. Through their sight, he keeps watch on the realm. They circle the skies of all Caelium at his command. He accesses their thoughts, seeing what they see and hearing what they hear. They can't pass through the Wall of Mist, but since you were beyond it, they have seen you. Now that Orm knows you're here, he will do everything he can to kill you, to speed his plan along. You're no longer safe." He hung his head.

Lina bent down beside him. She stared down at her hands for a moment, digesting his words. Then she held up her arms in question. "I don't understand what you mean," she said quietly. "Why am I not safe? Why does Orm even care that I'm here?"

Arturo paused, gazing toward the setting sun. When he looked back at her, his face as hard as stone. "Because, Lina, you are the daughter of the king."

Shock flooded her system at his words. A tinny, ringing sound began in her ears. Her stomach felt sick, and suddenly, she was faint. She sat down hard on the grass, tucking her knees to her chest. Her heart was pounding in her ears. She couldn't think clearly.

Bayard moved behind her, ruffling the top of her head with his muzzle. The horse spoke her name softly, worry in his voice. Lina swallowed convulsively, brushing his nose with her fingertips, and he nibbled gently at her shaking hand. Satisfied that she remained conscious, Bayard moved away, and she gazed at Arto, who was kicking at the dirt. Wrapping her arms around her knees, she rested her head on top, rocking softly on the ground.

Realization dawned on her as the events of her days in Caelium played back in her mind. She thought of her rescue from the trial in Meallta. How Arto had risked his life to pull her from the platform. How he had slashed fearlessly at the wolf beasts. Now it all made sense. The crows' attack, Arto's order of protection for her when he was away, Benjamin bowing in the stable yard,

Ita's shared glances with Arto, and the guarded secrets at the Timekeeper's Court. She was the daughter of the king.

It was almost too much for her to absorb. She had only just gotten used to the idea that there was an entire other world on this side of the gate. Now she had to grapple with the idea that she was royalty here? Tears threatened to overwhelm her, and she swallowed, clearing the thick lump in her throat. "My mother… She was the queen?" she asked.

Arto nodded. "Queen Astrid of Caelium. Wed to King Ard-Mathan…before her death," he murmured, hanging his head.

Lina's mind spun. She watched as the muscle in Arto's jaw feathered, and she narrowed her eyes. "You knew," she said. "You *knew* who I was. That's why you rescued me from the trial. Why didn't you tell me? *Why have you kept this a secret!?*" She threw up her hands in exasperation. "You just disappeared after that night in the library. And Ita wouldn't tell me anything. She said it wasn't her place. *So why?*"

Anger was blazing at her chest at the thought of what he had kept from her. She stood, stomping her foot, her hands gripping into fists at her side. There was no reason for him to keep the truth from her. Absolutely none.

Arto gazed up at her, his eyes full of regret. "There are things you do not understand, things you do not know." He blew out a breath, running his fingers through his dark hair. "Things I wish I could tell you…but…" He shook his head, stopping himself.

She shook her head. "You *lied* to me!" she said accusingly. "You didn't explain the situation. You didn't even tell me who I truly am!" She squeezed her eyes shut, then opened them, glaring at him with rage. "I wish I had never fallen through the gate! I wish I were back in the clock shop with Jacques, having rabbit stew!" she shouted. She pointed her finger at his chest, her eyes full of outrage. "I want to *know. What else are you not telling me?*"

Arto shot up from the stone, lifting his arms over his head. He half spun away from her then faced her again, his mouth a hard line. "Fine! That's just fine. If you want to go home so badly…to," He fluttered his arms wildly. "*Jacques* or whoever he is. Then fine! Just do it!" He stuck his palm out in front of him, drawing a large oval shape in the air. A quiet humming sound began as a wavering gate appeared before it. He stepped back from it, folding his arms. "Go. Just go."

She stood in shock, staring incredulously at the gate. "You— you said I couldn't go home! That there was no way to go back once I had gone through! That I was stuck here…with *you!*" She shook her head, chuckling mirthlessly. "Another *lie!*" She huffed, folding her arms. "I don't know why I'm so surprised. It's not like you've told me anything *true* since I've been here."

He spun toward her, his face inches from her own. His features were a sharp line, as hard and cold as she had ever seen them. But the edges of his eyes were tinged with fear and worry. "You want the truth? Then I'll give it to you," he spat. "Leave, if you must. But I'll warn you. Soon there will be no home for you to go back to!"

She shrunk back as if slapped, her eyes round pools. "What do you mean?" She frowned. "Have thieves broken in like before?" She shrugged. "I survived it. I…*we* can do it again. Jacques will help me get things back together."

Arto shook his head, peering at her with hard, dark eyes. "Thieves are the least of your worries. Soon, Time as we know it here in Caelium and in your world, the Mortal Realm, will cease to exist. Nothing and no one will survive it. There will be nothing left."

He turned away in defeat as Lina sat heavily on the stone, her face a mask of shock. She couldn't believe it. If everything Arto had said was true, then soon, everything she had ever known or loved would be gone. Her home in the forest clearing, Jacques in his clock shop, all of it. Silently, she scanned the landscape in front of her. Soon, Caelium wouldn't exist either. *Nothing and no one will survive it.* Isn't that what he had said? Her mind reeled, and she braced her fingers against her head, thinking.

Silently, Arto retraced the shimmering, oval gate with his outstretched palm, and its rippling shape disappeared beneath his hand. Then he sat down beside her, resting his elbows on his knees. Lacing his fingers in the front of his hair, he sighed. He turned his head to her face. "I'm sorry," he murmured. "I should have told you from the start. I shouldn't have lied to you…about who you are. Or about you being able to go back home…back to Jacques."

He looked away from her, gazing bleakly into the distance. "I'm sorry. For all of it," he muttered. He dropped his head, scuffing up a patch of dirt with the end of his riding boot.

Lina leaned back onto her palms, pursing her lips as she studied the landscape in the waning light. Arto's apology had stolen the heat of her rage. "It's strange," she said softly, after a few moments had passed. "The longer I'm here, the more it feels like…home." She shrugged. "In fact, my *other* home on the other side of the gate has gone quite blurry around the edges. This home feels more real to me than that one, now. The people feel more… real too." She dropped her eyes, and Arto whipped his head to her, raising his brows. Smiling with the side of his mouth, he relaxed, reclining back onto his palms. His fingers brushed her thumb and she flinched, pulling her hand away. He cleared his throat and readjusted his position, scooting slightly away from her.

She bit the side of her lip. "So why does the Court of Orm want me dead?" she asked.

Arto sighed. "It's a long story, but essentially, you are the key to Orm's defeat, or so the Book of Blessings reads." She frowned, leaning forward to rest her elbows on her knees. He continued. "There was a message, from the Eiks, that Queen Astrid and King Ard-Mathan had a daughter. The Eiks, ancient oak trees in the North Forest, are the Messengers of the Four Winds. It was said that the queen had escaped, while with child, to the Mortal Realm, after King Ard-Mathan's death. No one knew if it was true. We held hope, but we couldn't be certain. The Court of Orm intercepted this message and cut down the Eiks who had sent it. When the queen returned here, some cycles later, Orm ordered a lycanth to follow her back through the gate." Arto glanced at her sidelong. "Lycanths are the great wolf beasts you saw before the platform. She was captured by one of them, and then …" He trailed off, his jaw flexing.

"When I saw you on the platform in Meallta, I knew. You look just like her." He shook his head. "The golden hair…your eyes the color of the sea." He dropped his gaze, staring hard at the dirt. "When you heard Bayard's voice in the meadow, it confirmed who you were. Only Royals can hear animals speak like that." He paused. "Anyway…I'm sorry I didn't tell you."

Lina watched as deep grief skittered across Arto's face. She could see he was sorry for not telling her. Her mind drifted to his words, and she thought of her mother. It had been so long that she had almost forgotten what she looked like, but now, as if summoned by his memory, she remembered. Her mother's long hair and bright eyes matched her own. She could see how Arto had recognized her as her mother's daughter.

She thought of her mother's long absence as she had lain sick in the cottage. When she had returned, she had brought with her the sweet, healing wafer. Shortly after Lina's recovery, her mother had disappeared. She sucked in a breath, her eyes pricking with tears as she thought of the Tamarisk Cake. Her mother had gone back through the gate to get it for her. She had saved her life, and in the process, she had lost her own. The wolf-beast had taken her back through the gate, and she had been killed.

Lina pressed her eyes hard with her fingertips, willing tears not to fall. Taking a deep breath, she slowly exhaled and sat back onto her palms. "You knew her? My mother?" she said shakily. She turned to look at him. "What was she like? I was eight when she disappeared, and sometimes I think I've forgotten her."

Arto stared at the horizon, taking a deep breath. "She was strong, brave, and lovely…much like yourself." He turned to her, studying her face intently. The heat of his gaze pricked her skin, and Lina felt a flush rising from her chest. Her heart began to hammer as he leaned toward her, grazing her fingers with his palm. "Please, don't go," he whispered. He peered pleadingly into her eyes. "Just…just stay here. With me, okay?"

Lina searched his eyes, watching the deep ache of emotion in his dark gaze. She nodded mutely, her body frozen under his stare. Arto squeezed her hand. Then he dropped his eyes, moving away to rest his forearms on his knees. "Tomorrow we will head east. We'll meet with Chaeronne. He will tell you the rest."

Lina watched as a brief shadow passed his face, and then he stood, smiling down at her with softer eyes than she had seen since their moment in the library. He turned and began emptying his pack. Lina sat still, the heat of his palm still radiating on top of her hand. It was frozen in place. She watched as he started a small fire and tossed the materials for the tent up into the air. It drifted into a large circular shape, touching down near his feet. He lifted the flap and stepped inside, emerging a few moments later.

"If you don't mind, I'll sleep in here tonight," he said quietly. He watched her as she stared at him with hollow eyes, her face paling. He chuckled. "Don't worry. Cyrus and Bayard will alert us of any danger. And I've lowered the partition. So, your room will still be all your own." He grinned, pointing to the fire. "There's food in the pot when you're ready."

She nodded mechanically, and he smiled at her again before he disappeared behind the flap.

Slowly, Lina stood. She went to the fire and peered into the pot. A thick, rabbit stew was simmering. She frowned down at it, then rolled her eyes and placed her hands on her hips. "Very funny," she muttered. Arto's laugh boomed from inside of the tent, and she pursed her lips, holding back her own bubble of mirth.

Lina stared thoughtfully down at the stew. It did smell good. She spooned some of it into a bowl and returned to sit on the rock, enjoying her meal in the quiet twilight. When she had finished, she wiped the bowl clean and returned it to its spot by the fire. She wouldn't tell him, but Arto's stew was even better than what she had eaten in Jacques' shop. There was no need for him to know that, though.

Standing outside the tent, she crossed her arms over her chest and stared at it uncertainly. She was nervous about having Arto right beside her all night. She bit her lip, thinking. Really, it was no different than when he had slept on the opposite side of the fire from her in the forest that first night. Settled, she lifted the flap and let it fall behind her.

As he had said, Arto had rolled the partition down from the ceiling to the carpets, separating the large round shelter into two equal rooms. She paused in the doorway and glanced past it to his side of the space in surprise. She had expected that his room would be half the size, but his was just as large as her single room had been before. He was bent away from her, stoking the fire to a roar in the hearth. He stood barefoot on the stones, and he had rolled his white shirtsleeves to the elbows. The muscles of his shoulders and arms flexed with his movement.

She took a moment while his back was turned to survey his room. It was thoroughly masculine. A large flax rug sat below a dark blue armchair and wooden side table in the center of the room. Several books lay on top of it in a jumbled pile. She smiled, bending her head to try to read the spines. One of them read *Secrets of the Southern Sea.* A simple washbasin and small mirror were situated in the far corner, and a huge rectangular bed with a dark green coverlet was posted against the far wall. His sword and cloak were thrown haphazardly across it, and his boots lay in a jumbled pile on the rug.

She giggled at his messiness, and he turned, catching her appraisal. Clapping her hand over her mouth, she flipped herself quickly back against her side of the partition, crossing her arms over her chest and holding her breath. She could feel the warmth of color pinking the tops of her ears as his chuckle from rumbled from his side of the room, and she blew out her breath, fluffing the loose curls on her forehead.

Lina shrugged out of her cloak, hanging it over a chair with her bow and quiver. Walking to the mirror, she assessed her appearance. Her hair and dress were stiff with dried rain, and blood stained her forehead and back. She touched the wounds gingerly. She hoped that they weren't as severe as they looked. She needed a good soak and some fresh clothes.

She opened the trunk, pulling out a silver threaded nightgown and thick matching robe. She laid these along with fresh stockings and underthings across her mattress. Her washing tub sat waiting by the hearth. To her extreme embarrassment, Arto had already filled it for her. Sprigs of lavender floated on the water's surface. She paled as she studied them, then her face flushed a deep crimson. How was she supposed to bathe with him in the very next room? She sighed heavily as she sat on the edge of the tub and grazed her fingertips lightly across the top of the steaming water. It did look rather inviting. And truly, after all she had been through, she did need a soak.

Lina could hear him moving about his room. Just now, he had sat in his armchair and picked up a book, propping his feet on the small table. She felt self-conscious about undressing with him so close, but she was in desperate need of a bath. She bit her lip, gazing at the steaming water. If she didn't hurry up, it was going to cool. Then she would have to sit in tepid water. Though she had never had them at home, she had grown used to hot baths on this side of the gate. Now nothing felt worse to her than sitting in cooled water.

She moved to sit on the end of her mattress, unlacing her boots and slipping off her stockings. Standing, she lifted the compact out of her pocket and laid it on the nightstand. Unwinding her stays, she peeled off her stiff dress, letting it fall to the carpet. Then, as quietly as possible, she padded to the tub and stepped into the steaming water.

She scrubbed her hair and body, moving slowly so Arto wouldn't hear the slosh of her water. Even so, she finished within moments. Standing, she stepped out of the tub and stood before her fire, drying herself with the fluffy towel. She tried not to think about Arto's presence behind the thin partition. He turned a page, clearing his throat, and she jumped.

Hurrying to the bed, she shimmied into the nightgown, climbing swiftly beneath the coverlet. She tucked it tightly about her neck, laying her arms stiffly at her sides. Silence echoed in her ears.

Suddenly, Arto's book snapped shut. She heard him pad to the bed. Then he flopped onto his mattress. More silence. Lina waited, listening. "Did you enjoy your bath?" he said teasingly, in a low voice.

Her face and chest flushed, and she pursed her lips together. "Very funny," she said, fighting the smile in her voice. Arto chuckled, and she grinned. "Truly, it was very pleasant. Thank you," she said seriously.

More silence bathed the room about her until Arto's voice sounded again. "I'm glad," he said quietly.

"How did you—"

"Fill the tub?" he asked, his voice smiling. "I'll teach you. That and more. Good night, Lina."

She flipped onto her side, smiling against her pillow. "Good night, Arto."

CHAPTER 9

ARTO

On Lina's side of the tent, he started a fire in the hearth and filled her bathing tub with warm water, laying soaps and a thick towel beside it. Silently, he gazed at the floating lavender on the steaming surface. Unbidden images flashed in his mind, and he turned, making quick strides back to his side of the tent. He ran a hand through his hair. *Not good.* His face flushed and he shook his head, bracing his arm on the side of the hearth. "Get a grip on yourself, Arto. She's the daughter of the king," he muttered. He grabbed the poker, focusing instead on vigorously stoking the fire in his hearth. It was best to stay out of her space. Best for him and for her. She wouldn't want to be near him after tomorrow anyway.

Selecting a random book from the pile, he sat down in his armchair to read. He propped his feet on the small side table, opening it to his stopping place. Peering at the page, he willed his mind to focus. He scanned the words absently. It was no use. Thoughts of the woman in the room next to him filled his mind. He lowered the book and laid his head back against the seat. Grinning, he thought of Lina's curious blue-green eyes peering around his side of the partition. They had widened when he turned, and she had clamped a hand over her mouth as she leaped behind it. Sighing, he cleared his throat and lifted his book. Concentrating, he stared at the page. He scanned the words, sighing. He had read the same line three times, and he still had no idea what it said. Dropping the book in his lap, he pressed his fingers to his eyes.

He tried not to hear her now splashing in the water. His knee bobbed restlessly, and he tapped the spine of his book with his finger. She was moving slowly, trying to keep down the sound. He grinned to himself. She lifted out of the water, and he stood, snapping his book shut. *Good.* He tossed it on the table and paced in front of the fire, lacing his fingers behind his head. Now she was climbing across her mattress. It creaked with her movements. He held his breath, gazing up at the ceiling. At last, she was still, and her side of the tent was silent. He blew out his breath. There was no way he could have relaxed until now. He eyed his own bed. Maybe now he could get some sleep.

Stripping of his shirt, he fell across the mattress. He closed his eyes, then snapped them open, grinning as an idea occurred to him. Arto knew it would vex her. She had been embarrassed, trying to keep down the sound while she bathed. He crossed his feet, lacing his fingers lazily behind his head.

"Did you enjoy your bath?" he asked, struggling to keep the grin from his voice.

Her bed squeaked slightly, and she paused. "Very funny," she said flatly. Arto chuckled at her response. A few moments passed in silence as he tried to think of something more to say. Lina beat him to it. "Truly, It was very pleasant. Thank you," she said softly.

He grinned, happy he had pleased her. Flipping to face the screen, he propped his head on his hand. "I'm glad," he said, his smile widening.

Later, long after Lina had fallen asleep, he lay flat against the pillow and let his mind drift. Just as they had every night over the past several days, images of Lina dominated his thoughts. He remembered the delight on her face as he introduced her to Ita and showed her his home at the Timekeeper's Court. He thought about how she had looked in the emerald gown that night at dinner. How it tucked in at her waist and fell over her hips, her gold hair spilling in waves down her back. He blinked at the ceiling. He'd wanted to wind his fingers through it. She had taken his arm, and her touch had seared heat through his dinner jacket. If he thought much about it, he was sure he felt the weight of her palm even now.

His mind wandered, and he thought of wrapping his arm around her slim waist and pressing her body close as they rode Bayard. He smiled. She had yelped in spite of herself as they dove into the meadow that first night. Later, he had covered her trembling body with his cloak, hiding her from the Mumla. He could smell the fresh scent of soap in her hair as he bent over her head, whispering in her ear. The next morning, he hadn't been able to pull his eyes away from the sight of her in the light blue nightgown. He blew out a breath, crossing his arms over his chest. He was in trouble, and he knew it.

His memories shifted, and he was back in the library. Still, the memories were all of Lina. Her eyes had flashed anger when he pinned her small body against the bookshelves. She had gripped the shelf behind her with white knuckles, staring daggers. The fear in her eyes had made him soften. He couldn't stand to see it. He had been angry too, but it didn't stop him from wanting to be near her. She had looked so lovely in the lamplight of the library that, even then, right after he had met her, he couldn't help himself. The longer he had held her there, the more she had relaxed under his gaze. She had studied his face shyly from beneath her lashes and her cheeks had flushed. He grinned. *Pink.* An enticing color. He had wanted to lower his arms. To wrap them around her and kiss her full mouth, before she found out the truth and it was too late. But he hadn't. And he regretted it.

Arto laced his fingers behind his head, staring up at the ceiling. Tomorrow they would head east to the Court of Warriors. It was rumored that the court had been attacked. The male centaurs had been almost completely wiped out. Arto wondered what bleak scenes they would see when they arrived. He was sure the rumors were true. After all, the Court of Orm showed no mercy. Even so, he was eager to see Chaeronne.

Much Time had passed since he had seen his friend: the former general of the Court of Ard-Mathan. With the fall of the king, the male warriors had been hunted down, one by one. Orm had ordered them slaughtered, or worse. Arto had heard that some of them had been turned, the corrupted centaurs now standing with the Court of Orm. Understandably, the general stayed hidden. Chaeronne had lost his army and his king, and a bounty had been placed on his head.

Arto was worried for his friend. He knew what he must ask of him, and he also knew that Chaeronne would not deny him. Since he had rescued Lina, the pieces of his plan were falling into place, but he would need the general to complete the task. It would not be easy, and it might cost Chaeronne and many others their lives. But what choice did they have?

Tomorrow they would meet with Chaeronne, and then Lina would know everything. He flexed his jaw, frowning. As general, Chaeronne knew the Histories of Caelium better than anyone. And he knew Arto's history too. Enough of it to send Lina running back through the gate to her home and to Jacques. Then she would be lost, to him and to everyone else, and every created thing in the known worlds would soon follow. He sighed, turning onto his side. He hoped she could forgive him after she found out the truth. The truth of who he was. The *real* Arturo Elikai. Or who he once had been. And what he had done.

He grimaced. Who was *Jacques* anyway? Some man she had mentioned from back home. "Wish I was back in the clock shop with Jacques," she had said. Arto frowned. Probably, Jacques made her feel safe, which was more than he could say for himself at the moment. Even with his best efforts, she was still being hunted by the Court of Orm. He sighed. He doubted that Jacques had ever done her any wrong in his whole life. And, like she had said, he had protected her when she lived on the other side of the gate.

Truly, Arto knew he couldn't shield her from all harm, all hatred, and all worry, but that didn't stop him from wanting to. Pressing his eyes, he blew out a breath. He couldn't blame her for wanting to go home. Especially not after tomorrow, after she learned the whole truth. She would probably force him to open a gate for her on the spot. And he had already decided, he wouldn't deny her.

Still, she hadn't gone through the gate when he'd opened it last night. Surely that counted for something. Maybe it even meant she wanted to stay. He squinted. Or maybe she had only wanted to know the answers to her questions. About herself...and her mother.

His heart sank as he thought of the former queen. Queen Astrid of the Court of Ard-Mathan. The fair and gentle queen. She had shown him nothing but kindness, and he had repaid her in the worst way possible. His mind drifted, and he stood on a boat, peering over the bow. Her golden hair floated beneath the water, and her eyes, Lina's eyes, stared up at him, unblinking. His own pricked with tears, and he squeezed them shut, pressing them with his fingers.

He fell asleep soon after, drifting on thoughts and memories. In his dreams, Lina lifted an arrow, aiming at a huge clock. Its hands wound around its face faster and faster. She pulled the bow tightly against her jaw, her eyes narrowing in concentration. Filling her chest with a deep breath, she held it, releasing it with the arrow. It struck true, sticking in the center of the clock face. The giant clock shattered like glass, falling in glittering shards to the throne room floor. As the pieces struck the stone, they turned to blood. It ran red over the throne room, pooling in a large circle at Lina's feet.

Lina woke before him the next morning. He could hear her moving quietly around her side of the tent. He raised up onto his elbows groggily, catching sight of her as she lifted the flap and disappeared behind it. She was already fully dressed, her bow and quiver strung across her back. He lifted himself to the side of the bed, bracing his hands on his knees. He sighed, pushing up off the bed and splashing water onto his face from the basin. Running the excess through his hair with his fingers, he peered at himself in the mirror. Dark circles hung under his eyes, and his face was drawn. He looked as if he hadn't slept at all, and, in truth, he barely had. Night in Caelium was growing shorter with each passing day, and he had tossed and turned for most of the last one.

All of it was getting to him…the long stretches away from the Timekeeper's Court, the dwindling future, the guilt of his past, and the fact that she would *know*. Today, she would know all of it. His jaw flexed, and he dropped his eyes. It was an awful thought. Just when he felt he had made a little headway with her, everything was about to change.

Today was the day. He went to his trunk, pulling out a clean shirt and riding pants. Stuffing his legs and arms through the holes, he bent to lace his boots and fastened his sword on his side. Flinging his cloak around his shoulders, he waved his hand once over the fireplace. The flames went out beneath his hand. Then he lifted the flap of the tent, squinting into the morning sun.

CHAPTER 10

Lina crouched beside the firepit, stoking a small blaze. Coffee simmered in the pot above it. She turned to Arto, flipping her long braid over her shoulder. "Good morning," she said, smiling. She turned back to the fire, tending the flames.

"Morning," he mumbled, moving to sit opposite her on the smooth stone. "You're up with the sun, and you already made coffee. I'm impressed." He frowned lightly. "Though you probably did more work than I would've done." He smiled from the corner of his mouth, crossing his arms over his chest.

Lina flicked her eyes up to him, grinning. "I'm perfectly capable of starting a fire and making coffee," she sniffed.

He chuckled. "Well, how about we do it my way?"

He waved his hand over the fire, extinguishing it immediately.

"Hey! I worked on that all morning!" she huffed.

He smiled but didn't answer, moving the pot of coffee from where it hung over the fire and placing it on the ground. "Just wait. It'll be much less work this time. Watch." He stuck his hand, palm out, toward the logs. Rolling his fingers inward, he turned his palm toward his face. Orange flames ignited at his feet, crackling softly. He cut his eyes at her, smirking. "Easy," he said, shrugging. He waved his hands over the flames, and they vanished. "Now you try."

She huffed, dusting her skirt as she stood to her feet. "Show off," she muttered. Sticking out her hand, she concentrated on the logs. Arto watched her face with fascination as she furrowed her brow and bit her lower lip. He grinned at her over the firepit, his eyes drifting to her mouth. She glanced up at him, and he flicked his eyes up to hers, smiling wider. She smirked at him. "Stop it. I'm trying to concentrate," she said primly. Clearing her throat, she pursed her lips at him and readjusted her weight. Putting out her hand again, she retrained her gaze on the logs. She rolled her fingers into a fist, turning her palm quickly toward her face. Nothing happened. She dropped her hand. "It's no use. I can't do it."

"No, no. You can't give up that easily. Anyway, nobody gets it on their first try. You just have to move slower this time. Here. Just let me show you."

Arto moved to her back, placing one hand on her left shoulder and reaching his other arm around her right. The heat from his chest radiated onto her neck, and her bare skin tingled where his forearm touched. He shadowed the back of her slender hand in his large one and moved her palm to face outward. "Like this," he murmured softly.

Slowly he rolled his fingers inward on top of her own, gently twisting her wrist around toward her face. At once, orange flames sprang to life on the logs. Lina smiled down at the fire, giggling softly. Arto's breath tickled her right ear as he brought his lips close. "See? It's easy," he breathed. "Timekeepers and Royals can control the elements. It's how I filled the bathing tub."

His voice was like gravel. It caused her breath to catch in her throat. He lingered a moment, holding her fist in his palm. Slowly, he brushed his nose over the top of her ear, breathing in the lavender scent that clung to her hair. Then he pulled away, staring at her as he moved to replace the pot of coffee over the fire.

Lina couldn't move. The nearness and Arto's voice had made her forget how to do so. Arto peered up at her as he dipped some coffee into a cup, smiling from the corner of his mouth. Her cheeks were flush, and she dropped her eyes under the intensity of his gaze. He held the cup out to her, and she reached for it mechanically. The tips of their fingers brushed as he passed it to her, and she jumped, sloshing hot coffee onto her hand. She winced, ignoring the sting of it as she murmured thanks, furtively wiping her hand on the side of her cloak. Avoiding his gaze, she focused intently on blowing across the top of her hot drink. He kept his eyes on her as she sipped it, and she turned sideways, flustered by his continued stare. Why was he looking at her like that?

Finally, he looked away, and she relaxed, slumping against the trunk of a slim tree behind her. Her heart still throbbed in her ears, and her hand shook on the coffee cup as she lifted it to her lips. She held it out from her, afraid of spilling it again. Her heart was flying. She put her hand against her chest, silently pulling down a calming breath. Her heart rate slowed, and she swallowed, standing upright.

She had been alone with Jacques plenty of times. Day after day, she went to visit him in his clock shop, but it had never felt like this. Being near Arto felt a thousand times worse. She frowned. Or was it better? She wasn't sure. All she knew was that being with Arto felt something like losing control. With a soft smile, she realized she knew just what it felt like. It was like falling through the gate and being stretched past one's capacity. Scary, overwhelming, unsettling, but also new and exciting. She sighed, tucking her hair behind her ear.

She had to admit that thoughts of Arto had dominated her mind while he was away. Despite her best efforts to distract herself in the long days at the Timekeeper's Court, she hadn't been able to keep her mind off of him. It was a strange phenomenon she had never experienced before, and she wasn't sure how she felt about it.

Behind her, Arto raised his arms, lifting the tent into the air. It rolled inward, landing in a neat pile at his feet. He stuffed the contents of their campsite into his bag and turned to her, his eyes suddenly serious.

"Today we are riding east, to the Court of Warriors. There, we will meet with Chaeronne. The centaurs are loyal to the Court of Ard-Mathan. Once we are behind their Desert Door, we will be safe. But until we arrive, we are at risk. We're going to stay on the ground. After our encounter with the crows, I don't trust the skies. We will avoid Meallta, too. There are too many of his spies working in the village. The village is full of darkness now. Too many there are loyal to his cause. Instead, we will travel to the Haima Mountains in the northeast and head through Traveler's Pass. They won't be expecting us to come so close to Leyth Castle, so it's less likely we will be caught if we travel that way. Keep your eyes open, and stay close. Orm's foul beasts will be out in force. We will make camp at twilight in Traveler's Pass."

Lina nodded at his speech, gripping her bow. She tried to make her face a brave one, but truthfully, she was terrified. After all she had experienced, she hated to think what other horrors awaited them on their journey.

They wasted no time mounting up. Arto clucked softly to his horse, and Bayard pricked his ears, scraping up dirt as he galloped across the landscape. Cyrus cooed, turning his beak in her direction. She scratched his feathery neck. "Let's go, Cyrus," she said, patting his rump and whistling through her teeth. They took off, racing behind. Up ahead, Bayard strained his neck against Arto's hold, trying to gain speed. Lina could tell that they were moving slower than the horse would've liked. Still, they were nearly flying. The warm air pricked her skin as it whipped past, and she spurred her heels, urging Cyrus faster.

They raced at breakneck speed across the plains all day. Arto kept his eyes on the skies, keeping careful watch for the crows. Lina scanned the land around them, unsure what other dangers might lurk. Nothing moved on the ground. The surrounding landscape was still and quiet, as if nature were hiding in the wings.

In late afternoon, the outline of an ominous mountain range came into view. Thick, churning clouds rolled over top it, their shapes casting purplish shade on the sheer rock faces below. Large pieces of stone had broken off the sheer peaks in several places and now sat in a cascade of dark stone that spilled out onto the surrounding plain.

High in the cliffs, a sprawling stone castle sat among the dark rock. Its spires rose high into the sky, encircled by the heavy clouds above. The castle appeared abandoned. No one stirred on the grounds, and no light spilled from its dark windows. They yawned out at Lina like hungry mouths in a blank face. She stared up at them, shivering.

Bayard banked right before the mountain range, heading for a grove of evergreen trees at the mountainous base. As they flew toward it, a wide, cavernous opening beyond the trees in the base of the dark rocks came into view. Cyrus's wings stuttered, and he pulled back beneath her. She could tell he was frightened, and she understood the feeling. Her own heart skipped in her chest as she eyed the dark opening, and she bent to scratch his neck, urging him forward in low tones.

When they reached the shade of the trees, they slowed to a walk, their animals' feet silent on the hard earth. Bayard tucked back his ears and lifted his tail, moving stiffly ahead of her on wary hooves. Thick evergreen branches brushed against her sides as they followed the narrow grove toward the rock. The closer they came to the opening, the more her fear prickled at her neck. She took a breath, trying to steady her emotions as Arto turned his head to her, placing a finger to his lips. She nodded once, pulling up the hood of her cloak.

The air inside the cavern was close. Oppressive. Lina sucked in a breath, and the smell of soot tinged her nostrils. It conjured the image of the lycanth in the clearing and she shuddered, beads of sweat breaking out on her back. There was something dark in this cavern. Something evil lurked in its hidden places.

The passage was narrow, and the ceiling was too low. She tucked her head, gripping tightly on the reins. The walls of the tunnel brushed against Cyrus's wings, pushing them against her thighs. She flicked her eyes ahead, blinking. The pass was so dark that she could not see Bayard and Arto in front of her. She patted Cyrus's rump, trusting him to guide her. The air was still, and it was too quiet. Holding her breath, she listened for a sound from the path ahead. At one point, she thought she heard soft scraping on the stone above, but when she looked up, there was only empty silence.

Suddenly the air widened, and the rock expanded on her sides and above. Twilight peeked down at her from the evening sky, and she released her breath, glad to have left the oppressive cavern behind. They had come into a narrow pass between two sheer, dark cliffs. Traveler's Pass. It extended farther than she could see, weaving left and right through the dark rocks to an unknown destination. A small stream ran down the center of the pass. She wrapped her cloak around her nose. Its water was putrid and smelled like rot and decay. Bayard flicked his ears, his neck high and alert. Cyrus followed him, stepping in wary silence through the stones.

Darkness crept quickly in the pass, and Arto pulled out his lantern, lighting a small flame. He clucked, and Bayard pulled up in a curve of rock on their left. Sliding off his back, he moved to help Lina dismount. The animals went to stand with their rumps against the rocky cliff, dipping their heads to sniff hesitantly at the mossy ground. Arto spread some berries from his pack under their noses, and they munched happily, raising their heads often to scan the pass.

Suddenly Bayard snorted, lifting his neck to look down the passage behind them. His ears pricked and he stomped his right hoof softly. Cyrus shifted uneasily beside him. A wary coo gurgled in his throat, and he ruffled his feathers anxiously. Arto exchanged a glance with Lina, and they turned to face the way they had come, sword and bow drawn. Something was coming. Something horrid.

Just then, a scuffling and scrabbling sound came from their right, midway up the sheer rock face. Lina swung her bow towards the sound, but it disappeared, concealed by the darkness. She waited in the silence, and soon, it resumed closer to their heads. Lina flicked her eyes up the rock, but the lantern light didn't reach very high, and she couldn't see what was making the noise. She swung her bow in the sound's direction, but it disappeared again, and the pass was quiet except for the gurgling stream. Silence pressed her ears as Lina pulled her bowstring tightly against her jaw.

Just then, a soft clicking sound rose right above them on the rock wall. Arto spun toward it, lifting the lantern toward the sound. A long, spidery antenna extended toward him, brushing the hood of his cloak off his head. Lina stiffened, raising her arrow toward it. She fired and the creature recoiled, scrabbling backward up the wall, a raspy roar piercing her ears. The severed antenna fell, rolling into the stream. Arto swung the lantern higher, slashing with his sword.

Lina gazed up at the beast in horror. Crawling above them on the wall was a monstrous insect, like a giant form of the creatures Lina had seen on the underside of leaves at home. Rows and rows of sickly, pale-white body segments scrambled above their heads on a thousand creeping legs. A double-forked hook protruded from the creature's back end. It swung the hook out at them, slashing like a sword. The beast turned its head toward them, snapping at their necks with its massive jaws. It opened them wide, revealing two curved claws on either side of its mouth. These it sprung outward, attempting to spear them. The creature had no eyes and instead felt its way around the battle with its one remaining antenna.

Cyrus screeched, flapping his dark wings and flying up to meet it on the wall. He tore at the creature with his talons, scraping mounds of pale flesh from its segmented body. Greenish-gray blood oozed from the wounds, dripping down the dark rock wall. The creature roared, turning his face toward Cyrus. He opened his wide jaws and lunged, and as Lina looked on, it pierced the skin under Cyrus's right wing with his claw. "Cyrus!" she screamed. Greenish venom oozed around the wound, dripping onto the griffin's fur, as the wounded Cyrus fell to the ground.

The insect scrambled backward, roaring his victory, and turned to Arto and Lina. It lunged, and Arto swung the lantern toward its head. The insect recoiled, and Lina loaded her arrow, swinging it to follow the creature as it scrambled over the rock. She fired, and the arrow hit its mark, pinning the beast to the wall. The creature rasped a roar, tucking in his front legs. Arto came behind her and, slashing with his sword, removed the insect's head, which fell with a heavy thud onto the mossy ground. The creature's body went slack, its legs dangling as it hung in a long rope down the sheer rock face.

Lina dropped her bow, rushing to Cyrus's side. She put his feathered head into her lap, stroking his soft neck. The griffin's eyes were weak, and his chest heaved rapidly. She lifted his right leg. The skin around his wound was turning black, and dark blood oozed onto the ground. She pressed the hem of her dress to the spot. "Not again," she breathed. He cooed softly, lifting his weak head for her to scratch. She put her fingers into his feathers, and he dropped his head back into her lap, closing his eyes. Bayard muzzled the griffin's forehead, nickering softly. Lina knotted her hand into his soft neck as hot tears threatened to spill over her cheeks. It was Remus all over again. "Please, not again," she said, sobbing.

Arto brought the lantern close. He moved her hand, examining the wound. The black skin around the opening streaked up the griffin's side. He bent, pressing his ear to Cyrus's chest. He listened a moment then reached over Lina's lap and gently pulled up the griffin's eyelid. Cyrus's pupil was blown. "Blasted venom," he said grimly.

Lina swung her head to him, tears pricking her eyes. "What can we do for him?" she asked.

He lifted the pack off his back, shuffling through its contents and producing a small parchment, handing it to her. She opened the parchment, revealing a light wafer topped with cream. Lifting it from the paper, she placed it under Cyrus's beak. The griffin lay still, too weak to open his mouth. Gently opening his jaw, she broke pieces of the wafer off in her fingers and carefully placed them onto his tongue. She coaxed back his neck, helping him swallow each bite.

When the wafer was gone, Lina tore a long strip of linen from her underdress. Arto helped her, lifting the griffin's weight as she wrapped it snuggly around the wound. She placed her palm over the spot. Dark blood soaked it through almost immediately, and she tore another strip, wrapping it again. She stared down at the bandage. "What else?" she whispered, turning to face him. Cyrus gazed solemnly down at the griffin. "Now we wait. The Tamarisk Cake can only do so much. The rest is up to the Source."

Lina bowed her head, her eyes filling with tears. She didn't think she could take losing someone else. First her mother, then Remus, and Jacques, too. She hoped beyond hope that Cyrus would be shown mercy. She hoped the Source would see them in the mountain pass and have mercy on her gentle friend.

CHAPTER 11

Morning dawned, and Lina lifted her head. The side of her face was damp from lying on the mossy ground, and bits of dirt clung to her cheek. She wiped it with her palm. Sometime in the night, Arto had covered her in his cloak. Now he lay propped against the rock wall, his arms crossed over his chest. She pushed back the cloak, sitting up.

A small dark patch of blood stained the dirt where Cyrus had lain, but he was no longer there. Her heart leaped in her chest, and she jumped to her feet, whirling in a circle. The griffin stood across the stream below the rocky cliff face. He and Bayard were pawing at the ground. Cyrus lifted his feathered head, cooing in her direction. Lina blew out a relieved breath. She grinned at the griffin as Arto stretched behind her. He smiled when he saw

Cyrus standing, chuckling through his teeth. He reached into his pack and crossed the stream, throwing a handful of dried berries onto the ground. The animals nickered and cooed in appreciation.

Lina wiped her wet eyes with the back of her hand. "I guess the Source of All had mercy on this griffin," said Arto as he smiled and patted the griffin's rump.

"And on me," Lina murmured. "So I wouldn't have sorrow upon sorrow." She thought of Remus and his orange body lying limp on the soft earth. Tears pricked her eyes anew. A phrase her mother had said often echoed now in her mind. "The Source holds mercy that is new every morning." That day, in Traveler's Pass, it was so. Lina had seen it with her own eyes.

She moved towards Cyrus and lifted the linen strip, examining his wound. She gasped in surprise, letting the stained bandage flutter to the ground. The gash was closed, and the dark streak had vanished. Her fingers touched the soft skin under the griffin's leg. A jagged, silvery scar had formed it its place. She patted his feathered neck. "You're well," she whispered happily.

"We'd better get moving," said Arto. "The Court of Warriors is almost a full day's ride."

Lina nodded, slinging her leg over her griffin's back. She whistled, patting his rump. Cyrus lunged beneath her, and they trailed Bayard, riding swiftly through the narrow path of Traveler's Pass to the landscape beyond.

They followed the winding passage for a long while until its rocky outcroppings tapered toward the ground. As they reached the trail's end, Lina peered past Bayard's ears. Cold air blew into her face, biting her cheeks, and the air around her pulled and hummed. An odd sense of foreboding crinkled around her ears, lifting the hairs on the back of her neck. It felt a bit like standing before the gate.

Ahead, the trail cut off, and the ground was cracked in a long, jagged line, dropping off before them into a deep, wide canyon. The air above the canyon wavered and crackled, illuminated by a strange bluish haze. Beyond it, a landscape of snow and ice stretched far across the horizon. Arto stopped short, and she brought her mount up beside him. He turned to face her, his gaze piercing.

"This is the Chasm. It's best if you don't look down. Not that you can see the bottom, but still." He wet his lips, sucking in a breath. "The Chasm is the resting place of the Rotha-Am, or the Wheel of Time. After King Ard-Mathan was slain, the Rotha-Am fell from its place and cracked the earth. That is when the Chasm opened. All manner of fell beasts emerged, ready to serve their master: Orm. Some still lurk there in darkness, awaiting the day the Rotha-Am ceases turning and creation is no more."

Lina gazed at the buzzing, bluish air above the Chasm. She wondered what creatures lay at the bottom of it. She thought of the lycanth and shivered. They were probably none she would want to encounter.

Arto continued. "The Rotha-Am exerts a powerful force on all that approach it, bidding them to come. As the Wheel of Time is a creation of the Source, it moves the hearts of created beings, which in turn move the Rotha-Am. It craves this communion with the created. It's why Orm searches for beings to feed to it. He wants to control it for his own.

Often as you approach, you will hear and see what you most desire. You must not give in. Now that it rests in the Chasm, the Rotha-Am's force is corrupted, and it may pull you down into it. Once you go in, you can't come back out. Just focus on the path, ignore the pull, and don't look down. No one and nothing expects any travelers to pass this way. We should be safe."

Safe. Right. Lina nodded mutely, flicking her eyes nervously to the Chasm's edge. Already she could feel its pull on her body and mind. She imagined it would be worse when she was on the edge of it.

Arto turned, leading Bayard slowly onto a thin rock ledge above the Chasm's edge. Small pebbles scraped under the horse's hooves, bouncing down the dark canyon wall. They echoed as the fell further and further, until Lina couldn't hear them anymore. Lina and Cyrus followed closely. Her heart thrummed as they began scaling the narrow ridge, and her palms began to sweat.

The strange hum of the Chasm pulled at her ears, curling about her mind. Its deep blue darkness beckoned to her, willing her head to turn. She forced her eyes onto the rock ledge, closing her mind to the buzzing sound. She was right. The pull of the Chasm was much worse on the edge of it. Furrowing her brow, she gripped the reins, her knuckles turning white. She focused on Cyrus's neck, breathing slowly in and out. Once, his front talon slipped the ledge, and she pitched forward, her vision tunneling and sweat breaking out on her forehead. She sat upright, swallowing convulsively.

The bluish haze above the Chasm wavered and shimmered in her periphery, and the smell of soot and sulfur tinged her nose. Deep below, the rattle of heavy chains echoed through the canyon. Disembodied moans curved out of the darkness to her ears, and hissing whispers folded in on themselves, one over the other. She shuddered, leaning her body away from the canyon and toward the sheer rock wall. It was all she could do to keep from peering over the edge.

Halfway across the ledge, a melodious female voice curled up out of the darkness. Lina shut her eyes, focusing on the steady movement of Cyrus's body beneath her. The voice was singing. It was a voice she knew very well. Panic rose in her chest, and her arms tingled. Sweat dampened her back, and she slowed her breathing, calming her hammering heart. *Don't. Look.*

The voice continued its song, moving out toward her ear. It was the voice of her mother. Unmistakable. Real. The hairs on the back of her neck stood on end. "Evangeline," her mother's voice whispered. "Come to me. I am here. Look. Look at me." Intense fear gripped Lina, and a heavy weight pressed in on her chest, pushing against an old wound. She grimaced, pressing her palm to the spot as the wound threatened to open. The air was too thin, and her throat constricted. Panic rose. She couldn't breathe. She lifted her chin, gulping small down breaths.

In her periphery, strands of long golden hair floated in the bluish darkness. They wavered and rippled in the shimmering air. "Look at me. Please," the voice said, sweetly. "It's me, Lina."

"Not real," Lina whispered.

"I'm sorry," her mother's voice pleaded. "So sorry that I have been gone, but I'm here now."

Lina's eyes pricked and she squeezed them shut, gritting her teeth. It was more than she could stand. She *needed* to look. She wanted to, more than anything she had ever wanted in her entire life.

"Look at me!" the voice demanded. A growl was building in the voice's chest, and the urge to turn her head was almost more than Lina could contain. "Look!" it screeched.

Lina buried her face in Cyrus's neck, tucking her shoulders up by her ears. Hot tears streamed off her chin, dripping silently onto his feathers. All at once, the voice was gone. Only the hum remained. Lina blew out her breath, wiping her cheeks with the back of her hand. She peeked up at Arto. He had pulled his cloak over his face, hunching his shoulders.

Soon they reached the end of the rocky ledge. They walked silently through a grove of fir trees, leaving the Chasm and its horrid sights and sounds behind them. Lina gripped her neck, gulping in the fresh pine air. She pressed on her chest with her free hand. The heavy weight of the Chasm was gone, but the old wound of her mother's absence still burned at the edges. She inhaled, sucking down the fresh air greedily.

The sun was already dropping in the sky. The walk on the edge of the Chasm had taken almost the entire day. The animals were exhausted from the arduous journey, and so was Lina. Arto pulled Bayard to a stop, hopping down and patting his flank. He moved close to the horse's face, murmuring softly into his ear. Bayard nickered, nibbling at his palm. Lina slid from Cyrus's back, hugging his neck tightly against her shoulder. She breathed in deeply, pressing her nose into his feathers. He cooed, tucking his beak against her back. "We made it, Cyrus," she said softly. "Both of us."

Arto had led Bayard to a stream below them. Lina pulled Cyrus up behind them. Quietly, she and Arto dipped their own drink with their hands. Arto wiped the water from his chin with the back of his hand. "What did you see and hear, in the Chasm?" he asked her.

She paused a moment. "My mother," she said quietly, crossing her arms over her chest. "And you?"

He set his jaw in a hard line, squinting his eyes toward the horizon. "My mother too." He wet his lips. "And my father."

He turned then and moved to Bayard's side, mounting quickly. He clucked to the horse, patting his neck. Lina followed him with her eyes then lifted herself onto Cyrus's back. She wondered about his family. Who were they? And why had he never mentioned them?

They galloped over the landscape, gaining incredible speed. Lina's hood flew onto her back, and streams of loose golden hair trailed behind her head. She tucked her legs, crouching low on Cyrus's back. As they rode farther east, the landscape rolled and changed. The hills and valleys flattened, and they galloped headlong over dry, reddish dirt. The late afternoon sky stretched out above and before them, expanding as far as Lina could see. Scrub bushes dotted the landscape, taking the place of high grass and trees along the road. Dust kicked up from Bayard's hooves in a thin cloud behind him. Lina tucked her cloak around her nose and mouth with one hand, keeping the other tightly on the reins.

The desert landscape rolled on and on, and they rode through the flat, red dirt until the sun was beginning to drop on the horizon. Lina peered ahead, squinting her eyes against the dust. In the distance, several small red and tan rock formations began to take shape.

As they approached, the formations grew. She blinked at them in surprise. The rocks were gigantic, much larger than they had first appeared. They passed some on the left. The stones clung to each other in strange patterns, leaning as if they would fall. Large stones stacked precariously on top of small ones, and many were so tall that she couldn't see the tops. She craned her neck as they passed between two enormous rock columns. A flat, marbled stone connected them at the top like a massive table.

She squinted at the horizon. Ahead was an enormous, towering, tan rock with a flat top. Lina scanned her eyes from left to right. She could not see where it began or ended. She lifted off her seat to try to see over the edge, but the cliff was too high, even from her distance.

As they galloped toward it, the flat, red earth became disrupted by scattered debris. Lina looked down, examining a small, whitish object. It rolled out from under Bayard's hooves, tumbling on the packed dirt. Two large dark holes peered vacantly up to her from the white, oval shape. It was a man's skull. She shivered, pulling the cloak tighter about her face.

They had ridden into an old battleground. Countless bones of various shapes and sizes littered the earth around them. The remains had four legs, a large body, and a spinal column and skull. Lina's eyes widened. They were centaurs. Some were full skeletons, lying haphazardly in piles, whose bones had been scorched by the hot sun. Their arms were slung at odd angles, some still clutching their spears. Evidence of fire had charred the remains, turning portions of the bones dark. It was a gruesome scene. It turned Lina's stomach to see it. She looked away, training her eyes on Arto's back. He never turned, focusing his gaze on the steep escarpment ahead of them.

They raced through the battleground, straight toward the rock wall. The animals showed no fear, and Arto showed no signs of slowing. Lina hoped he would pull up, but they were too close to the cliff to fly over its top. Dust flew up from Bayard's hooves, and Cyrus craned his neck to keep up the pace. She gritted her teeth, closing her eyes tightly and bracing for impact.

Ahead, Arto muttered softly to himself. She opened her eyes just in time to see him raise one arm over his head and make a broad sweeping motion with his palm. The stone face gave way, and a large door opened out of the rock. They galloped straight into it, and the rock reformed, closing the door tightly behind them.

The inside of the rock was cool and dark. They pulled up, slowing the animals to a walk. Lina whispered gently to Cyrus, patting his soft feathers. Her voice reverberated against the stone walls, bouncing back to her. The low rock expanded, and she looked up, expecting the top of a reddish-tan cavern to soar overhead. Instead, the evening sky was visible. Purplish twilight reached down to her from the top of the narrow pass. Ahead, the rock walls fanned out and more light poured in. The sound of rushing water echoed off the stone. Bayard stepped out of the pass and onto a sandstone ledge, and Lina and Cyrus followed behind. She stopped beside them and peered over the ledge, her breath catching in her throat.

They were standing high above the ground overlooking an enormous, arched rock formation. A roaring waterfall flowed from under her feet into a deep blue pool spanning the ground below. Tan stone vaulted high above her head, its smooth dome curving outward over the water to form a single, large room. Cool, desert evening air wafted through the space from wide openings in the base of the stone at her left and right.

The pool lapped gently against the far shore. She followed it backward with her eyes, straining her neck to look under the stone ledge. The water below had a soft current. There it dropped down another fall farther behind the rock into a deep cavern she could not see.

Across the pool, settled against the opposite wall, a village was hewn from the sandstone face. Square and rectangular stone structures were stacked neatly one on top of the another, climbing up the wall. They stretched the length of the cavern, spreading wide on the rock below.

A woman with the body of a bay horse was bent at the waist, gathering water from the pool. Long, black hair fell in sheets around her face. Her tan, shapely arms were uncovered by a sleeveless leather vest, and a long, cerulean, sea glass necklace hung from her neck. She stood, tucking the water jar against her hip. Shielding her eyes with her hand, she peered up at them. Arto lifted his arm to her. She raised her hand and waved. Turning, she walked up a winding set of rock stairs fixed between the stone houses and turned left into a doorway at the top of the row.

A moment later, a man's torso emerged from the door. Long, gray-streaked, black hair shielded his face as he walked down the steps on horse's legs. He wore no shirt, and his taut muscles were visible even from her perch. Dappled, gray-blue swirls of hair covered his flanks, and his gray-streaked tail swished against his legs as he descended onto the ground before the pool. He raised his hand to Arto, smiling broadly.

Arto clucked, and Bayard pricked his ears and snorted, diving off the ledge and unfolding his wings as he glided to the ground. Lina followed, tapping Cyrus's flank and whistling low. She held her breath as Cyrus dove over the falls, her stomach dropping as he raced towards the wide pool below. He banked upward at its surface, skimming the water with his talons as he soared over the pool. He landed softly on the other side of it, right at the centaur's feet. Lina stared up at the tall centaur shyly. Proud, dark eyes peered back at her from the wrinkled folds of his tanned face.

"Evangeline Vasily, daughter of King Ard-Mathan and Queen Astrid, the Court of Warriors welcomes you. I am Chaeronne, general of the One True King and leader of the Court of Warriors." He bowed low at his waist, tucking his fist to his chest. His torso was crisscrossed with silver battle scars.

Lina exchanged a glance with Arto, who smiled encouragingly at her from the side of his mouth.

Arto turned to his friend, extending his hand. "Good to see you, Ronne," he said.

"Likewise, my friend," said Ronne, turning to clasp Arto's hand in his own. The centaur pulled him into an embrace, clapping his back. "It has been too long. I hear you have been traveling, of late." Ronne searched his features, his dark, almond eyes squinting at Arto's face. Arto nodded once, his jaw flexing. Ronne placed his hand on Arto's shoulder, squeezing slightly.

"Let us get you both inside. It will be nightfall soon. We are protected here, but we can never be too safe." Two young women with baskets of grain came to collect their animals. They had no trouble getting the hungry horse and griffin to follow. Lina watched them as they turned into a low stone stable near the water's edge.

Ronne led the way up the stairs, winding high up the wall through the stone houses. Curious female faces peered at her from the open windows. The women were lovely, with long dark hair, straight noses, dark, bright eyes, and sharp, tanned cheekbones.

One such woman passed her on the street, her dark horse body gleaming in the twilight. Her black tail swished as she folded her long, straight hair over her shoulder, adjusting the bowl she carried against her hip. She bowed softly to Lina as she passed, bending at her waist with a fist to her chest. Lina smiled, dipping her head in return. Then she turned away, frowning. Where were all the men?

Just then, Arto inclined his head, murmuring softly to Ronne, "The men…What happened to them? I've heard the rumors, but…We saw the bones outside the door."

Ronne paused on the stairs, turning his head toward Arto and speaking in low tones. "Gone. All of them." His face was as hard as stone. "We sent out a small hunting party as food was becoming scarce inside our court. First came the crows, then the drake."

Arto shook his head, his jaw flexing. Ronne continued. "We sent out reinforcements, the last of our Warrior men, but they were no match for him. He swooped in on his great wings and killed them all with his fiery breath." Arto placed his hand on Ronne's shoulder, bowing his head low.

Ronne turned into the last house on the left: a two-level sandstone structure with a flat open roof. A large wooden bed sat on top of it. Lina squinted up at it. She wondered who would sleep there.

They followed Ronne into the front room. Despite the stone interior, it felt cozy and warm. Heavy lamps sat on a large wooden table, and sconces lined the stone walls. A red, woven rug lay across the floor before a roaring fireplace to the right. The beautiful bay woman Lina had seen gathering water stood before it, stirring a mouthwatering stew in a large iron pot. Various herbs hung drying on a string above her, and a mortar and pestle sat beside her on a work bench. Lina furrowed her brow, scanning the table. There were no chairs. She pursed her lips, stifling a grin. But of course, what horse's body could fit in one?

The bay woman tucked her long black hair behind her ear, smiling over her shoulder. Her eyes were kind and friendly, and Lina instantly felt at ease in her presence. "Welcome, travelers. Soon we will eat. Please rest. It is our honor that you are here. Our home is your home." She dipped her head and put a fist to her chest, bowing low at her waist in Lina's direction.

Lina smiled, nodding in return. She already liked Ronne's lovely mate immensely.

Ronne led them to the back of the house where a wooden ladder stood against the far wall. A narrow incline led to the second-story rooms on her left and right. Arto seemed to know where he was going, and he took the ladder steps swiftly up and out to the roof.

Lina peered after him, craning her neck. Arto would be sleeping on the roof?

Ronne looked at her from the corner of his eye, grinning. "Arto told us he was bringing a guest. As we only have two bedrooms, he asked if my mate, Maria, would mind placing a bed on the roof. He thought you would like to have your privacy. With all his traveling, he is used to sleeping in the open air anyway."

Lina blushed, biting her lip as she peered up into the open air. *Of course.* "How kind of him," she said softly.

Ronne said no more and turned, leading her up the right incline to a dark wooden door. He pushed it open, allowing her to pass into the small bedroom as a question popped into her mind. "Where does Arto go when he's traveling?" she asked him.

Ronne nodded. "His travels span the length of the known worlds, but he came to see me most recently. He told me he had found you and that he would bring you here, to the Court of Warriors." He clasped his hands at his waist, smiling at her with kind eyes. "He came to ask me a favor. He wants me to recall the

Histories for you." He paused, tapping his fingers against the back of his hand as if he was puzzling out whether to continue.

"Sometimes he goes as far as the Mortal Realm." He paused, peering quietly down at her face.

"The Mortal Realm? He's never told me that." She frowned, crossing her arms. Why would Arto have any need of going there? "But why? What is in the Mortal Realm that he would be searching for?"

Ronne paused a moment, tightening his lips as if considering his words. He peered out the doorway, then returned his eyes to her face. "He was searching for you, Lina," he said quietly.

Ronne disappeared from the doorway, his hooves clopping on the stone as he descended into the front room. Lina threw off her bow and quiver, sitting down heavily on the thin mattress. She tucked her knees into her chest and wrapping her arms around her legs, considering his words. Arto had been searching for her? She thought back on their conversation, after the attack of the crows. He had told her that it was rumored her mother was with child when she escaped to the Mortal Realm. When Lina was ill, she had returned to Caelium for the Tamarisk Cake and had been trailed back to their forest clearing by a lycanth. According to Arto, she had been executed upon her return through the gate. Lina furrowed her brow, tucking her chin on top of her knees. Arto must have believed the rumors and come searching for her before she could be hunted by another foul beast. Before she could be killed, like her mother.

Arto knocked softly on her open doorframe. He peeked into the room, his eyes flicking over the mattress. "I thought you would want the room to yourself. There's only one bed and all." He pointed up. "Hence, my bed on the roof." He smiled at her with the side of his mouth, his dark hair falling over his forehead. He ran a hand through it, moving toward the mattress as Lina nodded mutely. She was still thinking about his visits to the Mortal Realm. She wondered why he hadn't mentioned them before.

He held his hand down to her, and she took it, standing up beside him.

"Come on. Let's eat. Maria has dinner ready. After, Ronne is going to tell you the Histories." He looked away, flexing his jaw. Wetting his lips, he met her eyes, his voice low. "Just …" He stepped toward her, his dark eyes peering pleadingly into her face. "Just please know that I'm not who I once was." Lina stared at him blankly, and he continued. "I know I probably should have told you myself, but…I think it's best that you hear the whole story from Ronne. He was there. He knows me. How it was. How *I* was." He blew out a breath, flicking his eyes to the ceiling and back to her. "Just try…try to find it in your heart to forgive me."

He closed the distance between them, resting his forehead on hers and closing his eyes. "Please," he breathed. He ran his free hand over her hair, trailing her ear and jaw.

Lina's heart thrummed, her skin tingling where he touched. His warm breath tickled her lips, and she craned her neck up to him instinctively. Her breath came in soft, short bursts, and she wrapped her free arm around his neck, tucking him closer to her.

"Lina, I—"

Maria's lilting voice called from the hallway below. "Come, travelers. Let's eat!"

Arto pulled back slightly, his dark eyes smoldering.

She gazed up at him shyly, her mouth forming a soft smile.

"Later," he said as he flexed his jaw. "If you can still stand to look at me." He dropped his arms, stepping back and staring at the floor. His eyes were full of grief, and Lina studied them in silence. She wondered what he meant. Why wouldn't she be able to look at him? Without another word, he turned and left her room in silence.

She gazed after him as confused as ever. Who was he, and what had he done? Why had he asked for her forgiveness?

Lina's stomach growled. The stew smelled delicious. She put the thoughts out of her mind and rounded the corner to the kitchen. She grinned down at the table. Maria had sat out two wooden stools while she was upstairs, and four heaping bowls of stew sat waiting at their places. Ronne and Maria took their seats at the ends of the table, reclining onto the floor, and she and Arto sat at the stools on either side.

Lina gazed shyly across at him, but Arto wouldn't meet her gaze. Instead, he kept his hard eyes trained on the bowl, eating in silence. He and Ronne shared a low conversation, something about a raid in the North Forest. She tuned out their voices, pushing the stew around her bowl. Once, he flicked his eyes up to her. They were all darkness and gloom. She studied his face as he dropped his eyes again. He was back to his old taciturn behavior.

She bit the inside of her lip, thinking of their exchange in the bedroom. Did he regret nearly kissing her? She flicked her eyes to his hard jaw and looked away, her heart sinking. Obviously, he did. She forced a bite, swallowing convulsively, but a bubble of disappointment had formed in her belly, and she put down her spoon. She couldn't eat.

"Is the food all right for you, Evangeline? You've hardly touched your stew." Maria placed her palm over Lina's hand, worry creasing her smooth brow. Lina smiled. "Yes, Maria. Thank you so much for the lovely meal. I think I am just overtired from our journey." She smiled a flat smile, lifting her eyes briefly to Maria then returning them her lap. She could feel Arto's dark gaze boring into the side of her face, but she refused to look at him. Ronne flicked his eyes from her to Arto in question, then he turned back to her, clearing his throat.

"Well, before you go to rest, allow me to tell you the Histories. After all, that is one of the reasons Arto brought you here. Is it not, Arturo?"

Arto kept his hard eyes trained on her. "It is." He folded his arms on the table, flexing his jaw. He turned his head to Ronne. "I have another favor to ask." Ronne nodded once, and Arto continued. "I know it's of great risk, but will the Court of Warriors stand with us, should it come to it?"

Lina flicked her eyes from Ronne to Arto. She wasn't sure what they were talking about.

Ronne stood, pressing his large hands on the table. His dappled horse's frame filled the front of the room. Clenching a fist to his chest, he lifted his shoulders, peering proudly down at Arto from his nose. "The Court of Warriors is ready. We stand with you." With that he turned, bowing to Lina.

Maria stood then, her face as hard as stone. "Though our men have been taken, we women are ready. We will stand with you, and we will fight!" She stomped her front hoof on the stone.

Arto stood, nodding once to them both. He flicked his eyes once more to Lina. They were sad and pleading. He opened his mouth to say something then closed it, clenching his fists at his sides. Then he turned and lifted himself to the ladder, climbing swiftly up and out into the night air.

Maria watched him go, a look of compassion on her face. She cleared the table and placed warm mugs of a dark, thick drink in front of Ronne and Lina. She waited as Lina tasted it, folding her hands at her waist. Lina sipped. "Mmm." The drink had a warm, sweet taste with a bitter tang at the end. She grinned up at Maria, who dipped her head. She had never had anything like it. "Hot cocoa for you, Evangeline," Maria said proudly.

"Thank you," said Lina. "It's wonderful."

Maria bid them goodnight, disappearing into the back hallway.

After she was gone, Ronne walked to the hearth, pulling two thick tomes off the shelf above it. He sat again at the head of the table, laying them reverently before Lina. "Your identity you already know: Evangeline Vasily, heir to the Throne of Mercy, daughter of King Ard-Mathan of Caelium and Queen Astrid of the Mortal Realm."

She knit her brows, putting her hand out on the table. "Wait. My mother was Mortal?"

Ronne nodded. "Yes. In fact, you and Arturo have that in common. His mother was Mortal also, and his father was fae."

She thought of Arto's ears, more rounded than a point. She reached her fingers up to touch her own. Her eyes widened. The tips of her ears were much the same.

Ronne smiled, crinkling his dark eyes. "Yes, your father, the Immortal King, wed your Mortal mother many cycles ago. She was known for her great beauty, her kindness, and her strength." He dropped his eyes, folding his hands. "You already know about her death." He peered up at her, his face a serious mask. "But there is much more you do not know."

CHAPTER 12

Ronne cleared his throat. "Allow me to start at the beginning." He tapped the cover of the emerald-bound book closest to her. "This is the Timekeeper's Tale. It is very precious and has been passed down through all generations, from the beginning of Time itself. Since the fall of the king, we have held it here, in the Court of Warriors, for safety, these many cycles. It begins with the story of creation, both of Caelium and the Mortal Realm, and all occurrences since creation are recorded here. We call these stories the Histories.

"The Histories read that the Source of All Things released the Four Winds upon the known worlds, which blew over the waters of the Southern Sea. So great were the swirling and powerful Winds that the center of the sea was pushed downward, sinking low into its place. There, the Source placed the main gate between the Mortal Realm and Caelium in the midst of the waters. As the sea fell, the earth rose above it on both sides of the gate, creating the landscape of Caelium and your Mortal home.

"Great goodness the Source breathed into the Four Winds that spread over the known worlds. In the beginning, there was no evil and no darkness to befall the creation, for the Source had made it so.

"The Winds blew across the earth, and all beings great and small, Mortal and otherwise, arose from the ground. The Source placed an Amloga, or Flame of Time, within each living being. The Amloga is very powerful. It is said that Amloga is a piece of the Source within us, and it gives us life. Amloga reflects the will of the Source, giving power to the Rotha-Am, or Wheel of Time, and it ensures that the Wheel of Time turns at the right speed and in the right direction.

"The Source placed the Rotha-Am in Caelium above the Haima Mountains. There, it hovered until the fall of the king. Its power extends to the ends of the known worlds. The Rotha-Am is what moves Time, both here and in the Mortal Realm. If not for the turning of the Rotha-Am, Time would stop, in both worlds, and finally, all creation would cease to exist.

"Inevitably, creation was corrupted with evil. Greed and hatred ruled the day. To ensure the protection of the Rotha-Am, the Source set the Order of the Flame in place as its stewards. The

Order is ancient and very sacred. It has been in existence since almost the dawn of creation. The members of the Order of the Flame are many, but each has a specific role.

"The first role is Royals of the Flame. Beings in this role hold very great Amloga. This is your family, Lina. After the death of your father and mother, you, Evangeline, are the last of these to exist. It is said that in the absence of the king, the daughter of the king holds the Mórloga. You *are* the Gerúla Mórloga, the Bearer of Great Flame. The Flame of Time inside you is very strong. It is the strongest in all creation. This is why Arturo has been searching for you so intently, and it is why Orm wants you dead. You are key to defeating the darkness of the Court of Orm and returning power to the Rotha-Am."

She considered this, silently resting her elbows on the table and her face between her palms.

He continued. "There is also a Mortal who is part of the Order. The Histories read that he is the Time Minder charged with the responsibility of watching Time in the Mortal Realm and ensuring it does not get out of balance with the Rotha-Am, as is the will of the Source. The Time Minder confirms that the Great Clock's balance matches the movement of the Rotha-Am. This balance is essential to ensure that Time moves synchronously in both realms and the will of the Source is done. This individual is blessed with extraordinarily long life, so that they can fulfill their duty to the Source."

Lina sat up, gripping the edges of the table. She thought of Jacques in the clock shop, hunched over a timepiece, listening for the *tick* he could feel in his chest. She remembered the large, ornate clock he had inherited from his father. It had frustrated him, its hands winding around its face at impossible speed. He could never mend it, and it sat covered in the back of his shop. Her eyes rounded in surprise. "The Great Clock…I've seen it! And I think I know the Time Minder! His name is Jacques. He found me! When I was a girl, he protected me. He has been as close as a brother."

Ronne nodded to her, taking her hand. "It was no coincidence you crossed paths. It was the will of the Source. There has always been a plan for your life, Evangeline Vasily, even when you could not see it." Lina's eyes brimmed. Her heart was nearly bursting at the truth of Ronne's words.

Ronne continued. "Last, the Source placed Timekeepers throughout Caelium and the Mortal Realm. We are the protectors of the Royals of the Flame, the creation, and the Rotha-Am. Arturo and I are two of these. Timekeepers and Royals whose blood is purely Caelian are Immortal. We carry great Amloga within us, which gives us great power and special abilities. Our power and loyalty to the Source and the king make us a target for the Court of Orm. He has spent much effort on hunting down our kind and sacrificing us at the Rotha-Am. Because of our great Amloga, our deaths are beneficial to him in the slowing of the Wheel of Time. Our Amloga serves to feed the Rotha-Am, bending it to his will. The goal of the foul Orm is to stop Time and, thus, control all creation.

"Those Timekeepers who were placed in the Mortal Realm have passed their Amloga through generations, unaware. You would consider them your most brave, most faithful, and most courageous individuals. Though not Immortal, they are extraordinary souls that pierce the lengthening darkness with an unrelenting light."

Lina sat back on the stool, folding her hands across the table. She peered up at Ronne's wrinkled face. "Arto seems nervous that I am learning the Histories." She looked down, wrapping her hands around her mug. "Something about his past, but he wouldn't tell me more about it. He said it would be best if I heard it from you."

Ronne shifted, resting his elbows on the table and folding his hands under his chin. He looked down at her, a soft sadness in his dark eyes.

"Yes. Arturo Elikai was not always on the right side of the Histories." He paused, taking her hand. "What I am about to tell you will be very difficult for you to hear. I want you to remember that we all have a chance for redemption, and Arturo has taken his headlong. He is not the man he once was, bless the Source."

She pursed her lips, sucking in a breath. "Tell me," she said in a small voice, but she was terrified of what Ronne was about to say.

"Arturo was born in Leyth Castle in the Haima Mountains. His father, Lionir, was Master Timekeeper to the king. King Ard-

Mathan trusted him implicitly. Lionir was a loyal Timekeeper and very strong in his abilities. He had protected the Royals of the Flame, the creation, and the Rotha-Am for his whole long life.

"Once, while in the Mortal Realm, he saw a beautiful maiden gathering water from a stream. So taken was he by her beauty that he whisked her through the Main Gate back into Caelium. There, he married her, with the king's blessing. Great love had Lionir for his wife, and he asked the king to bless her with Immortality. His wife became pregnant, and tragically, she died in childbirth before the Blessing was complete.

"Lionir was stricken with grief. His heart turned black and the Amloga within him became twisted and dark. Sadly, he allowed his anger and grief to drive him further and further into hatred and greed. He began to wish that it was he who sat on the Throne of Mercy, instead of the king. So, he crafted a plan to overthrow the king and take his throne, descending the known worlds into darkness.

"Lionir left his young son with the maid, Ita, who shielded him from much of his father's wickedness. That was, until he became of age and Lionir took Arturo under his care. He spun lies into a web of deception and persuaded the young man to join his cause. Arturo became Lionir's right hand, helping him to overthrow the Court of King Ard-Mathan. Together, they plotted the death of the Immortal king and Lionir took his throne.

Lina stuck out a hand. "So, Arturo's father is Lionir? Who is Lionir, and where is he now?"

Ronne smiled patiently. "Hold on. You will see."

"Before his death, King Ard-Mathan struck Lionir with blindness, ensuring he could not see the corruption of creation. Because of Lionir's deception, he became known as Orm, and he was cursed to slither upon the ground." Ronne ground his teeth, narrowing his eyes. "A fitting name for a spineless worm."

Lina blinked in shock. Arturo was Orm's son. She tucked her arms around her chest, afraid of what more she might hear.

"When King Ard-Mathan died and Orm sat on the Throne of Mercy, the slowing of the Rotha-Am began. As the king was the Gerla Mrloga, his Flame of Time was the strongest in all creation. Therefore, his death weakened the Wheel of Time. The killing of a Royal Immortal is corruption of the most sacred creation and thus is out of the will of the Source. This disobedience caused the Rotha-Am to fall from its place, striking the earth and creating a great tear in the fabric of Time. The Chasm was opened, and all wicked darkness that the Source had held there in chains was released upon the world. All manner of foul beasts emerged from the Chasm, free to do Orm's bidding. Some beasts, he created later, of lies and deceit."

Lina sipped her drink, swallowing convulsively. "How did they kill my father, if he was Immortal?"

Ronne shook his head from side to side. "Death is not what you think, Evangeline, especially not here in Caelium. An Immortal Amloga is more than just a body that can defy death.

It is an unstoppable force of creation. One is never truly *gone*. One's Amloga simply passes from one form to the next, from one location to the other, as if passing through a door. And that form can be reversed, if it is the will of the Source.

"Upon an Immortal's death from this body, their Amloga passes into a new form. That form communes with the Source, awaiting their next instructions. As the king is Immortal, the death that Orm wrought upon him was not a simple one, but his Amloga was severed from Time itself." Ronne frowned, lifting one hand. "I am not sure we will ever truly understand these concepts until death overtakes our bodies, too."

Lina nodded hesitantly and Ronne inhaled. "There's more?" she said weakly. "I'm afraid so," Ronne said, smiling kindly.

"Arturo spent much of his young life terrorizing all Caelium. Indeed, he was not searching for you in the Mortal Realm out of benevolence. At least not in the early days. The rumor had reached Orm's ears that Queen Astrid had fled to the Mortal Realm, and she was with child. He sent his son to find her... and you. He did not succeed, until she was seen by the crows, ten Mortal years ago, running along the shore of the Southern Sea. She was headed toward the West Mountains. No one knew why she had returned. Orm allowed her to pass back through the gate to the forest clearing, later sending his fell beast after her. The lycanth trailed her through the gate, returning her to Leyth Castle."

He paused, searching the ceiling for his next words. "When they returned her to the castle guards ..." He turned to her, his face full of sorrow. "Orm charged Arturo with her execution." Lina gasped, covering her eyes. She didn't want to hear anymore. She couldn't. Ronne bowed his head, uttering his next words softly. "He took her south, on the premise that she was going home. But he threw her overboard, drowning her in the midst of the Southern Sea."

Lina's heart sank like a stone. She held her forehead in her hands, gasping for breath. Her ears buzzed, and her stomach churned. She was going to be sick. The room began to spin, and beads of sweat broke out on her forehead. She laid her cheek against the cool wood. "Water," she said weakly. "I need some water."

Ronne stood at once, bringing her a cup of fresh, cool water and a cloth to wipe her tears. She sat up, drinking. Dipping the cloth, she wiped her cheeks with the cool rag and laid it onto her forehead. She leaned back, resting her head against the wall. She couldn't believe what Ronne had told her. She couldn't believe what Arto had done. Her mother was dead, and it had been at his hand. He was right. She didn't want to look at him, to even be *near* him after what he had done.

"I'm sorry," Ronne said. "I know it's not the news you wanted to hear. But you should hear the rest of the story."

Lina shook her head. "No, it's okay" she swallowed. "Please continue."

Ronne nodded.

"After her execution, Arto didn't go back to Leyth Castle. He realized that his father's treachery knew no bounds, and the lies he had been told were beginning to show holes. There was no one Orm would not kill and nothing he would not do to control the Rotha-Am and the throne. Arto resolved himself that the loyal Master Timekeeper Lionir was no more. His father's heart was a stone. No goodness, and no love for him or anyone remained. It was clear that his father's only goal was to stop the Wheel of Time from turning, thereby reversing all power and control over creation from the Source to himself.

"Arturo fled, and he was met on the road by the crows. They slashed at him with their claws, trying to pick him up and carry him back to the castle." Ronne tapped his neck. "That is how he got his scar. They would have carried him away if not for the great horse. He was saved by Bayard. He came swiftly from the North Forest, out flew the crows, and carried Arto to his new home, the Timekeeper's Court.

"This ancient court was set up as a training ground and home for Timekeepers at the beginning of the Order of the Flame. Arto rested there, creating the Wall of Mist to protect himself and the others while he healed and became a new man. Ita met him there and cared for his wounds. She had come home to the West Mountains and the Court of the Mountain Fairies after King Ard-Mathan's death."

"Wait. There is a Court of Mountain Fairies?" Lina asked.

"There was. Orm destroyed it, cycles ago. The mountain fae and satyrs that lived there were kind and full of loyalty and love for the king. Orm wiped out most of them, on a hunt to destroy Timekeepers and those loyal to the king. He knew that Ita had gone there too. She had formed a bond with his son, and Orm wanted nothing standing in the way of his plan for him.

"Ita and a few remaining mountain fairies fled to the Timekeeper's Court after the destruction of their lands. Though Arturo had been instrumental in that destruction, she accepted him back with loving arms. She baked the Tamarisk Cakes and helped him heal. If not for her love and care, he would not have lived."

Lina's head spun. Ronne's words were almost too much for her to absorb. She wondered how long ago these events had happened, and she pursed her lips as an another question popped into her mind. "How old is Arto?" she asked quietly.

Ronne chuckled. "Time in Caelium does not pass the same as your years at home. One cycle in Caelium is equal to seven Mortal years, and the aging process takes much longer, except in the case of the Time Minder. In this realm, his form has passed twenty-eight cycles." He flicked his eyes to the ceiling. "In Mortal years, that would mean Arto has passed to age 196."

Lina raised her brows in surprise. She didn't realize Arto had already passed so long a life. He didn't look it. In fact, he looked to be about the same age as Jacques.

"And now you know everything," Arturo's low voice said softly.

Lina spun toward him. She'd been so absorbed in the story that she hadn't noticed he was standing in the hall. He leaned against the doorframe with his hands in his pockets, staring at her with tear-filled eyes. He dropped his gaze, and one small tear slid down his cheek. He swiped at it with his sleeve, turning his heel and climbing the ladder to the roof.

Ronne patted her hand. "Go to him. He is not the man he once was. The Source has forgiven, and so shall you. Everyone deserves a chance at redemption."

Lina stood, smoothing the front of her dress nervously as she moved into the hall. She gazed up the ladder into the night air. She wasn't sure what to say to him, how it would feel to be alone with him, now that she knew. Slowly, she lifted her feet on the creaking ladder and climbed out into the night air.

Arto sat with his back to her, gazing past the cavernous opening into the night. She moved to his side, silently standing at his shoulder. The large moons illuminated his face with their glowing light. His cheeks were wet. He cut his eyes to her then turned his face away, wiping them with his sleeve. Lina sat next to him, dangling her feet over the rooftop. She didn't speak. She was unsure what to say yet, if anything. She watched as Arto sighed, staring hard at his toes. He opened his mouth to speak then closed it, shaking his head. Taking a deep breath, he tried again.

"I…I know what you must think of me, of what I've done." He shook his head. "There's nothing I can say. Nothing I can do." He turned his face to her, his eyes full of grief. "If I could take it back, Lina, if I could change it, I would. I would do *anything* to take it back. Anything, Lina. I'm so sorry." He hung his head. Thick hot tears dripped off his nose, and his shoulders shook.

Lina's heart squeezed at his words. Despite what he had done, her uncertainty melted away as she angled her body toward him, wrapping her slender arms across his broad chest. She laid her head on his shoulder. She was crying too. She was sorry for her loss, yes, but she was equally as sorry for the guilt Arturo had carried all these cycles. She wasn't about to let him carry it any longer. "I forgive you," she whispered softly.

He pushed away from her gently, dipping his head to peer into her eyes. "What did you say?" he asked, eyes widening.

"I said …" She turned to face him, "I forgive you." She smiled through her tears. "And what's more, I…I love you." She shook her head slowly back and forth, a small smile forming on her full lips as she realized the truth of her own words. "Love doesn't let someone carry a burden like this alone."

Arto leaned back slightly from her, studying her face in the moonlight. Wordlessly, he placed his left arm across her low back, scooting her closer to him. Relief and warmth washed over his face as he bent his head to her neck, resting his nose on her collarbone. He nuzzled her skin, trailing his lips lightly as he lifted his nose toward her chin. "Lina," he breathed.

He raised his free hand to the back of her head, curling his fingers into her long golden hair. Slowly, he moved his lips along the delicate skin of her jaw. Her heart hammered out of her chest. "I love you, too," he whispered, moving his lips to her ear.

"Arto," she breathed. Her heart was soaring.

He drew back slightly, drinking her in. Then his lips covered hers, her kisses answering his own. She wound her hands around the back of his neck, holding him to her. Her fingers found the raised skin of his scar, and, lightly, she trailed the old wound to his collarbone. He sighed, lifting her chin and covering her lips with his own once more.

As he held her, pouring all his love into her innermost being, a piece of herself she had not known was missing clicked into place. She had found the great love of her life. And surely, no love between two beings had ever been greater than this.

They pulled back slowly, holding each other in their arms. Arturo caressed her cheek with his fingers, his eyes drowning in her own. Finally, he stood, raking his hands through his hair. He held his hand down to her. "You should go to bed," he said as he grinned. "Tomorrow will come swiftly, and we don't know what it may bring."

She put her hand into his large palm, allowing him to lift her to her feet.

He pulled her onto her toes, tucking his arm around her back and tugging her body against his chest. He rested his lips on her head, kissing her crown. His lips smiled into her hair. "You're so small," he said. He tucked his large hands around her slim waist, running his fingers up her back.

She shivered, smiling against his chest. "No, I'm not small. You're just overly large," she teased.

She turned her head and pressed her cheek against him as his chuckle rumbled. His heartbeat thumped steadily beneath her ear. She closed her eyes, listening. According to Ronne, the Source had placed Amloga inside each living being. She wondered now if she could hear it. She squeezed her eyes, concentrating.

Arto's heart beat a steady thump. *Lub dub, lub dub.* She tuned it out, separating the heartbeat from something *more.* There it was. A faint, whirring hum, deeper and just to the left of the heart. A smaller, quieter form of the sound she had heard at the gate and near the Rotha-Am. The Flame of Time. Arto's flame. Lina lifted her face and smiled at him, and he gazed down at her with all the love and joy in his heart.

They held hands as they walked to the ladder. He climbed down first, and Lina followed. They moved quietly, being careful not to disturb Ronne and Maria. He lifted her down and walked with her to the bedroom door, holding it open. She paused as she passed him, looking up into his dark eyes. He grinned at her from the side of his mouth. "Good night, Arto," she whispered.

"Good night, Lina," he answered.

Chapter 13

Though the night was very short, Lina woke rested, having slept peacefully for the first time in days. She stretched and sat up on her mattress, gazing out the window. The morning sun shone through the rock opening in soft rays, warming the stone.

She got out of bed, carefully tidying the sheets. Maria moved about in the kitchen downstairs, laying breakfast. There was a soft knock on her door. *Arto.* She grinned, hurrying to answer it and pulling the door open wide.

Arto stood before her with one hand on his hip and the other balanced on the doorframe. "Morning," he said, his smile broad.

She studied his features. His face was serene. Happy. She smiled back at him. "Morning," she said happily. Lifting onto her toes, she planted a quick kiss on his lips and turned back into her room.

"I'll be right down," she called over her shoulder.

"Don't make me wait too long," he teased. She looked back at him, rolling her eyes. "But really, we have a meeting this morning with Ronne," he said.

She nodded, moving to sit at the vanity. She grabbed the brush, running it through her tangled hair. He pulled a stern face, reflecting mock seriousness at her in the mirror. "I mean it. Be fast." She giggled. "Alright, alright, I'll be right there," she said to his reflection.

She readied herself quickly, emerging from her room moments later. She carried her cloak, bow, and quiver to the kitchen, hanging them by Arto's on the wall. They sat at the table, and Maria poured steaming cups of coffee into thick mugs. The two books that Ronne had placed on the table last night still sat in their place. Lina held her warm mug, running the fingers of her free hand across their gilded spines.

Ronne reclined to her right at the head of the table, sipping his coffee. He sat down his mug, placing his hand on the emerald binding of the Timekeeper's Tale. "The Histories of the Timekeeper's Tale, you now know. What remains to be written is not yet seen. May the will of the Source be done." He moved his hand to place it on top of the other book. "This, Lina, is a gift for you." He lifted the book gently, placing it reverently in her hands.

Lina ran her fingers over the dark red binding, tracing the gilded script. At first, she could not read it. She frowned, looking to Ronne in question.

He gestured to the book. "Look again," he said quietly.

Lina returned her eyes to the cover, tracing the words. The text wavered, and suddenly, she understood the words. "The Book of Blessings," she said softly.

Ronne smiled, placing his hand over hers. "Only the one bearing the Mrloga is able to read it, to recite it, and to give the Blessings of the Source. That is you, Evangeline." He peered down at her with joy-filled eyes. "I have kept it for you and held hope that one day you would come to my door. Carry this book with you. Its words are a light in the darkness and provide hope where all hope seems lost."

She opened the cover and read the inscription on the first page softly to herself.

Gerúla Mórloga:
Bearer of the Great Flame,
Daughter of the king,
Thy destiny was, is, and shall remain.
Strengthen thy heart.
Steady thy hand,
For the day grows dark and Time is corrupted.
But let the will of the Source now speak.
Let hope rise on the wings of the Four Winds.
Let Time fly true,
And the Rotha-Am be restored.

When she finished, she brushed the sacred text with her fingers, lifting her head. She could feel the words throughout her body, warming from her heart outward. Maria's eyes were filled with tears. She dabbed them with the corner of her apron, turning back to the pot of coffee on the fire. Ronne stood, his right fist raised to his chest and his eyes fixed on a distant horizon. Arto placed his arm around Lina's shoulder, squeezing gently. She closed the book reverently, placing her hand on the cover.

Maria stepped into the back hall, returning moments later with a dark leather pack. She took the book and placed it gently inside, fastening the golden clasp. She handed the bag to Lina, who placed it over her back.

Arto took the seat to her left. Ronne reclined, eyeing them both, his face a serious mask. Arto spoke first. "Now that Lina is here, we must discuss our plan to overthrow the Court of Orm." Ronne clasped his hands in front of him on the table. "Yes. Orm has stolen so much Amloga and has corrupted many. The Rotha-Am is moving slower than ever. So many foul beasts have come up from the Chasm, and still others await the fall of Time. He has killed countless Timekeepers, and wickedness lurks in every shadow. We will need every living being we can gather to fight. It will take much Amloga to overthrow his court. Many may die in this fight, but we must not fail." He furrowed his brow, peering deeply into their faces.

"Arto, you have been searching far and wide for the Mortal Timekeepers. Their Amloga is strong. We must have them to dare a chance of defeating the Court of Orm."

Arto hung his head. "Yes, but they are scattered to the far reaches of the Mortal Realm. I went again to search for them over the last few days, but so far, I've had no success in finding them."

Ronne nodded confidently. "The Source will provide. You will find them when the moment is right." He reached to unfurl a rolled parchment Maria had placed on the table. It was a map of Caelium. He placed his finger over what appeared to be a door beneath the waters of the Southern Sea.

He looked pointedly across the table at Arto. "First, there is another matter for you to address. You must go to the Court of Merrows," said Ronne. Arto's face paled, and his shoulders went slack. Ronne peered at him seriously. "We obtained a message from the river that the Lady Sirena wishes to speak with you."

Arto swallowed convulsively, his jaw flexing. "Do you know what she wishes to discuss?" he muttered.

Ronne peered over the table at him apologetically. "She did not send word, but I am sure one could guess."

Arto nodded, sighing deeply.

Lina wondered at their words. She looked from Arto to Ronne. Both men's faces were hard, worried masks. Whoever Lady Sirena was, both of them were scared of her.

Ronne continued. "After you speak with her, you must go to

the North Forest." He tapped the map over the trees near the top. "The dryads there are many and loyal to the king. A great number of the ancient trees in their home, the Grove of Eiks, have been struck down, cut to the roots by the Court of Orm for carrying messages from the Four Winds.

"The great wish of the dryads has always been to protect the Eiks, who were placed by the Source into their charge. They are fierce and mistrusting of travelers in the North Forest, and they will strike at you before you have time to speak. You must convince them of Lina's identity. Show them that she will fight for their cause." He turned to Lina. "After much loss and sorrow, the dryads have nearly lost hope of Orm's defeat. You must show them who you are. Give them hope before all their hope is lost."

He turned to Arto. "As for us in the east, the Court of Warriors is ready." He placed his arm around Maria, who stood at his side. Gazing up at her, he said, "We have too long been here in hiding."

Maria raised her right fist to her chest and lifted her chin. "The Court of Warriors will fight."

Just then, a female centaur appeared in the doorway. She carried a small pot of water that she passed to Maria. Maria dipped her head in thanks, then she brought the pot to the center of the table. As she placed her hand over the top of the pot, a curl of sparkling steam began to rise from the water, swirling into Maria's palm. She shut her eyes, closing her hand around it. Holding her fist above the pot, she paused for a moment, deep in concentration. Her fine brow furrowed, and she inhaled, her lips becoming a hard line.

When she opened her eyes, they rested on Arto. "A message comes through the river from the roots of the Eiks. The Source of the Four Winds has caused the Mortal Timekeepers to gather at the Main Gate. However, they have forgotten who they are. Their minds have been poisoned by the Court of Orm. Daily in the Mortal Realm, they have been fed the Elixir of Oblivion." Ronne and Arto locked eyes. A small smile formed on Ronne's lips. "The Source has delivered," he said.

Lina's mind spun as she remembered the bird-woman and the drink in the chipped, blue china cup. Lina had taken the elixir willingly, enjoying every drop. Soon after, her mind had gone fuzzy, and her limbs had become slow and weak. Dizziness and confusion had overwhelmed her, and the bird-woman had nearly led her to her death on the platform.

She tucked her hands under her chin, considering. The elixir had a curious way of filling one up, but the feeling didn't last, and she had craved the drink soon after. Despite its ill effects, the world had felt softer somehow. Easier to bear. She understood what it was to drink it. To forget. And after, to be weak and powerless under someone else's control. It was a difficult trap to escape. If not for Arto's rescue, the elixir may have been her end. Certainly, a daily dose would cause one to forget one's true self entirely. How would they convince the Mortal Timekeepers of their identity if they had drunk the elixir every day?

Arto spoke. "We must visit the Mortal Realm and retrieve the Mortal Timekeepers first. Ronne, you will come with us. You can lead them back through the gate. Then, head for the West Mountains and the Timekeeper's Court. Ita will meet you there. The Mortals will be weak, having so long drunk the elixir. Ita will bake the Tamarisk Cakes. When the Mortal Timekeepers eat them, the strength of their minds and bodies will be restored. When this is done, you can train them for battle, along with the remaining mountain fairies."

Lina remembered the Tamarisk Cake. For her, it had been the bread of life. A sweet manna that had restored her body, that had purged the venom from Cyrus, saving them from certain death. She was sure it would do the same for the Mortal Timekeepers.

Ronne nodded. "Let us go. Maria, ready the warriors. I will send you a message when the moment has come." He turned to Arto and Lina. "Your winged mounts will be safe in our care while you travel. The merrow patrols will monitor your situation and alert Maria when you have need of them. She will ensure they are brought to you expediently." With that, he kissed Maria's cheek, and the three walked out of the house.

When they reached the pool at the bottom of the stone steps, Ronne turning to face them. "I must warn you. Many of those in the Order of the Flame with the pure blood of Caelium are Immortal, but neither of you carries this blessing. As both of your mothers were Mortal, Immortality has not yet been extended to you. You are both in grave danger in this fight. In the event of your death, your final form is permanent. Be on your guard, and may the Source go with you."

Across the water, Lina caught a slight motion from the corner of her gaze. A dark figure was moving slowly toward them from behind the falling water. She shielded her eyes with her hand, peering across the pool. The figure broke through the fall, and the bow of a small, wooden boat came into view. Lina grinned. Its crooked captain stood at his post on the stern, rowing slowly in their direction. He hummed his tuneless song from his throat and pulled the boat close to shore, nodding to them. All three climbed aboard, and he began rowing back toward the waterfall.

Lina took her seat near the bow, and Arto sat next to her. Ronne reclined behind them in the floor of the boat. She gripped the side, gazing fearfully at the dark opening behind the fall. The idea of falling over it in the small boat was terrifying, and she had no idea what awaited them on the other side of it.

Arto placed his large hand over hers. "The fastest and safest way for us to travel is the underground rivers. They reach all corners of Caelium, from the North Forest to the mountains in the west and all the way to the Southern Sea. We will travel this one to the main gate first. From there, we will go to the Mortal Realm. Don't worry. They river is swift, but our guide is skilled."

Lina nodded uncertainly. She peered backward at the strange

captain, who still hummed his tuneless song. He gazed down at her with his blue eyes, nodding once in her direction.

The cavernous opening of the underground river yawned before them, and the current pulled hard against the hull of the boat. There was nothing but darkness past the falling water. Lina pulled her cloak over her head just as they passed beneath the upper waterfall. Cool water splashed her hood, dripping onto her nose and clinging to her lashes. She gripped the side of the boat and gritted her teeth, anticipating the drop of the fall beneath them as they floated into darkness. Arto tucked his arm around her back, holding her closely to his side.

The boat creaked and groaned as the bow tipped over the fall, and then they were falling headlong into the abyss. Lina's bottom lifted off her seat and her stomach reached her throat, forcing her breath up and out in a *whoosh*. She counted to herself as they plummeted downward. *1-2-3*. The bow splashed into the river, sending a torrent of water over them all before the boat righted itself and the world came back into balance. Arto patted her shoulder, and she sucked in a breath, relaxing her grip on the side.

The current at the base of the falls was calm, and they floated dreamily in darkness. The only sounds were the row of the captain's oar and his tuneless hum mingled with the sounds of their breathing. Lina assessed the size of the cavern by listening to the echoes bouncing off the walls, finding it to be quite narrow. She reached out her hand, touching the damp stone wall. The bluish-purple light she had discovered in the tunnels above the beach flared beneath her hand. She trailed her fingers on the stone, and the light blazed. It circled over their heads and down the cavernous tunnel that stretched long before them until it turned left and out of sight. She followed the trail of light, craning her neck to see the around the turn.

As they rowed toward the riverbend, an iridescent pair of lavender eyes peered up at them from the water. Lina squinted. The eyes were set in a woman's face, with long, flowing hair streaming about it in the current. The tip of her fine nose was submerged, and her winged brows flared delicately upward from her large eyes toward iridescent scales trailing up her temples. Lina remembered a similar face from the man selling sea creatures in the market.

As they approached, the woman raised her slender arms and dove, submerging her head and exposing a magnificent, flowing tail, its shimmering scales matching the ones on her temples. Her fluttering tail fins flicked once above the water, and she was gone.

Lina looked to Arto, her eyes wide.

He chuckled. "She's a merrow. From the Southern Sea. They are beautiful, intelligent beings. And sometimes deadly." He swallowed, flexing his jaw. "They are a fiercely loyal and proud people. Mostly friends to those who are friends to them." He shook his head. "Not a group you want to cross. And they are excellent spies. They patrol the subterranean waterways, ensuring that they are safe for passage."

Lina nodded to him, considering. *Deadly*. Was that why he had paled when Ronne mentioned a meeting with Lady Sirena?

The current was picking up in earnest as they approached the riverbend. "Hold on," said Arto. "The ride to the Sea Door can get pretty rough."

Lina gripped her seat as the water swirled and pushed against the boat. They sped through the tunnel, faster and faster toward the turn.

When they reached the bend, the captain turned his oar rapidly, banking them sharply left. The boat groaned in protest, tipping sideways, and water sloshed over the sides. Arto gripped her side, tucking her head into his shoulder. The captain kept his post, his bare feet standing solidly on the stern. He righted the boat, and they sailed down the corridor at incredible speed. Lina gripped her seat as the current sloshed them left and right, high onto the curved walls. She peered ahead. There was another bend. She gritted her teeth and gripped the seat with all her might. The wooden boat could not stay upright much longer.

Suddenly the captain turned the oar rapidly, holding it against the current. The boat spun backward, and they rushed along the tunnel, headed for the bend stern first. The captain hummed, turning to peer behind his shoulder, his sinewy muscles flexing as he pulled the oar against the water. Lina gazed over her shoulder, and her heart dropped into her feet.

The river dropped beyond the bend into another fall. She

gripped her fingernails into the wood of the seat, tucking her feet against the sides. Arto tightened his grip, tucking her tightly against him. Then they were tipping backward, falling into the darkness.

The drop felt endless. She forgot to count, but certainly this fall was much greater than the first. Her lower body lifted into the air, and she would have lost her seat if not for Arto's grip. Groaning, she squeezed her eyes shut. Her insides turned out and her hair and dress billowed over her head. She opened her mouth to scream, but her voice was silenced in her throat.

Finally, the wooden boat splashed into the water. The impact jerked their bodies forward, and they fell into a heap on the floor of the boat. Arto grunted, pulling himself upright. He reached down, feeling for Lina's hand. "Are you hurt?" he asked, reaching out his fingers to feel over her face and arms.

She took his hand, sitting up. "No, I'm fine. Are you?"

"Fine," he answered. He swung his head to Ronne. "Ronne? You alright?"

Ronne was still seated on the boat's floor, but his hands gripped the sides. "Just fine, Arturo," he said placidly.

They lifted themselves back onto their seats. The water had stilled, and they floated quietly in the darkness. "Tell me it's almost over," Lina said in a small voice. She didn't think she could take another dip over the falls.

Arto chuckled low in his chest. "Yes," he said. Pulling her against him, he kissed the top of her head. "We are almost there."

The stalwart captain rowed them left around a curved rock wall. Soft light spilled through the cavern, and waves crashed in the distance. Around the corner, the vine-covered opening of the beach emerged and the river spilled out over the stones, its shallow water meeting the Southern Sea beyond it. Lina heaved a sigh of relief at seeing land, but Arto put his hand softly on her arm, gesturing to the sea beyond. "I'm afraid our way still lies in more water." She couldn't help but glare at him, and he chuckled. "But I'm sure we can take a moment on dry land."

They stood, stepping onto the beach. The captain moved the boat deftly over the shallows from his perch on the stern, pausing to wait for them when he reached the seawater. Smooth pebbles and glass fragments sparkled in the midday sun, and the cool sea breeze blew softly through Lina's hair. Her legs wobbled after the turbulent boat ride, and she held out her arms for balance. Arto reached for her hand, pulling her close against his chest. She gazed up at him, wrapping her arms around him inside his cloak. He grinned down at her, ducking his head to kiss the tip of her nose. She giggled, squeezing her eyes shut. He pulled away, gazing intently into her face. "I love you, you know," he said softly.

"I know," she said, smiling. "I love you, too." She still couldn't quite believe it after all that she had learned. But it was true. She did love him.

He dipped his lips to hers, kissing her softly. Then he tugged her hand, pulling her toward the boat, where Ronne and the captain sat waiting.

Down the beach, a dark gray horse galloped in their direction. Its hooves made no sound as they hit the glassy stone. Lina frowned, staring at its feet as it approached. Small, round crustaceans dotted its hooves, and bits of seagrass wound their way up its ankles. It stopped in front of her, standing in the shallow, lapping waves. Various shells, kelp, and sea moss were woven through the dark, grey hair of its mane. It shook its neck, chuffing, and stared at her with its clouded grey eye.

Lina's hearing muffled as she gazed back at it. She stared into the stormy eye, and she found she couldn't turn her head. Her arm moved of its own will, and she reached out her hand. Her fingers trembled, and an overwhelming urge to lace them into the horse's mane and climb on its back slithered through her mind. Warning bells trilled in her head, but she blocked them out. She stepped one foot toward the horse, wetting the hem of her dress in the shallow water.

Vaguely, she heard Arto yelling in her direction. He was coming toward her, sloshing through the water. A fresh, sea breeze blew through the horse's hair, and she inhaled. The scent was heavenly. She wanted nothing more than to ride on his back in the shallow waves. Her vision tunneled, and her head filled with an ethereal sound. It tugged at her ears, urging her forward. Her leg moved of its own accord, and she took another step. She was nearly touching its mane when Arto jerked her from her feet. He carried her sideways, dropping her heavily into the floor of the boat.

She fell onto her back, the impact pushing the air from her chest. Gripping the wood, she blinked up at the sky, struggling to inhale. Arto's face appeared above her. His mouth was moving, but she couldn't hear any sound. He frowned down at her, shaking her shoulders. Just then, her chest moved, and she gulped a mouthful of air. Distantly, she could hear him calling her name. "Lina! Lina? Can you hear me?" The sound grew closer and closer until his voice was loud and clear. She sat up, looking back toward the beach for the strange grey horse. He was gone.

She breathed heavily, staring at the shoreline. "Where's the horse?" she asked him.

He peered backward, then met her gaze. He shook his head. "It's not a horse. It's a seahorse. And believe me, riding on its back isn't the best way to enter the Court of Merrows. It's an apparition placed by the court to guard the shoreline. If you climb on its back, you cannot climb off. It will gallop headlong into the sea, pulling you down, down into the depths. Unwelcome visitors often drown before they reach the court and can stand trial before Lady Sirena." He gazed over the water, his jaw flexing. "Better to enter the Court of Merrows invited."

Lina looked past him, keeping her wary eyes on the water. Images of a dark horse galloping under the waves filled her mind. She shivered. What was worse: a horse that pulled her to her death or the giant vortex that had nearly sucked her beneath the waves? She scanned the water, searching for other horrors. She saw none, and soon the captain stopped rowing and they floated in the open water.

Arto grinned down at her mischievously. "Want to open the Main Gate?" he asked. She looked at the empty air before them uncertainly, remembering the shimmering shape she had fallen through. "Fair warning: the Main Gate is pretty tough to open." He pursed his lips and looked past her, leaning back casually on his palms. "Of course, it's easy for me. So, I'll help you, if you need it." He crossed his feet, smirking at her from the corner of his eye.

She grinned, standing up in the boat. "I don't think I'll be needing your help," she said teasingly.

Before he could say more, she stuck out her palm and closed her eyes, concentrating. Her actions felt almost familiar, in a bizarre way, like she had done them a thousand times, like knowing the way back home. Inhaling, she steadied her feet, waving her hand once over the open air. She felt the hum before she heard it, and the air in front of her fell away. A large, shimmering gate opened in its place. She grilled down at Arto, who sat gazing at it with his mouth open. She giggled. "Easy," she said, folding her arms over her chest.

He chuckled and stood, running a hand through his hair. "I should have known you would be a natural. Royal blood, and all." He tucked her against his side, planting a kiss on top of her head.

Ronne stepped forward first, putting one leg through the gate before looking back to them and nodding. Then he stepped forward and disappeared through the wavering air. Arto braced his foot on the side of the boat, reaching his hand to Lina. She grasped it, glancing back at the captain, whose tuneless hum garbled from this throat. He nodded once at her, his blue eyes crinkling at the edges. She smiled and nodded back at him. She turned, and together, she and Arto stepped through the gate.

CHAPTER 14

Lina kept a tight grip on Arto's hand. This time, the fall through the gate was longer. Time stretched out in an eternity before her, and the pressure on her body was enormous. The colorful kaleidoscope wavered and shimmered, the patterns flickering in and out. The melody of voices was muffled, like listening underwater. Faces and figures blurred past her, and her body stretched and lengthened into an impossible ribbon shape.

She forced her head to turn to Arto, pushing against the incredible weight. He was tunneled in her vision, strung out from where their hands connected by a long string. She could force no more air into her lungs as her body spread long and thin in the flickering light. For a moment, she was suspended, stretched beyond what was survivable. Time seemed to hover at a standstill within the passage, and she was suddenly fearful that they might never escape. They were doomed to hover forever between their two worlds, in a place where no living being can linger. Her brain wanted to scream, and she forced her mouth to open against the crushing pressure. The passage stuttered, and all light and sound flickered out.

Suddenly the passage reappeared, and she rebounded into her original shape. Arto squeezed her hand, and they floated in soft, white nothingness. The silence held them in a delicate hammock of Time and space. Relief flooded Lina's chest, and she sucked in a sweet breath. Like before, a familiar peace swirled around her body, and she wished she could stay here, free from worry and harm.

Too soon, they were sucked backward from their soft cocoon and thrown headlong through the other side of the gate. The sound of shearing metal ripped about her ears as they dropped into the forest clearing. She rolled onto all fours, expecting to be sick. Ronne had managed to land upright, his hooves steady on the ground. Lina closed her eyes, heaving, as a fine sheen of sweat broke onto her brow.

Heavy snow banks flanked the clearing. Their biting cold numbed her fingertips and wet her knees. She sucked in a breath as Arto sat up right behind her, dusting snow from his cloak.

"We must not linger here," said Arto. The gate is collapsing as Time is stretched. It will be impassable in a few Mortal hours. There will be no way back...or out."

Lina blinked her eyes rapidly, sucking in deep breaths. She pressed her hand to her middle, trying to calm her churning stomach. She sat with her back against the ash tree, nodding to Arto. "Okay," she said uneasily. "Just give me a few moments." Arto didn't answer. He stood above her, staring in disbelief into the clearing.

She turned her head to look in the same direction. Her eyes widened, and she scrambled to her feet. The forest clearing was full of people. Men and women, young and old, from all across her Mortal Realm had gathered by the Source at the gate. Some were from her own village of Jalda, but others wore clothing from some faraway land. They stood in little pockets, speaking indistinctly to one another.

One young woman with fiery red curls and freckles that marched across her nose approached her, peering deeply into her face with bright green eyes. Her voice was strong as she asked, "Excuse me, miss, but do you know why we are gathered here?"

Lina exchanged a glance with Arto. She smiled at the young woman and nodded. "Yes, but it is better for you to pass through the gate and learn the reasons why on the other side. You must hurry. Ronne will lead you through. He will show you the way." She gestured to Ronne, who stood to the left of the open gate beneath the ash oak, his hands clasped at this waist.

The red-haired woman eyed him dubiously, but nodded, gesturing for her group to follow. Lina imagined it was even more shocking for the woman to see Ronne in his half-horse form here than it had been for her to see him on the other side of the gate. Still, the woman followed him. Lina marveled at her nerve.

The brave young woman was the first to pass through the gate, and her friends followed closely behind her. Lina traveled around the forest clearing, speaking softly to each group of people and providing encouragement for the journey. Arto stood waiting beside the gate, guiding each Timekeeper through the shimmering surface. Though many were fearful, and often uncertain, the Source had given them courage, and they followed one behind the other through the gate and into a strange, new world.

When they had all gone through, Arto waved his hand once in front of the gate. It closed swiftly, and they stood alone in the clearing. The land was eerily silent. There was no wind, and Lina did not hear a single animal sound. She surveyed the land about her, hugging her cloak tightly about her shoulders. Mounds of snow blanketed the forest floor and lay heavily on the bare limbs, bowing them low. Though she felt it should have been midday, the light was already waning, and the dimming sunlight appeared somewhat gray as it sank below the horizon.

Time was drawing short in her Mortal Realm, and the landscape blurred at its edges. The forest flickered in and out from the side of her gaze, like shadows dancing in candlelight on the wall. Small pockets of trees had lost their shape entirely, and a smudged void of darkness hung in their place. She blinked her eyes, turning toward the disturbances, but when she faced them, the landscape appeared as it had always been. She shivered, turning to Arto and motioning for him to follow her. She needed to see Jacques before Time ran out.

They arrived at the village of Jalda just as the sun had completely fallen below the trees. The air was frigid, and Lina shivered, holding her hood tightly against her ears. Her breath came out in clouds before her face. She breathed heavily, kicking her feet as they trudged through the packed snow. Flecks of ice rose before her in a cloud, hovering in the air. She stopped, moving around them in a circle, watching the crystals float before her face. Reaching out her hand, she swiped at them, sending them left and right. They hovered there. *Strange.* She swung her cloak, making a current of air, and watched as they traveled slowly toward the ground.

As they crossed the bridge into the village, Lina furrowed her brows, her mouth grim. The village was completely dark, and the market stalls were empty. Silence pressed close about her ears. She moved through the front square, peering into the dark shop windows. There was no one here. The village looked deserted. Everyone had gone. Or worse, they were dead. Her heart began to race. *Jacques.* What if something had happened to him?

She arrived on Jacques's doorstep and cupped her hands, placing them against the glass of the front window. She peered inside. There was no fire in the hearth. She wrapped heavily on the door with her fist, placing her ear against it. There was no sound. "Jacques? Are you there? It's me, Lina. Let me in." She paused to listen, but there was no answer. She looked helplessly to Arto, who pushed her gently behind him. He threw all his weight heavily against the wooden door, and it crashed inward, swinging on its hinges.

A cold gust of winter air blew into the workshop, scattering wood shavings across the floor. The waning twilight dimly illuminated the shop, and Lina searched the room with her eyes. There was no sign of Jacques. She rifled through a nearby shelf and found the flint, then she lit the lantern. Holding it aloft, she cast a glowing light over the workshop.

The entire shop floor and walls were stacked floor to ceiling with broken clocks. It was even more stuffed than when she had last seen it. Lina shone the light on the cuckoo to the left. Its hands were not moving. The cuckoo door was sprung open, and the yellow, wooden bird hung haphazardly from its spring. Glass fragments, wooden doors, spilled paint and stain, and various mechanical clock parts lay strewn across the floor. She held the light high, stepping through the broken clocks toward the back of the shop.

A faint rustling sound came from her left and she swung the light, peering into the back corner. A linen sheet lay tangled across the floor, and a small orange lump was wound in its middle. A pair of green, glittering eyes shone back at her in the lantern light. Her heart leapt into her throat. "R–Remus?" she cried.

The little orange cat stretched luxuriously, curving his tail at the top. He scampered toward her and sprang from the sheet, landing deftly in her free arm. Remus purred and nuzzled her chin, and she giggled, tears filling her eyes.

"Oh Remus, I thought you were gone. I missed you. The lycanth…you saved me." She bent her head, tucking his nose against her neck.

Remus mewled softly, pushing his head against her cheek. He hopped to the floor and padded over the sheet, squinting behind him as if asking her to follow. She stepped gingerly behind him, weaving through the mess on the shop floor. There, in the corner, lying propped on his side with his head resting against the Great Clock, was Jacques. She squinted, holding the lantern high. At least she thought it was Jacques. He appeared much older than when she had last seen him. Much, much older.

She gasped, falling onto her knees and cupping his sunken cheek in her hand.

He opened his watery eyes weakly, peering at her over a pair of round spectacles perched on his nose. His hair was completely white and lay in a shock over his wrinkled forehead, and a white beard covered his chin. He reached his quavering hand up to her face, cupping her chin with his large, gnarled fingers. "L–lina?" he croaked.

Tears sprang into her eyes, "Yes, Jacques, it's me." She helped him sit with his back against the Great Clock, wiping her cheeks with the back of her sleeves. "Jacques, what happened to you?"

She frowned up at the Great Clock. It appeared old and tired. Dust gathered over the wooden carvings and the glass covering over its face was cracked. Its hands were barely moving. As she watched, the *tick* paused, hovering over the same spot for several seconds.

Arto kneeled next to her, and she turned to face him. "What is happening to him?" she whispered.

Arto's jaw clenched. "As Orm's power grows and the Rotha-Am slows its turning in Caelium, all of the Time in the known worlds is affected. Time here in the Mortal Realm draws shorter and shorter, until there is no Time left." He peered up at the Great Clock. "The Mortal Realm will be left as nothing but an endless void, its creation gone forever. Because Jacques is the Time Minder, his Time draws short also. Normally, Time Minders have very, very long lives, in order to fulfill their task from the Source. But because of Orm's corruption of Time, Jacques has become old before he's due."

Lina ran her hand over Jacques's white hair, her eyes full of sorrow.

Arto continued. "It is particularly difficult for a Time Minder to survive the corruption of Time. His service to the Order, you remember, is to ensure that the Great Clock is in balance with the Rotha-Am. Because of the treachery of Orm, the Rotha-Am and the Great Clock are out of balance. Time in Caelium stretches longer, while Time in the Mortal Realm draws short. This process will continue until, the Source forbid, the Rotha-Am stops turning.

"The danger is that Jacques will die too soon, and we will be unable to restore Time in the Mortal Realm, even if we do restore the Rotha-Am in Caelium. If a Time Minder passes to the Source before he is due, and before there is an heir to his position, there will be no one left to mind the Great Clock. It will be forever out of balance, and Time in the Mortal Realm will be forever corrupted, regardless of what happens with the Rotha-Am."

He peered up at the Great Clock, its hands stuck in the same spot. "Thank the Source, it appears we have a small gap of Time in which to work." He turned to Lina. "Jacques is too old and frail to stand and mind the Time. He will never make it until we restore the Rotha-Am. He needs the words from the Book of Blessings to make him strong."

Lina nodded, lifting the leather bag off her shoulder. She reached inside, pulling out the Book of Blessings. She brushed her hand over the crimson cover, opening it in her arms. Standing, she sifted through the pages, searching for a passage to help her weakened friend. Her fingers landed on a heading marked "The Time Minder's Prayer." Pausing, she smoothed the page. She cleared her throat and began to recite in a clear, strong voice.

Let thee, Jacques Thomas,
Time Minder of the Order of the Flame,

Hear these words that the Source now speaks:
Mind the day.
The sun doth rise.
Mind the night:
Moon, stars, and skies.
Mind the Time,
The Keeper's piece,
In hand, you hold.
The Mortals' peace.
Let twins,
Of unbelief and faith
Be torn in two,
As darkness fades.
Let strength return,
To proper place.
And let hands on,
The Great Clock's face,
Be one in Time,
As you find the way.

As she read, Jacques's countenance strengthened, and he began to lift himself off the floor. He turned to face the Great Clock, placing his crooked fingers upon its face. Upon the end of her prayer, he closed his eyes, and pressed an ear to the timepiece. A faint smile hinted at his lips. "Yes, it is there," he whispered.

"It always has been, and always will be." He pointed to his chest, grinning over his glasses at Lina. "The *tick* in the chest." Chuckling, he patted the Great Clock. "Lina, hand me my tools," he said.

Arto reached behind him and gathered a toolbox from the workbench. Jacques peered at him over his glasses, fixing him with his dark, watery eyes. "This must be him." He glanced at Lina. "The man who took you away?" Lina patted his hand, smiling through tears. "No one could ever take me from you, Jacques." She sniffed. "You're as close to me as a brother."

He smiled at her, chucking her under the chin. "I am at that," he said.

Arto passed him the tools, and he took them with shaking hands. Turning, he knelt, opening the belly of the Great Clock. Lina knelt beside him, peering inside. The mechanics were staggering. Metal gears, glass pieces, and wooden parts were inlaid in complicated arrangements. Jacques's gnarled fingers reached inside, expertly removing and replacing parts, occasionally reaching to the workbench behind him for additional pieces.

As he worked, he murmured excitedly to himself, and the old light began to return to his eyes. He turned his head, peering at her over his glasses. "You three better get going. The light is already gone, and Time draws short. I'll mind the Time, in the Mortal Realm." He turned back to the Great Clock, chuckling lightly. "Time Minder…yes," he whispered. "I can see that now."

Lina hugged his back, reaching to place a soft kiss on his wrinkled cheek. "Until we meet again," she said softly. As she turned to go, she sent a prayer to the Source that she and Arto would be successful in their quest. She prayed that, indeed, she and Jacques would meet again.

Lina tucked Remus tighter to her chest. He purred against her, wrapped snugly under her cloak. Arto held the lantern high, lighting the way as they trudged back to the clearing through the drifts of snow. He placed it down by the ash tree and waved one hand firmly over the air. The gate opened with a hum, its surface shimmering in the lantern light.

Lina adjusted Remus to the crook of one arm. She bent her head, scratching his scruffy neck. "The passage will be over soon," she cooed. Remus squinted up at her with his green eyes, pushing his nose against her chin. Lina's heart squeezed. She still couldn't believe her Remus was alive.

Arto reached for her free hand, bringing it to his lips to brush a kiss over her palm. She smiled up at him, and he nodded once, smiling from the side of his mouth. "Ready? he asked.

She turned to face the gate. In her periphery, she saw the world flicker, a dark emptiness wresting for control. "Ready," she said, a shudder running through her core. Together, they stepped through.

The gate snapped closed behind them, leaving the solitary lantern on the floor of the forest clearing. Its flame cast a golden circle on the snow, pushing back the gathering night. Just then, the ground beneath the lantern wavered, tipping the lamp onto its side. Its flame went out, and the oil spilled onto the snow. The air around it quavered and shook, and the landscape beyond dissolved into a dark void. Then the lantern was gone, and nothing remained but hollow darkness.

CHAPTER 15

Lina held Remus tightly against her as they tumbled through the passage. The pauses were greater this time. Their bodies stretched long and thin, their extended shapes suspended between two worlds. The faces and colors swirled, blending into inky darkness, and the muffled voices stretched flat in the yawning abyss. The passage shook, and the light flickered in and out. Its shape bent and wrinkled, threatening to fold in on them and collapse. Lina braced herself. She was sure they had crossed too late.

At last, they rebounded. Their bodies rested in brief white silence before they tumbled through the other end of the gate and landed flat on their backs in the wooden boat. Lina grunted, blinking up at the sunny sky. Despite their long travel, it was still midday on Caelium's side of the gate.

Momentarily, the sun was shaded, and she blinked in shock, scrambling for the side of the boat. Standing over her was a massive gray wolf, his tongue lolling out of the side of his mouth. She gripped the edge in terror, her heart hammering in her chest, but the wolf just crouched onto his stomach, swishing his tail and covering his nose with his great paws. He whined, peeking up at her with twinkling, green eyes.

Suddenly she realized Remus was missing. She stood straight, looking frantically about the floor of the boat. There was no sign of the little orange cat.

"Hello, Lina," said a male voice to her mind. She blinked in surprise, staring at the green-eyed wolf.

"*Remus?*" she gasped.

The wolf lifted his head with a tilt. "Yes, Lina?"

She smiled in disbelief, sitting down hard on her bottom. "It *is* you!" She bent over the wolf, ruffling his furry head in her hands. He lifted his paws onto her shoulders, knocking her flat into the boat and licking her chin. She giggled, swiping at his fur. His nickname made sense to her now. "Okay, Okay, I love you too! Get down, you little wolf!"

Remus obediently sat, his tongue lolling over his jaw.

Arto laughed, patting Remus's head. He lifted his hand, closing the gate, and turned to the captain. "Take Remus ashore and send a message through the river to Ronne. Tell him to send Benjamin on a griffin. Have him fly Remus west, through the Wall of Mist, to the Timekeeper's Court." The captain nodded once from the stern then resumed the tuneless hum in his throat.

Arto extended his hand to Lina. His face was grim as he stared over the water. "Ready to meet the Court of Merrows?" he asked flatly.

Lina nodded, wholly uncertain. She wasn't sure what danger lurked beneath the waves, but she was certain by Arto's expression that it was nothing good. She patted Remus goodbye and turned, placing her hand in his. Together, they stepped onto the wooden seat and jumped into the salty sea.

Lina held her breath as she sank beneath the waves. Her dress billowed over her head, and she pushed it down with her hands. She kicked her legs and pulled herself up with her arms, until she burst from the surface. Arto was close behind her. He gasped for air, brushing the hair off his forehead and blinking. Lina turned, searching for the boat. It was already out of sight. They floated for a moment in silence.

"What now?" she asked.

"Now we wait," Arto said grimly. He searched the surface, turning around in a circle.

Lina wondered what he was looking for. She peered down beneath the waves. The water was so dark she couldn't see her feet. How far down was the Court of Merrows? And how would they get there? Her throat constricted, and she became acutely aware of the depth of the water. She lay on her back, letting her feet float to the surface. Somehow, being able to see her toes made her feel safer.

Suddenly she felt the familiar tug of a current pulling at the hem of her dress. She brought herself upright, looking fearfully to Arto. He smiled a small smile, nodding at her encouragingly. "The way to the Sea Door," he said. He grabbed her hand as the water began to swirl, wider and wider, in a massive circle. It pulled her sideways, casting her around and around in the whirling water. The bottom dropped out, and she gasped at the gaping vortex beneath them. It looked even deeper than it had last time. Her heart hammered and panic rose in her chest. She kicked and pulled her arms with all her strength, but she was no match for the swirling water. Gasping, she pulled in a breath as the whirlpool pulled them slowly down beneath the waves.

The whirling water was disorienting. Lina tumbled end over end in the darkness. She was spinning at incredible speed, and the turbulence broke her grip on Arto's hand. The swirling vortex dragged her down, down beneath the dark water. The air in her chest was growing thin, and her thoughts became hazy. She frowned. Surely this was not the way to the Sea Door. It was more likely that this was her way to death. Unable to suppress it any longer, she opened her mouth to take a deep breath, swallowing seawater. Her chest burned. There was no more air in her lungs, and her limbs felt weak. This had to be the end. She was going to die. The way she had come into Caelium was the way she was going out. She closed her eyes, letting her muscles relax. The vortex flung her outward, and she floated freely in dark, ethereal silence.

Suddenly a thin, tenuous melody streamed toward her through the water. She opened her eyes to slits. The melody grew, softly blossoming into a beautiful, disembodied song. She turned her eyes toward the enchanting sound, somehow breaking through her haze. The voice was coming from the mouth of an iridescent-eyed merrow. The merrow smiled a small smile, moving toward her through the dark water. She paused before Lina, and her long, dark hair billowed softly around her beautiful, porcelain face.

The merrow touched her face with delicate webbed fingers, placing her mouth to Lina's ear. There, she whispered the song. The melody floated inside her head like a wisp of smoke and lingered there, caressing her mind with soft strokes. Immediately Lina exhaled, and water pressed out of her lungs. She sucked in again and found that she was breathing clean, dry sea air. Relief flooded her, and she pulled it down greedily.

At once, her limbs felt lighter, adept to the depth of water. She tested their motion, kicking her legs out in front of her and waving her arms left and right. She felt as if she were moving through air instead of thrashing about near the sea floor. She gazed in wonder at the young merrow woman, who floated before her, smiling. The long lavender curve of her tail flicked upward between them as she hovered, its long, lacy edges fluttering like wings. Lina smiled at her in return, and joy bubbled up inside her chest. She laughed and was shocked to hear the sound clearly, not muffled as she had expected.

The merrow turned, motioning for her to follow. Lina kicked her legs, trailing her shimmering tail through the inky darkness. As they swam, her eyes adjusted to her surroundings. A few moments before, she could see nothing but a yawning abyss of dark water all around her. Now the blue-tinged sunlight filtered down from the surface, creating a waving, golden glow on the underwater world. The bright sand of the ocean floor below her undulated, shaped by the rolling waves. Clusters of large stones created hiding places for a menagerie of sea life, their surfaces bursting with purple and orange coral and deep red and dark blue marine plants. They waved with the tide, and strange, colorful creatures peeked at her from the rocks as she swam over them.

She followed the merrow through a grove of waving green seagrass higher than her head. Lina reached her arms through it, lacing her fingers between its blades. They slipped through her hands like long strips of silk. Tiny colorful fish wove in and out of the grass, their delicate, glittering scales shimmering in the sunlight. They stopped to inspect her, curiously hovering before her face.

To her right, the ground dropped off into a steep canyon. A fish as wide as a village street glided slowly above it. Its dark blue eye met hers, and she shrank back, hiding among the seagrasses. The merrow woman, however, was not at all concerned with the giant fish and swam toward it, caressing its large blue scales with her fingertips. The creature ignored her and swam placidly on.

They wound their way through the sea depths until they came to an underwater cave hidden in a cleft of rocks. They swam inside, tunneling through the dark stone until they emerged on the other side. There, before them, stood a large underwater arch. It towered high above on weathered gray stones. Sea moss peeked from between the rock columns and overhung the arched stone overhead. They swam to its base, floating before it on the sand. Lina peered around the stones, craning her neck to see what lay beyond them. She squinted. There was nothing but open water.

The merrow faced the arch, stretching her hand out flat before her. She opened her mouth, singing a few rising notes. As she sang, she lifted her other palm toward the surface. A soft *whoosh* sounded in front of her hand, and the water before it began flowing upward. This continued until a wall of shimmering water filled the opening of the arch, like a door. The merrow dropped her palm and moved through the wall of water. Lina followed her, stepping onto dry, aged stone on the other side.

Lina smoothed her hands over her dress and hair. Despite her swim, she was completely dry. The merrow paused, facing the arch, and raised her right arm above her head with her palm facing down. She lowered her hand, and the wall of water on the outside of the arch collapsed into the surrounding sea while the interior wall stayed upright.

Lina looked at her in surprise. The merrow now walked on two slender, shapely legs. Her feet were small and arched, and delicate translucent membranes spanned between her toes. Farther up her leg, iridescent scales trailed up her outer thigh from the base of her knee. She wore a simple, gauzy, blue garment that covered her midsection and chest, leaving her abdomen exposed. She turned, walking down a stone corridor. Lina studied her back. The thin strip of a delicate, lavender fin trailed up her spine like a blade.

Lina followed her, looking about in amazement. Ancient rock columns towered over her head, creating a large stone passage. The top of it was open, and she lifted her chin, gazing toward the surface. A shimmering dome of water soared high above her, spreading wide before dropping down to the sea floor. The sunlight glittered through it, casting rays of golden light on the stone. The merrow turned left down another corridor, passing a large glass window. Lina stopped before it, her mouth opening in awe.

In the valley below her lay a sprawling underwater city covered by the shimmering dome. She knew at once that this was the Court of Merrows.

The enchanting city was encircled on all sides by high, rocky cliffs creating a large stone fortress. Pools of water and small streams wove their way through the valley, and cypress, river birch, and willow trees grew in their midst. Many homes were hewn directly from the rock, but some were towering glass structures that glittered in the golden sunlight.

In the distance, a waterfall spilled over a high cliff. Two towering, weathered, stone columns marked its edges. At its base stood a glittering, domed castle made entirely of cerulean glass. A tall, dark-haired man stood on the glass steps before the castle. Lina squinted. His hands were bound, and he was being ushered into the front door by two Merrow guards.

Lina's heart leaped into her throat, and she pressed her hands to the glass. "Arto!" she screamed.

Her merrow guide turned, fixing her glittering gold eyes on her face. "Come," she said softly, extending her hand. "We go to Lady Sirena, now."

Lina stepped reluctantly from the window, cautiously taking the merrow's hand. *Lady Sirena.* Ronne had said she wanted to meet with Arto. That must be where the guards were taking him.

She followed her guide down the stone corridor and out into the city streets. Curious merrow faces paused to stare at her as they climbed the winding path to the glass steps of the castle. At the top of the stairs, they paused before the large glass doors. The merrow guide stood quietly to her left, her hands clasped at her waist. Two sentries stood guard by the doors. They never moved from their post but examined Lina with their large, glittering eyes.

Her guide turned to her. "I must ask that you leave your weapon with me. I shall have it taken to your rooms. It will be waiting for you after you return from the Lady Sirena."

Lina hesitated, moving her eyes from her guide to the guards. The two men dwarfed her in size, and their long spears were taller than her body. Reluctantly, she removed her bow and quiver, handing them to the young woman. She accepted them, bowing low at her waist with her palm fisted at her chest. "The Court of Merrows welcomes you, Princess Evangeline Vasily. My name is Sevika. I am honored to be your helper and guide." Lina flicked her eyes to her in surprise. The young merrow straightened, smiling softly. Then she turned and walked down the glass steps, disappearing under a stone bridge on her right.

Lina watched her go then turned back to face the tall doors. The sentry on the left rapped his spear once on the portico, and both men moved to pull the doors wide. Lina straightened her shoulders. She was uncertain what awaited her inside. Drawing a deep breath, she stepped into the throne room.

Intricate glass columns lined the expansive hall and soared high overhead into a cathedral ceiling. Rows upon rows of armored sentries stood at attention in front of the columns to her left and right. Lina glanced at them sidelong as she moved toward the dais. They didn't acknowledge her and stared straight ahead as she passed. At the end of the room, Arto kneeled between the two guards, his head hanging low.

Lady Sirena sat before him on an ornate, ammonite throne, its large spiraling curve towering above her. She peered down at Arto regally from her high nose, fixing him under her iridescent green gaze. Dark, flowing hair reached down to her waist, and translucent silver scales trailed up her high cheekbones. A silver dress was cut high on her leg, exposing matching scales on her thigh. She wore no shoes, and her feet perched delicately on the glass of the dais. To her right, an opaque blue glass orb rested on top of a scepter beneath her palm. Though her fair skin was smooth, Lina got the impression that she was much older than her appearance suggested.

Lady Sirena kept her eyes trained on Arto as Lina approached and stood close behind him. She placed a hand on his sagging shoulder, and he turned. He gazed up at her helplessly, a weak smile forming on his pale face. Whatever was happening, it couldn't be good. She squeezed his shoulder with her palm, wishing she could wrap him in her arms.

Lady Sirena stood, tapping her scepter once upon the dais. "The Court of Merrows will now hear the trial of Arturo Elikai. Arturo, you are charged by the Court of Merrows for crimes against the Royal Order of the Flame. As Timekeeper, you are committed by the Source to protect the Order and all it holds dear. However, you have failed gravely in your duties. You are named by our spies as the one responsible for the death of Queen Astrid of the Court of Ard-Mathan.

"This court understands that because of this treachery, you have left the daughter of the king an orphan lo these ten Mortal years. As you are well aware, the murder of a Royal member of the

Order is punishable by death, and your sentence would normally include such measures." She paused. "However, the Court of Merrows has decided to extend you mercy."

Arto snapped up his head in surprise, and Lady Sirena leveled him with her green, glittering gaze.

"For though it seemed to all that the queen had died, she yet lives. After she was thrown into the sea, she was rescued by our Forces and returned to us alive, here at court."

Chapter 16

Lina's knees felt weak, and she sank to the floor, tears pricking her eyes. Lady Sirena continued. "The queen lived with us here in safety, until the longing to see her daughter became so great that she bravely traveled to the surface. She was intercepted by the Court of Orm on the beach and is now held in the dungeons of Leyth Castle." She paused, flicking her eyes to Lina. "It is our belief that she is being held there to lure out the princess, whom the Court of Orm wishes to see dead." Lady Sirena nodded once to Arto. "If you, Arturo Elikai, can retrieve the queen and return her to us safely, you will be hereby absolved of your crimes." She tapped her scepter once on the dais. "Go. We will speak more of many things when you return." She put her fist to her chest, bowing low to Lina from her waist, and turned, disappearing down a long, glass corridor to her right.

Lina pulled Arto to face her, holding his head lovingly between her palms. She kissed his lips once then pulled back to look in his eyes. Her face was streaked with tears. She couldn't believe it. Her mother was alive. She had to go with him. She had help him saver her.

"When do we leave?" she asked quickly. Arto peered down at her, hesitation wrinkling his brow. "You can't come with me, Lina," he said slowly. "Lady Sirena is right. Orm is holding the queen to lure you out. If he catches sight of you, he will kill you on the spot. I have to do this alone. It's only right." Lina shook her head. She opened her mouth to protest, but he cut her off. "It's my place. My redemption at stake. You see?"

Lina pressed her lips as tears welled. She understood what he meant. She didn't like it, but she understood. "Please. You have to save her Arto," she breathed.

He nodded, tears spilling onto his cheeks. "Yes. Praise the Source I have the chance. I'll save her for you…and for me."

She brushed back his hair, wiping his tears with her thumbs.

The guards lifted him from the floor, escorting him away. He turned his head, speaking to her over his shoulder. "Wait for a message from the Eiks. They'll tell you how I am faring." She nodded, clasping her hands at her waist. "I love you," he called.

"I love you too," she cried, but the guards had already pulled him forward, disappearing down the long corridor.

An entire, long day had passed, and still no word had come

from the Eiks. Lina sat in the alcove of the large window in her rooms, overlooking the undersea landscape. She sighed, sitting her head on top of her tucked knees. She couldn't wait much longer. Time wouldn't allow it.

Just then, Sevika knocked and entered her rooms, carrying a silver tray heaped with breakfast. She set the tray near the window on a small, round table. Lina stood, stretching her back. She hadn't slept well the night before. The bluish light from the sun had filtered through the water long after it should have been night. Time was stretching longer and longer. It was almost always day now, in Caelium. Soon, Time would pull to a thread so long and thin that no one and nothing in all creation would escape. She sighed, staring down at the overfull tray. She didn't have an appetite.

Sevika moved about the room, straightening the bed and fluffing her pillows. The room was small, a cavern hewn into the rocks high in the stone walls of the fortress. Protection for the daughter of the king, or so the merrows had said. But with no word from Arto, it felt more like a prison. She turned, staring around the room. At least it was beautiful.

Her bed was made entirely of a great opalescent seashell. It faced the window, and she had a lovely view of the sea floor. The sheets were soft gauze, woven to appear like waves. Their fabric was cool and slid past her skin like silk. A delicate glass vanity sat in the far corner, and a seagrass rug lay beneath two upholstered coral chairs, facing the window. She sat in one now, picking at the plate of sea scallops and leaf greens that served as her breakfast.

She put down her fork, settling instead for hot tea. Sevika filled her shell cup from a decorative opalescent pot. Then she placed the pot on the table and stood with her hands clasped at her waist. "You've a message, Your Majesty, from the Lady Sirena. She wishes that you meet her in the palace."

Lina's chest leaped. Quickly, she placed her cup on the saucer and stood, equal measures of excitement and dread bubbling in her chest. Surely this meant there was news. Maybe Arto had even returned with her mother. She put on her cloak, gathering the mirrored compact into her pocket and slinging the leather pack, quiver, and bow across her back. She nodded once to Sevika, and they hurried down the winding stone corridors until they emerged under the bridge at the castle steps.

In the throne room, Lady Sirena stood upon the dais, her hand on her scepter. Lina stood on the glass floor, fixed under her iridescent gaze. "Your Majesty, we've had a message from the Eiks. In the midst of his rescue mission, the Timekeeper Arturo Elikai has been captured. He is now held in the dungeons of Leyth Castle."

Lina's heart sank into her stomach. "I must go to him," she pleaded.

Lady Sirena peered down at her, her lips a hard line. "I do not recommend you leave the Court of Merrows. Here, you are safe.

As the Grula Mrloga, you are wanted by the Court of Orm. He is luring you to the castle for your demise. If you are captured and executed, all hope of the restoration of the Rotha-Am will be lost."

Lina clenched her fists at her sides. "Arto saved me in the village of Meallta when I first arrived in Caelium. I owe him my life."

Lady Sirena eyed her, unblinking. She frowned, her delicate brows scrunching slightly.

"You would risk your life for a murderer such as he? The man who is a traitor to your father, the king, and has cast your mother into the sea at Orm's bidding?"

Lina put one hand to her chest. She shook her head. "I do not fear for my life, for it is not Orm's hand that holds it. And Arto is not the man he once was. The Source has forgiven, and so have I. Please. Let me go to him. When we return, with Queen Astrid, we will discuss the restoration of my father's kingdom."

Lady Sirena paused, her face a still mask. Then she put one fist to her chest, bowing low from her waist. She stood, tapping her scepter once on the glass floor. "Do as you say. Go. Take my chariot to the surface. And may the Source go with you." She raised her free hand, summoning Sevika. The woman appeared at Lina's side and led her through the glass palace to a platform set high in the outer stone fortress.

Sevika stood on the platform and placed two fingers to her lips, whistling three high notes. From a cavern in the base of the stone, two large, ancient seahorses appeared. They were dark grey with clouded eyes, just like the one from the beach. They lifted through the air from the sea floor, pulling a glittering, glass chariot with an opalescent shell seat. The horses thundered onto the platform, stopping the chariot on the stone at Lina's feet. Sevika moved to stand by the seat, bowing low to Lina and gesturing for her to climb aboard. Lina gazed sidelong at the seahorses, remembering Arto's warning. "You have nothing to fear, as long as you don't climb on their backs," Sevika said. She smiled, extending her hand.

Lina pursed her lips, grasping it and lifting onto the high seat.

She had scarcely climbed aboard when the horses pulled against the reins and shot through the air, heading for the dome. A wide section of the dome before them opened in a large shimmering oval. The galloping horses raced through it, and the opening snapped shut behind them. They thundered through the open sea as Lina gripped her seat, the bluish, hazy light of the sun glittering down on them through the water.

Lina floated on the seat as the horses glided toward the shore. They lifted their heads high, their dark manes shimmering in the sunlight. She shielded her eyes with her hand, scanning the shoreline. There, near the mouth of the underground river, stood Cyrus. The griffin cawed to her as she floated toward him, lifting off his massive paws and flying out to meet her. She stood on the seat, gripping onto his feathered neck and swinging her leg swiftly over his back. He was off in an instant, gliding up and over the high cliff above the shoreline.

She guided him swiftly over the rolling landscape, urging him to gain speed. They flew high above the village of Meallta, and the tall, stone buildings with their sloping roofs looked small from Lina's place in the sky. To the northeast, far in the distance, the stark peaks of the Haima Mountains rose high into gathering, grey clouds. The ominous outline of Leyth Castle hovered among them. Lina urged Cyrus towards its darkened doors, behind which the Court of Orm held captive two of those she held most dear.

Chapter 17

Dark clouds gathered heavily over the mountains as she approached the foothills of Leyth Castle. Cyrus swooped left and right, avoiding the fat raindrops pelting their heads in the gathering gloom. Lina peered over his neck at the castle's tall, dark towers of forbidding stone. The structure seemed to rest under a heavy weight, and an oppressive feeling pressed on her chest as she approached. She swallowed against a lump of fear as she peered at the stone steps leading to the front door. In a moment, she would scale them, and who knew what evil lurked inside of the castle. She braced herself, sure she would meet with foul horrors behind its doors.

Suddenly from behind a cloud bank above her head, two dark, winged shadows swooped toward her. She sucked in a sharp breath, pulling hard on Cyrus's reins as the crows materialized overhead. They descended, cawing and scratching at her with their sharp claws. Cyrus flapped his powerful wings, pushing backward as she readied her bow. She loaded and took aim, firing two arrows rapidly in the crows' direction. The birds zigzagged above her, her arrows narrowly missing their marks.

One crow swooped towards them, glaring hard with his glittering, black eyes. He slashed at Cyrus's neck with his sharp claws, ripping out a swath of soft feathers and leaving claw marks on the griffin's skin. Cyrus banked right, screeching in agony. The other crow descended, and the two pecked at his eyes, their dark wings flapping hard against Lina's head. She shielded herself with her arm as Cyrus retaliated, pulling up with his front paws, slashing at the birds with his long talons.

In a flash of fury, Cyrus let out a booming call, his large paw batting one crow to the side. As the remaining crow squawked, Cyrus grasped it in his front paws, pressing its rib cage between his talons. The crow fought against him, flapping his dark wings hard against the griffin's head. It struggled as Cyrus squeezed, and then the crow's bones cracked. Its eyes went flat, its head hanging limply to the side. Cyrus released it, and it fell through the clouds. It tumbled end over end, its dark wings hanging limply from its crumpled torso. then it landed in a twisted heap on the earth.

The other crow screamed, its eyes flashing in anger. It lunged at Cyrus's throat, but the griffin was too fast. He flapped his great wings and carried them upward, through the clouds, higher than they had ever flown. Lina held fast to his back as Cyrus spun. She could feel by his movements what he was about to do. She gritted her teeth, bracing herself as he tucked his wings. He angled downward, and then he was diving. Lina's stomach reached her ears as he dove headlong through the clouds, his talons reaching toward the remaining crow.

Lina held tightly to the reins, shutting her eyes as he collided with the large bird. Cyrus wrestled the crow, tumbling end over end in the open air. Further and further, they fell. Lina flattened herself against Cyrus's neck, holding his feathers in a death grip until they made impact with the ground.

Meanwhile, in the throne room, Orm slithered across the floor toward the Throne of Mercy. His useless, shriveled legs lay limply at the sides of his serpentine body that undulated as he trailed up the dais. He paused on the steps, turning his milky, opaque eyes toward the minds of the crows. He scanned their field of vision, accessing their thoughts. They were engaged in a midair battle, with a griffin and a girl. His thin lips widened with glee, and his pale, translucent skin quivered with delight. It was Evangeline, and she was deliciously close to the castle.

It was exactly as he had hoped. He would send the basilisk, and then, she would be no more. He crept over the white stone, a slick of dark mire trailing in his wake, and seated himself upon the throne. He watched with bated breath as the crows lunged at the neck of the griffin and pelted Lina with their powerful wings. He smiled, his thin, pallid lips pulling over yellowish-gray teeth. He might not even need the basilisk. The crows might rid him of her first.

The first crow tumbled, and he hissed, his tail slithering over the stone in agony. He reached a twisted hand to his hairless crown, squinting his lidless eyes. He watched as the griffin tumbled with the other crow toward the earth, crushing its neck between his talons. Orm recoiled, roaring from deep in his throat. He brought his other hand to his neck, heaving, his sickly, worm-like body wracked by pain.

Suddenly, the griffin was still. Lina opened her eyes. She sat up right, peering below. Cyrus stood on top of the crow, his talons gripping its black neck flat. The bird's eyes had gone dark, and its wings lay crumpled at strange angles. Cyrus released him, stepping down onto smooth, flat stone. Lina looked above her. They were standing on the stone steps of Leyth Castle.

With his spies now dead, Orm turned his pale eyes, searching for another creature with which to see. Hunting deep within the belly of the castle, he found the eyes of the basilisk who roamed the dungeons. He hissed a laugh, pressing his gnarled fingers on the arms of the throne. The basilisk was sleeping, his dark eyes closed. But Orm knew where Lina was headed. Soon, she would step inside the walls of the castle. And soon, the beast would wake.

Lina tucked Cyrus into a cleft of rocks, bringing his feathered neck to her jaw. "Be still and silent until I return. I won't be long," she whispered, patting his head. He cooed, closing his great eyes, then sat down on his haunches to wait.

Lina scanned the dark rocks as she climbed to the stairs. In her mind's eye, she imagined a lycanth stepping from behind them into her path at any moment. She shivered, struggling to push the thought away. The ominous pressure she had felt in her chest was worse now that she was near the castle doors. Fear nipped at her neck as she gazed up at them. In a moment, she would step inside, and then what horrid evil would she meet? She tried not to think about the lycanth or what other horrors lay before her as she crept her way silently through the rocks. Then, at last, she came to the great, white stone stairs.

Her breath came in short bursts by the time she reached the top of the steps. Near the front doors, a beast lay sleeping on the stone. Lina gazed at it curiously, her mind signaling an extra burst of fear. Its head was like a lion, and it had the body of a bear. A great pair of folded wings lay at its sides. She drew her bow, pointing it at the beast's head.

Her feet were silent on the stone as she moved towards the strange creature. Lina wondered if she could slip past it without causing it to wake. Warily, she studied the large talons at the tips of the beast's claws. She was certain she didn't want it to. Silently, she slipped forward, but to her great horror, the beast stirred when she was mere footsteps away. Her heart trilled, and she aimed at it with her bow as it woke, peering at her lazily with one eye.

A jolt of shock shot through her arm as a deep laugh rumbled from the creature's throat, and it stood, prowling. The beast, grinned, pulling lips over long, sharp fangs.

"Your weapons have no power here, Evangeline Vasily," said a feminine feline voice. The beast began to circle her, baring sharp teeth in a menacing grimace. "You have come for the queen, Astrid the Fair, and the Timekeeper, Arturo Elikai." The creature paused before her, her face towering above Lina's head. She raised one long, sharp claw. "But first, you must solve my mysteries. All travelers who pass this way must answer these tests. All who answer correctly may pass, but those who do not …" The beast sat back onto her haunches, lifting her front paw and examining her long, gleaming claws. "Well, I rather enjoy …" She flicked her eyes up and down Lina's body with disdain. *Mostly* Mortal flesh." She smiled wide, showing her wide rows of gleaming fangs.

Lina stood still, her eyes even with the beast. Her legs were trembling with fear, but she steadied her voice. "I accept," she said, her hands forming fists at her sides.

The she-beast stood, prowling around in a circle. Her claws clicked against the stone with her steps. "Goood," she purred. She stopped by Lina's left shoulder, whispering a low hissing voice into her ear. "What starts lying flat, then kneels, then stands, only to end lying flat again?"

Lina considered, her fists tightening with her frown. She thought for a moment, then her brows raised. She knew exactly what it was. "The body," she answered steadily.

The beast hesitated. "Yes," she conceded grimly. The creature turned, circling her. "What ages hard but rises soft, is grown, then baked, and eaten oft?"

Lina thought for a moment. *Think.* If she didn't, she would never reach Arto or her mother. She bit her lip, then smiled slightly as the answer came. "The bread," she answered.

"Correct," the beast growled. Lina could tell she was irritated. She prowled angrily, then stopped behind Lina's right shoulder. "What is first contained that once released cannot be put back in a beast?"

Lina hesitated, searching her mind. *What is it? What can't be put back in a beast?*

Relief washed over her as an answer formed. "The blood," she replied.

The beast swiped at the stone furiously, sending sparks tumbling across it. "Yes," she roared.

Lina stepped forward. She had given her the answers. The beast had promised to let her pass if she did. But the creature stuck out her large paw, blocking her path. The beast circled in front of her then sat back on her haunches, scowling down her feline nose. "One last question," she seethed. Lina stepped back, folding her hands at her waist to stop their trembling. She hoped she could answer it. The lioness snarled, her fangs inches from Lina's nose. "What sours the vine that first was sweet and is made by crushing for the drink?"

Lina searched the skies, pursing her lips. The answer was on the tip of her tongue. At last, it came. "The wine," she answered softly.

The creature roared in her face, blowing back the hair from Lina's forehead. Lina shut her eyes against the blast, grimacing. She braced herself for what she knew was coming. Despite her promises otherwise, the creature was going to eat her, right here on the castle steps. After all she had endured, she was going to die. She sucked in a breath, steeling herself for the pain of sharp fangs around her neck. But to Lina's surprise, the creature held up her end of the bargain. Lina opened her eyes, watching as the beast lifted her great wings and took flight, leaving Lina alone by the castle doors.

Lina peered up at them warily. The dark wood seeped some strange liquid. It ran down the sides of the frame, like dark red blood. She pulled her eyes from it, shivering as she squared her shoulders. Then she took a deep breath and pushed them open.

The doors creaked on their ancient hinges as she peeked her head around them, scanning the high room. Wall lanterns dimly lit the dark wood of the main hall. She blinked, letting her eyes adjust. A set of ornate wooden doors marked the end of the hall in front of her. To her left, a dark stone corridor led to a set of steps that descended into darkness. Fear curled around her ears as she examined it. She headed in that direction, keeping her back against the wall.

Silently, she crept down the slick, stone steps. Strangely, she met no one. There were no guards here, and there had been none in the main hall. She frowned, wondering at their absence. Surely someone was guarding the prisoners and castle halls. She reached out her hand as she descended, steadying herself against the damp stones. Water trickled from the overhead rocks, dampening the top of her hood, and darkness pressed her heavily before and behind. Distantly, rattling chains echoed in the darkness.

A lantern hung from a wall hook at the bottom of the steps. She took it, holding it aloft to light the dark dungeon corridor. Pressing her back against the wall, she crept to the end of the first hall and looked down two more corridors to her left and right. She held the lantern high, peering past the light into the right hallway. A yawning abyss gazed back at her silently. To the left were rows upon rows of iron grates. She tiptoed toward them, moving silently past the bars. Each cell she passed was empty, and panic rose as she continued forward. What if she couldn't find them—her mother and Arto? What if they weren't in the dungeons at all?

There was only one set of iron grates left at the end of the hall. From inside, she heard the faint rattle of chains. Relief flooded her as she hurried to the sound, casting her light past the bars. Arto sat with his back against the right wall. His eyes were closed, and he had a deep cut across his lip. A trickle of blood had run down his chin, staining his shirt. A woman lay opposite him on the cold stone floor. Long golden hair hung loose over her face, and her knees were drawn in. Her dress was dirty and torn, and she was very thin. The woman rolled weakly onto her back, and Lina's heart leaped into her throat.

For a moment, she lay as still as a stone. Lina watched her chest, willing it to rise. Her mother sucked in a breath, and Lina rested her forehead heavily on the grates. She was still breathing.

Lina tapped the iron bar closest to her, whispering, "Arto. Arto, it's me, Lina. Wake up."

Arto opened his eyes to slits, squinting at her through the bars. He scrambled to stand, his eyes going wide. Frantically, he held out a hand to her, placing one finger to his lips. "Shhhh, Lina. Be quiet. He will hear you. You shouldn't have come. It's not safe!"

Lina frowned, shaking her head. "What do you mean? Who will hear me? There weren't any guards on my way in."

Just then, a chuff of warm breath tickled her shoulder. Lina froze. There was someone behind her. Or something.

Arto snapped his eyes shut. He stumbled over his feet, rushing to meet her at the grates. "Lina! Lina, shut your eyes! Keep them shut! Don't look into his eyes. Don't look!"

Lina had already partially turned her head, catching a sidelong glimpse of the horrifying beast.

An enormous reptilian creature with slick black scales stood in the dark hallway behind her, its rows of gleaming teeth glittering in the lantern light. The terrifying creature stepped toward her, its long purplish claws scraping the stones. Its powerful back legs were in shackles, and they rattled with its movement. The beast growled deep in its throat, stretching its membranous black wings. They fluttered as Lina snapped her eyes shut.

She spun, grunting as she swung the lantern hard toward the creature's head. He screeched, recoiling out of the light. A long, slithering tail flicked into the air as the beast raised itself up on two legs and opened his jaws in a deafening roar.

Orm watched from behind the basilisk's eyes as Lina swung her lantern. "Kill her!" he screamed. Lina pulled a single arrow with her free hand, jabbing it wildly at the basilisk's head. It recoiled, swiping its claws down the length of her arm. She screamed in anguish as her flesh tore beneath them, and Orm chuckled with glee. "Yesss," he hissed. "YES!"

Just then, he heard Queen Astrid's voice, weak and rasping, through the grates. "Lina, my darling, what Arto says is true. Keep your eyes tightly shut. Those who look into the basilisk's eyes are sure to meet their death. But there is one way to defeat them, or so the Histories say."

Lina swung her lantern again, causing the basilisk to roar. She kept her eyes squeezed tightly shut. "What do I do?!" she shouted.

"The basilisk's gaze will cause death to any who look upon it, even the basilisk himself."

Lina paused, holding the lantern in midair as her mother's words registered. She had an idea. Dropping her arrow, she reached deeply into the pocket of her dress, retrieving her mother's gilded, mirrored compact. The beast roared in warning, its sharp claws scraping on the stones as it lunged. Lina screamed as she felt the hot breath of the basilisk at her throat. She dropped the lantern onto its side and swiftly opened the compact, holding it up before her face like a shield.

The mirror reflected the basilisk's gaze.

"Nooo!" Orm screamed. His milky eyes burned, and he shielded the lidless orbs with his twisted hands. The light behind the basilisk's eyes had gone out. Orm sagged against the throne, roaring in angry defeat. Once again, he sat alone, in darkness.

Lina's hands shook as she held up the compact, shielding her face in her shoulder. Her heart was pounding in her ears, and she did not hear the heavy, scaled body drop to the floor. Silence cloaked her as her mother reached a gentle hand through the grates, touching Lina on the shoulder. "Lina, open your eyes. It's safe. The basilisk is dead."

Lina didn't move her head. She squinted one eye, peering sidelong at the beast. The creature lay on the floor, its massive, horned head at her feet. She stepped back from it gingerly, dropping the compact to clatter against the stones. Swiftly, she turned, embracing her mother through the bars. Arto gazed down at the creature, grinning from the side of his mouth. "Who needs guards when you have a basilisk?" he said teasingly.

Lina's mother put a hand lovingly to her cheek. She peered weakly through the bars.

"We must hurry," said Queen Astrid. "I have no doubt more of Orm's foul beasts may be lurking in these shadows."

Lina studied the iron grates. She had no idea how to get them free.

Arto read her mind. He pointed at the basilisk through the bars. "The key," he said. "It's around the basilisk's neck."

Lina peered over her shoulder. A braided leather rope was tied around the creature's neck, and on it hung a large iron key. Gingerly, she stepped over the beast's great head. She watched its large, closed eye warily as she bent to its plated neck, untying the leather strap and retrieving the key. Thankfully, the basilisk remained still. She placed it in the lock, turning the latch and opening the iron grates.

Silently, the three hurried out of the dungeon. To Lina's relief, like before, no one stirred in the main hall. They escaped through the doors unseen.

Outside, Arto whistled low. Bayard appeared from the sky in moments. He landed swiftly on the stone portico, his hooves raining sparks as he skidded to a stop. Bayard shook his grey mane as Arto placed Lina's mother gently on his back. Lina reached out and held her hand. Queen Astrid may have meant royalty to the realm of Caelium and redemption to Arto, but to Lina, she was simply her mother. Simply, wonderfully, incredibly, her mother. Queen Astrid squeezed her hand as Arto clucked to Bayard. "I'll see you soon, my daughter," she said softly. "I promise."

Lina smiled, joyful tears streaming freely down her face. "Soon," she agreed.

Bayard took off, galloping over the foothills before taking flight. Lina watched her mother's golden hair trail behind her as they rose into the air. She still couldn't believe it. Her mother was alive. Quickly, she retrieved Cyrus from his hiding place, and they followed, heading south for the Court of Merrows.

When they arrived at the beach, they dismounted and stood waiting in the shallow waves. Lina spoke softly to the animals, guiding them into the cavernous opening of the underwater river. She hid them there under the overhanging vines. Patting their necks, she whispered, "We'll return for you soon. Wait here, out of sight." They nuzzled her hand, cooing and nickering in turn.

In a moment, the dark seahorses appeared in the shallow surf. They tossed their high necks, pulling the chariot to rest before Queen Astrid's feet. Sevika surfaced, smiling broadly at each of them from her delicate face. She dipped her head. "Welcome, Queen Astrid, Timekeeper Arturo Elikai, and Princess Evangeline Vasily. Lady Sirena will be most pleased with your return. As am I." She motioned for each of them to approach and, in turn, whispered her song into their ears. Then the trio climbed onto the opal seat, holding fast as the seahorses galloped beneath the waves.

They reached the dome quickly, passing through and landing on the platform outside the fortress. Two merrow guards met them there and escorted Arto ahead of them directly into the throne room. Lady Sirena bowed her head low in the presence of the queen, a small smile on her lips. "You are most welcome in our court, Queen Astrid. The Court of Merrows is glad of your safe return. Please rest here as you recover. We will be thankful to supply all your needs." She turned her head to Arto, her green eyes glittering.

"Arturo Elikai, Timekeeper of the Order of the Flame, the Source has seen fit to redeem you of your crimes. You have shown yourself worthy by risking your life in the rescue of the queen. It is clear to me that you are no longer a slave to the twisted plan of destruction of the former Master Timekeeper, Orm. The princess has forgiven you for your past shame as has the Source—and as have I.

"It is because of the love of the daughter of the king and her willingness to risk her life for your rescue and the rescue of Queen Astrid that you are now absolved of your crimes. The Court of

Merrows hereby releases you of your charges. May you live a life worthy of your redemption." She tapped her scepter once on the glass dais, and the guards immediately moved away from Arto's side.

Lady Sirena raised her hand, summoning Sevika. "Now please take Queen Astrid to her rooms. Here she shall remain, in safety, until the defeat of the Court of Orm." She nodded once to Queen Astrid, who smiled softly up to her. "Thank you, Sirena," she said weakly. "But first, let me tell my daughter one thing."

Lina looked at her mother, into the eyes that were just like her own. "Mother, you should rest. I'll be here when you wake," she said softly. Her mother smiled. "Lina. My daughter, my heart, my beautiful gift. For the sake of the two worlds that you are a part of, you must go." No words came to her, and Lina could only stare. She wanted to stay, but she knew her mother was right.

"I would love to promise that we will have Time together that was stolen from us. But as the Rotha-Am slows, that Time may no longer exist." Queen Astrid put one unsteady hand on Lina's cheek. "My brave, beautiful gift to the world. You have saved me. And now you must go and save us all." Tears brimmed in her eyes. "I love you."

"I love you, too," Lina said softly, her voice catching in her throat. And with that, Sevika led her mother down the castle steps.

Lady Sirena watched her go with a smile. Then sat on the throne, addressing Arto and Lina. "Now we must discuss other important matters." She folded her hands regally onto her lap.

"It has come to my attention that the Rotha-Am will not long turn in its fallen place and that Time will soon draw to a close. Foul beasts terrorize the land, and so many created beings have already met their death. Creation is corrupted, and deception runs rampant in the Mortal Realm and Caelium, alike. Indeed, my own father, Lord Dolion, betrayed our selkie neighbors, bound in deception to Orm's will. He sold Lord Ronan of the Selkie Court, passing his Amloga into Orm's hands. Lord Ronan was a Timekeeper and had pledged his life to the Court of Ard-Mathan and the Order of the Flame. His Amloga was much desired, a piece of power to be fed to the Rotha-Am to cease its turning, and in payment for his life, Lord Dolion gained dominion over Lord Ronan's people.

"After Lord Ronan's death, my father stole much from the Selkie Court. He took their lands, driving them farther south to the Selkie Isles. I understand Lord Ronan's mate and daughter still grieve his loss after so many cycles, as does the entire court. It is hard to lose those whom one loves, as I well know.

"As a result of his treachery, Lord Dolion lost his life. He was eaten by Nathair, the great serpent who dwells at the bottom of the sea." She paused, gazing at the floor, then lifted her iridescent eyes. "As Lord Dolion's daughter, I wish to atone for these wicked actions against our selkie neighbors. As part of that atonement, our court will join your great cause. The Court of Orm has long defiled the Throne of Mercy, but no more." She stood, tapping her scepter against the floor. "The Court of Merrows will stand with the Court of Ard-Mathan, and we will fight."

With relief at Arto's pardon, Lina and Arto bid Lady Sirena goodbye. Lina was sure that they would soon meet the merrow ruler again. They left the glittering castle beneath the sea, once again carried to the surface in the glass chariot. Once there, they headed for the mouth of the river, where their animals waited behind the hanging vines.

Lina greeted Cyrus, scratching the feathers under his chin. She swung her leg over his back, following Arto and Bayard up over the rocky cliff. It felt good to fly again, without fear of the crows. She and Arto soared up through the whisps of clouds, savoring the heat of the midday sun on their backs.

Lina shielded her eyes with her hand, peering up at the sky. Except for the dark, oppressive space around Leyth castle, the sun still perched high over her head. It had not changed its place for a long while. In fact, this was the longest day she had experienced in Caelium.

She wondered about Time in the Mortal Realm. The hours of sunlight there grew shorter and shorter, sped along by the winding hands of the Great Clock. She remembered the wavering landscape of her forest clearing, how it flickered and faded in her periphery. Soon, it would all flicker out. There would be nothing left of the cottage in the clearing, the village, or her beloved Jacques. *Jacques...*He had become old before he was due. He wouldn't last much longer. She furrowed her brow, spurring Cyrus with her heels. They must hurry. Time was running out.

Just then, the air in front of her sucked inward and she involuted into a dark, blank space. Her ears rang, and she blinked her eyes against the blackness. Lifting her hands, she grasped for something solid. There was nothing to hold and no hands with which to hold it. She frowned, panic rising in her chest, kicking and punching where her arms and legs should've been. Realizing her limbs were missing, her throat constricted. Her breathing hitched, and she clawed frantically at the darkness. It was no use. She floated, a mind with no body, in a great black void. Opening her mouth, she tried to scream, but there was nothing with which to make the sound. She was trapped, a mind with no body, and there was no escape.

Suddenly the black void flickered, and the surrounding landscape stuttered in and out around her. In a moment, she rematerialized, her hands still gripping Cyrus's reins. Tucking her knees against his sides, she swallowed convulsively, sucking in deep breaths of the cool, open air. Cyrus felt her distress, and he flapped his great wings at double speed. Smoothing his neck, she wondered if he too had been trapped in the dark void. She studied the back of his head. She hoped not.

She whistled low, bracing against his back as he sped across the sky. Lina peered past his neck. The North Forest of Caelium sat on the horizon. Soon, they would meet with the dryads. Ronne's warning about the dryads' mistrust weighed in the back of her mind. So many of their beloved Eiks had been cut down, and their hope was almost lost.

She hoped that she and Arto could convince them of her true identity. They needed the strength of the dryad's Amloga to defeat the Court of Orm and raise the Rotha-Am. They needed the dryads to be willing to fight. Lina frowned. She hoped they could restore their hope, before Time ran out.

CHAPTER 18

As far as Lina could see, the great trees of the North Forest spread out before them. Bayard had already landed below her in the meadow. He stood waiting by a large arch near the edge of the forest. It was made of two large trees, twisting roots, and vines. The structure towered as she clucked to Cyrus, pulling him down gently to rest on the ground beside Bayard.

Lina slid from Cyrus's back, craning her neck to examine the massive doorway. Two great trees served as columns for the opening. Twisted roots sprawled from their bases, winding out over the forest floor. Their leafy crowns laced together in intricate patterns, creating a natural arch high above the ground. Floral vines overhung the arch, twisting onto the tree trunks and trailing to the ground below.

Arto turned to her. "It's best we pass through the Forest Door, or the dryads may see us as a threat. Their scouts are always watching, and they'll soon know that they have guests. You probably won't see anything on our way in, but keep your eyes and ears open. They are masters of disguise. If you do suspect company, it's best not to draw your weapon because the scouts spook easily.

"We will hike to the heart of the forest. There, the Grove of Eiks encircles a central clearing. It is the home of the dryads. They make their shelters in the Eiks, protecting the ancient trees with their lives. Because the Court of Orm has felled so many of the Eiks, the dryads will be nervous about our appearance in the clearing."

Lina nodded. Quietly, she and Arto left their mounts beside the Forest Door and stepped through the arch. Above them, a high canopy of tangled limbs and green leaves rustled softly in the breeze. Sunlight peeked through the cracks, creating a dappled golden pattern on the lush undergrowth. Great ferns and toadstools marked the path to the clearing, and small forest creatures scampered up and down the trees and across the forest floor. A wide, iridescent-winged butterfly floated gently beneath the low limbs. Lina followed it with her eyes as it fluttered away. More than once, she caught a flash of movement from her peripheral gaze, but when she turned her head, the movement was gone.

Above her head, a small brown bird sat on a limb, chirping a measured, melodious song. Lina peered up at the cute little sparrow, grinning at his tufted wings. He turned his beady black eye, gazing down in her direction. As quick as a wink, he lifted from the limb and flew over the path ahead of them. Arto turned his head to her, smiling from the corner of his mouth. "A scout," he whispered.

Arto followed the sparrow out of the canopy and into the bright sunlight. He turned to her, raising a finger to his lips. Then he walked to the center of the clearing with his arms raised, sitting down quietly on the grass.

Lina followed him warily, lowering behind him and resting silently against his back. She lifted her eyes, examining her surroundings. Encircling the forest clearing was the Grove of Eiks. The oak trees were ancient and enormous. Their great crown of leaves reached high above her head, and the limbs cascaded one over the other to fold softly toward the ground. Hanging moss fell over their branches, and patches of crusting lichen stuck to the sides of their wide trunks. Thick, winding roots sprawled from their bases, overlapped with each tree beside, connecting one to the other.

To one side of the clearing, however, Lina could see through the Grove, into the woods beyond. Many of the Eiks there were cut down close to their roots, their remains charred by fire. Forest plants had filled the area with green, but the blackened stumps felt like an open wound upon the clearing. Lina studied them as she placed her hand onto the grassy carpet. In the spot, a soft undercurrent of emotion ran over her skin, raising chills on her arm. She squinted her eyes, turning the side of her head toward the ground. A whispering voice trailed up from the earth, tickling her ear. She blinked in surprise, pressing both palms flat to the ground. Closing her eyes, she listened. A sad, moaning sound groaned up through her arms.

"Sorrow upon sorrow, we have suffered. How long shall the Source tarry? How few must we be, before the end?" a creaking whisper groaned.

Her eyes pricked, and she opened them, gazing up at the Eiks. Great sadness permeated the remaining members. She could feel it, like a rushing current running through the ground.

Suddenly a great Wind blew through the North Forest. An ethereal peace blanketed the clearing as the Wind stirred the great leaves of the Eiks. Lina sat still, basking in the peaceful feeling that had overtaken the sorrow from a moment before. The tightness in her chest at the emotions of the Eiks softened, relaxing with the Wind's swirling path.

As the Wind blew, a faint tinkling sound began at the back of Lina's head. It raised the short hairs on her neck, and she shivered. The sound spread, flowing out into her hands and feet and curling about the sides of her mind until her whole body was filled with a soft warm glow. The glow pulled inward, retracting itself to the center of her chest. It lingered there, a slow gentle burn to the left of her heart. She brought her hand to the spot, pressing her palm flat. The glow swirled about her belly and bubbled up into her throat. Great joy flooded her, and she laughed out loud. She listened to the sound, and tears pricked her eyes. Then she was crying in earnest. She wasn't even sure why. Soft, flowing tears dripped off her chin, wetting the front of her dress.

Arto choked out a grunt, and she sat upright, wiping her face. She gazed over her shoulder to see what had happened. There, a slender forest creature stood behind him with fingers wrapped in his hair and a rough blade placed to his throat. A dryad. The creature looked as if she was part of the forest herself, her oaken skin patterned with wood grain. Her small feet were bare, and her body was covered with patches of tree bark and moss. Wildflowers grew among her long brown hair, and winding green vines covered her midsection and chest. Her ears were pointed at the tips, and a circlet of tiny yellow mushrooms grew over her left upper arm.

Her piercing emerald eyes squinted down at Arto's face. "Who dares enter the sacred Grove of Eiks?" she growled. She flicked her eyes to Lina, who slowly turned to face her, kneeling with her hands raised. Despite her small size, the dryad was menacing.

Arto swallowed convulsively. "It is I, Arturo Elikai, Timekeeper of the Order of the Flame." He flicked his eyes to Lina. "And this is my companion, the daughter of the King Ard-Mathan, Princess Evangeline Vasily."

The dryad squinted her eyes at Lina, tucking the blade tighter against his throat. It was a wooden blade with a keen edge whittled on one side, drawing a thin line of blood. "Blasphemy!" she yelled.

More dryads had begun to gather at the edges of the clearing, emerging from under roots and holes in the ground and leaping down from the limbs of the Eiks to watch the display. Lina cast her gaze warily in their direction. There were so many of them. She was sure she and Arto would be in trouble if the small dryads decided not to trust them.

Arto swallowed, his angular throat bobbing. He flicked his eyes up to the frowning dryad above him. "Ask them if what I say is true. Ask the Eiks to prove it to you."

The dryad woman flicked her eyes to the watching crowd and paused, considering. She nodded once, and the dryads immediately snapped to attention. As Lina watched, they formed a large circle. Closing their eyes, they whispered a soft humming sound. Then they placed their hands upon the large trunks of the Eiks. The Four Winds blew through the leaves, shaking the canopy of trees above the winding limbs.

Moments passed, and no one moved or made a sound. The Wind swirled, once more, through the clearing, and then, all at once, it stopped.

Finally, the dryads dropped their hands from the Eiks and turned to face the clearing. One by one, they brought their right fist to their chest, bowing low before the daughter of the king. The dryad woman released Arto's hair, dropping her wooden blade to the ground. She knelt before Lina, bowing her forehead low.

"Forgive me," she said quietly. "You are most welcome in the Grove of Eiks, Evangeline Vasily. The Eiks, the ancient tree messengers of the Source of the Four Winds, greet you, as do I. Long have we awaited your coming. Long have we awaited a message of hope. Too long. Much too long." She sat upright, bringing her right fist to her chest as low murmurs sounded among the dryads around them. "Long live the court of King Ard-Mathan! Long live the one true king!" The crowd of dryads echoed her words, and Lina dipped her head, smiling quietly as they looked on.

The dryad woman stood then, offering Lina her wooden hand. "Please come stay in my home." She bowed once more. "I am Willow. You, and your Timekeeper, Arturo Elikai, will be most welcome."

Arto and Lina followed Willow's wood-patched legs to the far edge of the clearing. There, she stopped before a dirt path in front of the largest and most ancient tree in the Grove. Moss blanketed the ground beyond the path, creating a soft green carpet below its branches. Clusters of large toadstools grew in rings at the tree's base, and flowering vines hung heavily from the crown. Their blooms blew in the soft breeze, giving the air beneath the tree a heady floral scent. On the side of the large trunk, a trio of circular windows reflected the dappled sunlight.

Lina followed Willow up the path to a set of exposed root steps. A small, green wooden door was fitted into the side of the tree above them. Willow hopped agilely up the roots and pulled open the door, standing aside for Lina and Arto to enter. Lina ducked her head, stepping over the low threshold.

Inside the tree was a large, circular living space. The furniture was small, dryad sized, but the room was cozy and warm. A round, rough-hewn table and four stools sat atop a mossy rug in the center of the room. Wildflowers in a small clay vase decorated the table. A kitchen space stood on the right wall, and a small, cozy fire roared in the dugout hearth beside it. A pot of stew simmered lightly above the flames. A series of shelves were fixed to the left wall with a menagerie of collected items atop them. Lina smiled as she studied them. Interesting rocks, large acorns, colorful leaves, and dried flowers were arranged on the shelves in display.

In the back of the room, a set of root stairs wound their way up the wall to the second floor. Beneath it, a small round window overlooked the clearing. Beneath the window, in an alcove under the stairs, was a dryad-sized bed and a bookshelf hewn from the wall. The books stacked on it were quite small, and the lettering inside was sure to be even smaller. Lina wondered who had written them.

Willow led them up the wall steps to the second floor. She stepped into the room, motioning to Arto with her slender hand. "This can be your room. It's the largest space in the house." She chuckled a musical sound. "But I'm afraid you'll have to sleep on the floor." She turned to look at the tiny bed in the corner. The walls of the tree's wooden trunk curved around it, making a cozy, circular sleeping space. Arto squatted down on the edge of the mattress, his knees hitting his chest.

He laid back, curling into a tight ball. Mocking sleep, he pretended to snore. His feet hung off the end of the mattress, and his head was situated at an odd angle. Lina and Willow glanced at each other and broke into peals of laughter, hugging their midsections. Tears squeezed out of the sides of Lina's eyes as Arto flopped onto his back, letting his long legs drag the floor.

She wiped the corners of her eyes, smiling a broad smile. She had forgotten how good it felt to really laugh. It made her think of Jacques. How often had they laughed like this in his clock shop? Her smile faltered as she thought of his aging body and the dwindling Time.

The mirth was extinguished as worried thoughts and doubts swirled in her mind. What if they couldn't stop the Court of Orm? What if the Rotha-Am never rose? What if Jacques passed away before they were able to right it? Then, the Rotha-Am would never turn in harmony with the Great Clock again. If they failed in their quest, it would all be gone. She looked around her, at the trees, and Willow, and Arto. This Grove, these lives, Jacques, and even herself. Everything in all of creation would be no more. Her smile had vanished as the enormity of her task yawned before her. What if she was not enough? What if the task was too great?

Her joy tamped down deep, and she was quiet, suddenly hugging her arms across her chest.

Arto sat up, eyeing her soberly, his dark hair sticking up in all directions. He ran a hand through it as he stood. Moving across the room, he wrapped her in his arms, nuzzling the top of her head. She held him tightly, tucking her cheek against his chest. She wondered how many more times she would hold him like this before it was all over. Before the end of all things.

He pulled back, lifting her chin with the tip of his finger. She gazed up at his tender face. As if he could read her mind, he said, "We will defeat him, Lina. Have some faith."

She nodded, feeling hollow inside. She hoped he was right. But she was just a girl. And what could a small, half-Mortal girl from a forest clearing do to save Time? He brought his lips to hers, kissing her soundly. Tears squeezed from the edges of her eyes. She wondered how many more kisses they would share.

Wordlessly, she gripped his hands, pulling slowly away. Fear was gripping her across her chest, and she didn't know how to force its release.

Willow turned and climbed the stairs to the attic. Arto gave her hands a squeeze, and then Lina turned away, following after the dryad. When she reached the top step, she blinked in surprise, and a small gasp escaped her lips. Her spirit lifted slightly as she turned in a circle.

The attic was situated high up the trunk, near the tree limbs. Leafy green branches cascaded down around the circular windows, providing cool shade to the room. The ceiling was vaulted, and thick, green vines wound down the walls from between the wood. Little purple flowers hung in clusters from vines, creating a light floral scent to the air.

In the far corner, an enormous nutshell had been halved, creating a small bed. Its top was covered with a thick moss blanket. A fern sprouted from the corner opposite it, next to a wicker rocking chair and side table. Lina cast her cloak and weapon across the back of the chair, sitting in the seat to remove her boots. She stood, stretching her arms over her head. The room was warm from the fire below, and the bed looked soft and cozy. She hadn't slept since before the castle rescue.

Suddenly she felt very drowsy. Without warning, her knees gave way, buckled from exhaustion, and Willow caught her arm, guiding her swiftly to the bed. "Rest, now," she whispered softly. "There is Time."

Lina's lids grew heavy as Willow tucked her under the moss blanket, her rough fingers brushing the hair back from her forehead. Curling onto her side, she tucked the blanket under her chin, allowing fatigue to pull her under. Her breathing grew even almost immediately, and she slipped into a silent and dreamless sleep.

She awoke sometime later with dappled sunlight streaming onto her face. A tiny butterfly had landed on her hand, and she raised it to the light, examining the pattern on its shimmery, blue wings. It fluttered off her hand and floated down to the moss blanket where it perched. Arto and Willow were talking quietly in the great room below. Lina pushed back the coverlet carefully, so as not to disturb the beautiful insect who sat on top of it. Softly, she padded down the steps.

Arto and Willow sat around the table, the remnants of stew in clay bowls before them. Willow stood when Lina entered the room and filled her bowl from the pot. She sat down the bowl in the space before her as Lina sat on a low stool. Steam wafted to her nose from the bowl. It smelled delicious. Soft bits of root vegetables and fragrant spices floated in the delicate broth, and Lina lifted the bowl to her lips, savoring the hearty medley. She looked at Arto across the table. His face appeared troubled. The flat mouth and drawn brows had returned.

She sat down her bowl. "What's the matter?" she asked him.

He flicked his eyes up to her. "Willow says that since the felling of the Eiks, the dryads have lost hope and become fearful. They do not believe that Orm can be defeated, having seen his evil and might firsthand. They have refused to fight. They prefer to stay hidden, here in the Grove, until Time is no more. I don't know how we might convince them." He looked up at her in defeat.

Willow kept her eyes downcast. A tear trickled down her rough cheek.

Willow wiped the tear with her mossy forearm. "Long I have cried for hope in this land, but there is none. The Source is silent. We are abandoned. The Eiks send messages from the Four Winds to all Caelium, but the Source has no message for us here.

Even when the Eiks were felled by giants and the dark fire came, we cried out for help, but there was no answer. The Source has forgotten us." She bowed her head, tears dripping onto the vines at her chest.

All at once, Willow scooted back her stool and stood, fleeing the house out of the little door. Lina and Arto followed her down the raised root steps. They trailed her into the clearing. There, in the center of the Grove, Willow dropped to her knees, her fingers digging into the dirt. Bitter tears dripped off her chin and onto the ground. She cried out with a loud voice, saying, "All of Caelium knows your voice, but we, those in the Grove, protectors of your messengers, the Eiks, and lovers of peace, we hear not of your love and mercy but of fear, death, and destruction. We have pleaded with You for a message from the Four Winds, but the Eiks have grown silent. How long must we suffer at the hand of Orm? How many more Eiks must be destroyed? How long must the Rotha-Am be fallen and the Throne of Mercy defiled? Do you not hear our cries or notice our despair? Must we remain to the end in fear and without hope? Have you forgotten those you have created?" She bowed her head, sobbing onto her chest.

Countless dryads gathered at the edges of the clearing. Many bowed their heads low, and tears filled their eyes.

Lina knew how they felt. Fear filled her chest, and her hope waned. She moved to stand by Willow, placing a comforting hand on her shoulder. She wasn't sure what to say to her.

Just then, from the corner of her gaze, a large white shape moved into the clearing. The dryads cleared a path, pointing toward it and whispering one to another in awe. Lina turned her head to see what had caused the commotion.

In the midst of the grove stood a great white stag. He reached two heads above her, and his towering antlers were covered in hanging moss. Many touched his white coat as he walked toward her in the middle of the clearing. As he passed, the dryads hugged one another, speaking softly.

Lina flicked her eyes to them as the white stag stopped before her, his soft brown eyes fixed on her face. Then he bowed his head low at her feet. "The Source of the Four Winds greets you, Evangeline Vasily," the stag spoke to her mind. He raised his great head. "It is you the Source has chosen, a half-Mortal girl from the forest clearing, for such a dark day as this."

Lina reached out a trembling hand. She touched his white face softly, tears springing into her eyes. "A message," she whispered, "from the Source." She turned to look at Willow, who nodded, a light in her eyes through her tears.

"The Source has heard us," she breathed. "The white stag is our most sacred creature. He only comes in times of deep despair and most need. The Histories say he is a visible symbol from the Source of courage, hope, and coming peace." She gestured around her. "Many here have never seen him." She smiled at Lina thoughtfully. "Perhaps he has waited for your appearance here in the grove,

Princess Evangeline, to give our people hope. And to show you that you have been created by the Source for such a dark day as this."

Lina nodded, wiping her tears. She thought so, too.

The dryads gathered about her, holding hands in a great circle before the Eiks. In harmony they began to sing a song that Lina had never heard.

> The Source of peace,
> Brings hope to thee,
> And from the Four Winds blows.
> How sweet to see,
> Evangeline,
> To bring us joy and hope.
> The Grove of Eiks,
> Our home will be.
> Forever it will stand,
> For soon the king,
> Will rise to be,
> Our savior,
> Once again.

Willow stepped toward her, grasping her hand. The white stag had given her courage. "We have known grief in the Grove. We have seen loss. And we can take no more of it. We will fight with you, not for our own mercy, but to preserve the known worlds from such a grim fate. We will stand with you, strong like the mighty oak, and we shall strive not to fear Court of Orm's dark shadows."

Lina embraced her, holding her new friend close.

Suddenly a rushing Wind filled the clearing. "A message from the Four Winds," said Willow. She went to the nearest Eik and placed her small hands on its rough wooden surface. Closing her eyes, she listened, her hands pressed against the bark. She paused for a moment, as still as a stone. Suddenly she stepped back, whipping her head toward Arto and Lina. Her face was a worried mask. "There's been a breach at the Wall of Mist in the West Mountains. You must hurry. Foul beasts have begun to enter the Timekeeper's Court."

Lina and Arto hurried from the woods, mounting Bayard and Cyrus and flying high over the land. Lina whistled low, spurring Cyrus's flanks. They were moving slower than usual, despite their best efforts. The air felt like a heavy weight, pressing against her and Cyrus as they flew, forcing them to slow.

In her periphery, the landscape flickered in and out, just as it had in the Mortal Realm. Bits of darkness cut into the grass and trees at random. She shuddered at the thought of falling into a black void like she had on their way to the North Forest. Surely, the same thing was happening with the Wall of Mist. It was flickering in and out as Time drew to a close. That must have been what caused the breach. She frowned, hunching low over Cyrus's neck. Time was stretching so thin it was fraying at the edges.

Chapter 19

In the distance, the jagged rift in the thick wall flickered in the sunlight. From her perch, Lina watched as the Mist stuttered and disappeared, revealing the sheer rock of the West Mountains behind it. The Timekeeper's Court was now exposed, unprotected and at risk. Arto spurred Bayard, and Lina whistled low to Cyrus, pushing for speed. They had to hurry.

They flew between the mountains, banking left and following the river. Lina peered over Cyrus's back, searching for signs of trouble. The landscape below was eerily still, but she couldn't see anything amiss. Yet.

They crossed the lake, into the valley of the Timekeeper's Court. The estate sprawled silently in front of them. No one stirred on the grounds, and no lights shone from the windows. Silently, she searched toward the stables. There was no sign of Benjamin or the other boys, and no griffin's call echoed against the mountains' sheer walls.

The animals touched down in front of the house, and Arto and Lina dismounted in silence. Lina brushed her hands gently over Bayard's and Cyrus's necks, whispering soothing in each of their ears. The animals chuffed and stomped nervously, but she guided them to stand against the house, where they waited, their necks held high and alert.

Arto crept around the right corner of the estate, toward the sweeping, circular walls that surrounded the courtyard and gardens. His sword was drawn, and he held it aloft, his head on a swivel. Lina moved her feet silently behind him, pulling her bow taut against her cheek. Her heart thrummed in her ears as they ducked beneath the picture windows, worried they might be seen from anyone or anything lurking inside.

Lina peeked cautiously above one frame. No one moved inside. There was no sound.

A rounded archway marked the middle of the wall several feet ahead. Arto went to it, pressing his back against the wall. Turning to her, he reached his free hand to her face. He paused to peer into her eyes, brushing her chin lovingly with his fingers. Then he turned and ran through the arch.

Lina followed him, holding her bow taut in defense. She rounded the corner, stopping short as her heart dropped to her feet.

Arto stood still before her in the courtyard. He had dropped his arms, and his sword scraped the dirt. His knees hit the ground, and he hung his head. Lina lowered her weapon as she moved beside him. The bow and arrow slipped through her fingers as she scanned the courtyard, and she dropped onto her knees on the ground beside him. The devastation was more than she could handle.

Ronne stood in the center of the courtyard, his spear stuck through a lycanth. He pulled it free, black blood spattering his face and chest. The foul beast dropped heavily to the dirt, its black eyes flat. His body began to disintegrate upon impact. Heavy gray ash floated on the breeze. Lina followed it with her eyes, watching it drift up and over the mountain.

Ronne wiped his blade and stood, leaning heavily on the spear. His breathing was labored, and black blood mixed with sweat dripped off his chin. He looked up at them, sorrow on his weathered face.

Lina stood, her hands fisted at her sides. The ground ran red with blood. Men and women lay strewn about the courtyard, their arms and legs mangled at odd angles. She stepped gingerly through the bodies, looking for signs of life. Glassy eyes stared vacantly up at her out of their pale faces.

Her heart sank. The Mortal Timekeepers were dead. All of them were lost.

Just then, she came upon the fiery, red-haired woman, her face laying toward the ground. She bent, gently turning her over. Tears spilled over her eyes as she looked on the face of the brave woman who had approached her in the forest clearing. She had been the first one through the gate. Lina held her head in her lap, pushing the long, red curls out of her face. Rocking back and forth, she cried loudly for the lives lost. There had been so much death. So much destruction. The centaur men from the Court of Warriors, the Eiks, the Court of Mountain Fairies, and so many others. And now the Mortal Timekeepers were gone, too.

Anger seared at her chest. *Why?* Why would the Source gather the Mortal Timekeepers at the gate just to see them slaughtered by the Court of Orm? It made no sense. It wasn't right. A just Creator would do no such thing to his creation. She sucked down a breath, swallowing her angry tears.

Time was wearing thin. Already in Caelium, the landscape flickered, and daylight stretched on infinitely. Surely the Mortal Realm was now held in unrelenting darkness. Lina sighed wearily. Without the Mortal Timekeepers and their Amloga, how would they defeat Orm and raise the Rotha-Am before Time ran out?

Looking at the estate, she thought of Ita, Benjamin, and the others. Where were they?

She hurried to check the remaining bodies, searching every face, until she reached the last one. Relief washed over her, and she released her breath. They weren't among them.

Arto and Ronne sat behind her in the garden, speaking in hushed tones. Arto had his hand on the wearied centaur's shoulder. Lina grabbed her weapon. Silently, she walked past them, pulling open the door to the sitting room. She would search for the others inside.

The house felt vacant. The air was still, and dust motes sparkled through the picture windows, floating to the floor in silence. She scanned the entry hall and searched the kitchen, holding her bow and arrow ready. No one was there. She wove her way through the dining room and the front halls, making her way to the library. The wall sconces were still lit, and she backed her way around the bookshelves, raising her bow toward the upper stories. The only sound was the rushing waterfall coming from the hidden alcove. She lowered her bow, frowning. Taking the main staircase, she searched her own room, then Arto's.

She moved inside his room cautiously, scanning with her bow drawn. She jumped as a clatter sounded in the back corner and the night table turned onto its side. Something was there. She swung her bow as a great grey wolf leaped toward her, his tongue lolling out of the side of his mouth. He smacked into her chest, pushing her up against the wall and licking her face with his slick tongue.

Lina lowered her weapon and rubbed the scruff of his neck. "Hello, Remus. I'm glad to see you too, little wolf." She pulled his face away from her. "I almost shot you, you know." He bumped his nose against her chin, and she pushed him down. He sat on his haunches, looking up at her expectantly with his green eyes. "Remus, where are Ita and the others?"

Remus dipped his head. He sniffed at the door, looking at her over his shoulder. "Follow me," said his voice to her mind. She opened the door, and he bounded down the steps.

Remus sat waiting for her by the front doors. She pulled them open, and he sprang outside, turning left toward the stables. Lina pressed her back against the house, scanning the landscape with her bow drawn. She rounded the corner, creeping toward the stable doors where Remus had disappeared.

The sunlight was muted inside the cool stable. Lina blinked, letting her eyes adjust. The griffins were still in their stalls, and they shuffled their wings and cooed at her nervously as she passed. Bayard, Cyrus, Remus, and the other boys stood solemnly near the end of the stable, circled around the last open stall. Inside, someone sniffed. Lina frowned as a shuddered breath reached her ears. Someone was crying. She lowered her bow and hurried toward them, squeezing between Cyrus and Remus to get a better look.

Ita lay on the floor of the stall with her head in Benjamin's lap. Her small, still frame was covered with a green stable blanket. Tears streamed down Benjamin's face, landing softly on her short, gray hair. Sobbing, he held her limp hand to his cheek, kissing her palm. Lina knelt to her, placing her head on Ita's still chest. She listened, but there was no sound. Lina sat back onto her heels, covering her mouth with her hand. Tears sprang in her eyes, and she let them run unchecked down her cheeks. Their beloved Ita was gone.

The Timekeepers were left where they lay as they prepared for Ita's passing. Ronne insisted that they not be moved, despite Lina's insistence that their deaths somehow be marked. Still, he resisted. She didn't understand why, so she took it upon herself to pick flowers from Ita's garden, laying one on each of their still bodies as she whispered a prayer.

Later, sadness hovered over Lina like a heavy cloud as she sat in her room, preparing herself for Ita's ceremony. She searched through the armoire, hunting for the emerald gown she had worn on her first night at the Timekeeper's Court. Ita had loved her in that dress. "Lovely," she had called her. Lina's eyes brimmed as she pulled the gown over her head. She gazed at herself in the mirror, touching the delicate fabric.

Ita had been lovely, too. Kind, thoughtful, loving, and generous. She was a mother to the motherless, having taken Arto, Benjamin, and the boys under her wing. Lina had since learned that Ita was Benjamin's grandmother. His pain at her loss was acute. She had been the only family he had left after Orm's raid on the Court of Mountain Fairies.

So much joy and life went with her, so much knowledge and wisdom. She had been a woman of honor and great faith. Lina peered absently out into the garden and wondered. *Now that Ita is gone, who will make the Tamarisk Cakes?*

Lina's thoughts were broken by movement in the courtyard below. Benjamin was gathering fresh flowers from Ita's garden.

Their sunny blooms made a sharp contrast to the gruesome scene behind him. Lina remembered the night Ita had sat in the garden with her instrument. Her hands had lovingly touched the strings, bringing forth a beautiful sound. Lina had sung along with Ita's sweet melody, remembering the words from long ago. "These words you sing are good news, Evangeline," she had said. Lina's eyes pricked, and she turned away.

Later, they gathered at the edge of the lake to say goodbye to their beloved Ita. The captain appeared from beneath the falls, rowing the small, wooden boat to rest before them at the shore. Benjamin and Arto walked solemnly from the house, carrying Ita gently in their arms. Her body was wrapped in a white linen sheet, and Benjamin had woven a circlet of flowers to place on her head. They lowered her reverently into the boat, and Benjamin tucked the bouquet from her garden at her chest. Her face was serene, facing the sky. The group gazed down at her silently, bowing their heads in deep respect. Then the captain turned his oar, rowing the boat and its precious cargo beneath the falls.

A gentle Wind began to blow through the valley, creating ripples on the surface of the lake. It rustled through the leaves and whipped Lina's golden hair about her face. Closing her eyes, she lifted her hands, allowing the Wind to swirl around her frame. She smiled, lifting her face to the sky. A feeling of hope and a peace that she could not explain curled inside her chest. She was sure, now, that death was like Ronne had said. Ita had only passed through a door. She wasn't *gone*. She just lived somewhere different.

Above her, an eagle soared high in the clouds. Lina followed its path as it glided majestically over her head and came to roost in safety, high in the rocks.

Chapter 20

Unrelenting sunlight had persisted since Ita's death and the slaughter of the Mortal Timekeepers. The house at the Timekeeper's Court was heavy with mourning. Lina sat in her room with her back to the door. Her tray lay untouched on the table. Arto had been doing his best to get her to eat, but she had no appetite. Her hope was worn thin, and she just couldn't stomach it. He rapped gently at her door, opening it a crack. "May I come in?" he said softly.

She nodded, not turning to face him.

He sat beside her on the bed, lacing her fingers in his own. She turned to him, searching his features. His face was drawn. Dark circles cut low beneath his eyes, and the buttons on his shirt were unevenly fastened. She sighed, reaching for his shirt and refastening the buttons one by one. He studied her face, bringing his hand to her ear and curving her golden hair behind it. Lifting her chin, he searched her eyes, his face tender. "I miss her too," he said.

Her eyes pricked, and she closed them, pursing her lips. "I know," she murmured.

"She was the best of us," he said.

"Yes, she was," Lina whispered.

He lowered his face, kissing her softly on the mouth. She melted against him, as tears ran down her cheeks, wetting his chin. His lips tasted of salt, and she tucked her hands over the back of his neck, holding him to her. He wove his fingers into her long hair, sighing her name against her lips. They remained there for a few more moments, comforting each other in their sorrow. Then, slowly he pulled away, wiping her cheeks with his thumbs. He smiled down at her, folding her hands in his own and resting them in his lap.

Wetting his lips, he stared at her hands. "Ronne wants us to meet him in the garden," he said. He lifted his eyes to her. "He's asked that you bring the Book of Blessings."

She gazed up at him quizzically. "Why?" she asked softly.

Arto shrugged, meeting her gaze. "He didn't say."

Lina stood, smoothing her dress and hair. She went to the chair and reached inside the leather pack, pulling out the heavy book. She brushed her hands over its gilded cover, wondering what Ronne could mean. What good would it do her to speak a Blessing now?

Ronne was waiting for them in the garden. He faced the courtyard, his hands clasped behind his back. Lina and Arto stepped up beside him, surveying the battleground. In the short Time since the slaughter, the bodies of the Mortal Timekeepers had swiftly withered in the constant midday sun. Now only white, sunbaked bones remained.

Ronne looked to his left, gazing down at Lina. "The Book of Blessings—did you bring it?" he asked her. She nodded, lifting the book from her side and cradling it in her arms. "Open it," he said softly. "Recite the Blessing to these dry bones that they may live."

Lina whipped her head to his profile, her brows creasing in confusion. Surely Ronne didn't think a Blessing could raise the dead. She searched his features but found his face a hard line. He stood motionless, staring at the skeletal remains of the Mortal Timekeepers.

Lina looked to Arto for an explanation. He shrugged, then nodded once in her direction. She gazed down at the crimson book, running her fingers softly over the gilded script. Taking a deep breath, she lifted the cover, letting it fall open to a page. Her lips parted in surprise at the words written there. She squared her shoulders and recited in a loud, clear voice.

The Source of the Four Winds Speaks to These Now Slain
Let those that lie,

In sleep arise.

Return, the soul to stand.

Secure the sinew.

Mend the bone.

Restore flesh, once again.

Let Mortal wounds,

Immortal be.

Oh, hear, Amloga flame.

Let warriors rise,

From valley low,

An army for Your name.

A whispering Wind had begun to blow about the valley as Lina recited the Blessing. It gathered speed until it whipped the hair around her face and lifted the hem of her skirt. A buzzing hum followed the Wind, swirling in a circle over the courtyard. The air was charged in the Wind's wake, and the flowers and tree limbs bent low with the Wind's path. The grass around Lina's feet pressed flat against the earth as Arto reached for her arm. She linked it with his and Ronne's, widening her stance to avoid toppling beneath the gale.

The Wind whistled through the hollow bones until it became an almost musical sound. Suddenly the bones began to lift off the earth, floating in midair. Lina watched them as they swirled in a circle, and the hum became a chorus of ethereal voices. Bones that had broken fused back together, creating completed frames. Lina gazed on in amazement as flesh began forming upon them, first at the center and then flowing outward, until each body was restored.

Just then, a fiery flame appeared in the midst of the bodies, and the chorus of voices grew louder until musical shouts filled the courtyard. The flame rose in the Wind, which whipped it into a vortex. The fiery whirlwind spun over the courtyard, concealing the bodies within the flame. Suddenly the vortex involuted, and a resounding *boom* shattered the air of the courtyard. Lina, Arto, and Ronne fell flat, slammed to the ground by the impact.

The flame separated, and now miniature flames perched above the chests of the Mortal Timekeepers who lay fully clothed upon the ground. The Wind was gone, and the courtyard was quiet. Lina, Ronne, and Arto stood, staring at the bodies that lay still and silent.

As they watched, the flames melted into the chests below the Mortal Timekeepers clothing. The fiery Amloga, imparted by the Source, was taking its rightful place. Lina watched the Timekeeper lying closest to her, her eyes focused on her chest where the flame had disappeared. The woman's hand lay flung out, her palm facing the sky. Slowly, her finger began to twitch, and then she parted her lips and took a deep breath. Her chest rose, and her eyelids fluttered open. She sat up onto her palms, blinking.

All over the courtyard, the Mortal Timekeepers drew breath. Soon they began standing, walking, and talking with one another. In moments, they gathered into groups, practicing the skills Ronne had been teaching them. Some twisted their fingers, bringing flames to life above, while others whipped the air into a vortex around them. To Lina's left, Timekeepers gathered water into orbs above their palms from the air, while a group to the back pounded their fists on the ground in unison, opening a large chasm beneath it. Lina watched as they sealed it over, and Ronne chuckled low under his breath, casting a sidelong glance at her. She stared on in amazement, and he patted her shoulder. "Gerúla Mórloga, the Source is on our side."

He turned, moving through the house and out the front door. A merrow was waiting for him in the water by the shore. He instructed the scout to take a message through the underground river to the roots of the Eiks. The day of Orm's destruction had come. Ronne bowed low and spoke softly in the silver-haired merrow's pointed ear, relaying the plans. The Court of Merrows, the Court of Warriors, the dryads, the Timekeeper's Court, and all other able beings of creation were summoned to march on Leyth Castle posthaste. The merrow nodded once, his iridescent blue eyes glowing above the water. He dove, his glittering blue tail flipping up as he disappeared beneath the falls, carrying Ronne's message to the four corners of Caelium.

In the valley, Time weighed heavily on Lina. It tugged at her limbs and pressed down on her head, creating the sensation that she was moving through deep water. She fought through the dense air, gathering her weapon and heading for the stable yard.

Arto met her in front of the house. He smiled at her from the corner of his mouth, gathering her into an embrace. "I'll meet you after," he said. He tipped her chin, kissing her softly on the mouth.

She returned his kiss then pulled back, placing both hands on the sides of his face. She studied him desperately, trying to memorize his features. He pulled a face, and she grinned, ruffling her fingers through his hair. She pecked him once more on the mouth. "After," she whispered. "Promise me."

Arto nodded. "I promise."

They flew hard through the dense air, pushing for speed over the flickering landscape. Heavy clouds gathered in the distance, casting a purplish haze on the earth below. Benjamin had insisted that they take the whole fleet of griffins for the journey. He flew ahead of them, and many Timekeepers sat in twos or threes on the griffin's backs. On the ground, Ronne lagged on his four horse legs, pushing through the weight of slowing Time. Lina peered past Cyrus's neck. Up ahead, a great army had gathered in the plain below the foothills of the Haima Mountains. Dryads, merrows, centaurs, and fae stood in large numbers, sharpening their weapons and conversing with one another in hushed tones.

They touched down, and Lina brought Cyrus to a walk. She milled slowly through the crowds, smiling at familiar faces and nodding toward others. Often whole groups brought their fists to their chests, bowing low in reverence for the daughter of the king. She stopped, dismounting before Lady Sirena, who was conversing with a young woman Lina did not recognize. Lady Sirena bowed to Lina, gesturing to the lovely woman beside her.

"Princess Evangeline Vasily, may I introduce Lady Elysia of the Selkie Isles? She is the daughter of the Selkie leader, Lady Malca." Lady Sirena touched the young woman's slender arm. "I am honored by her presence here today and her willingness to fight side by side with the Court of Merrows."

Lady Elysia smiled softly at Lady Sirena. "The honor is mine," she said softly.

The young woman turned to Lina, bowing her head low. Her dark brown curls touched the grass, and the sunlight danced off the strands, giving it a deep red hue. She stood, meeting Lina's gaze. Her large green eyes turned up at the edges and held flecks of gold that shimmered in the sunlight. She was enchantingly beautiful with porcelain skin and fine features. Lina knew she must transform when she touched the water, but seeing her in this form made it hard to imagine.

Elysia grinned broadly, grabbing Lina's hand. "And it is an honor to meet you, Princess. I met your mother briefly in the Court of Merrows. She speaks of you so often I feel as if I already know you."

Lina smiled broadly, squeezing her hand. She liked the young woman immensely. "The honor is mine, Lady Elysia. May we meet again." She waved goodbye, leading Cyrus through the winding crowd.

Near the front of the gathering, Ronne stood talking intently with Arto. Lina stopped beside them. Soon Lady Sirena, Lady Elysia, Maria, Willow, and Benjamin joined.

Ronne's eyes flashed as he addressed the leaders in the circle. "We have gathered here today for this great cause: to defeat the Court of Orm and return the Rotha-Am to its rightful place and its right turning. Too long have we hidden in shadow and gloom."

The crowd behind them had begun to push in, listening to Ronne speak. He stepped up with his four horse legs onto a flat rock and raised his voice, addressing the king's army with his fist placed over his heart.

"Too long have the wicked tormented and the evil won. Too long have our sons and daughters lived in fear and in bondage. Too long have our peace, our joy, and our hope been stolen. Too long has our faith wavered and our light been hidden in darkness." He raised his fist above his head. "But no longer! Today is the day we reclaim the lives of all created beings in the known worlds, both in Caelium and the Mortal Realm. Today we push back the darkness and reclaim the light. Today, by the will of the Source, we shall see the restoration of Time before our very eyes." The crowd murmured assent, and he lowered his fist, beating his chest. "We bear the power of the Source in our Amloga! Yes, we, the created, have the Creator on our side! Let all who are with me give a shout! Today we claim our victory!"

A deafening roar filled the plain as all created beings, great and small, Mortal and Caelian, lifted their voices to the heavens and raised fists in unison. The sound was one that Lina would never forget. It was the sound of hope. The sound of victory.

Chapter 21

As the crowd rejoiced in their battle cry, another roar, louder and harsher, overtook the shouts in the plain. Lina turned to the noise, her heart sinking into her feet. From the mountain pass, a monstrous three-headed drake emerged. The beast lifted its middle head to the sky and roared, the sound reverberating off the rocks. Its two other heads followed suit, creating a paralyzing cacophony that echoed across the plain.

For a moment, no one moved, and then Arto sprang into action, raising his sword and crying with a loud voice as he charged the dark beast. The trio of heads screeched as Arto took flight on Bayard's back, lifting onto their hind legs. Bayard circled behind the beast's three necks, and the drake roared in deafening anger, swiping at them with his claws. Arto swung his sword as the right head of the drake snapped with its large jaws. He sliced off the center head with a deep slash. The remaining heads screamed in agony, and the dragon fell forward onto his front claws. The king's army charged the creature, pelting it with swords, arrows, and spears, as Timekeepers threw balls of flame from their fists.

Only a moment passed before the central head's wound sealed over, and a new and identical head grew in its place. The new head hissed, opening its mouth and spewing fire upon all who had dared to come close. The warriors fell to the dirt, their bodies lost in flames. The drake opened its mouth once more, ready to release its fiery breath. Lady Sirena stepped into its path just as the flames emerged, tapping her scepter on the ground. The orb atop it glowed, and water gathered toward it from the surrounding air. The water spread out in front of her like a large shield, and Timekeepers brought their own water to meet it, extinguishing the flame. The beast roared in anger, swinging his great spiked tail.

Chaerrone was upon the dragon now, his spear aimed at its chest. Arto whistled low, and he and Bayard charged on the ground behind him. Chaerrone wove on his horse legs left and right to avoid the fiery breath of the monster. When he was directly under the beast, he threw his spear, sticking it in the soft flesh to the right of its chest. The dragon recoiled, roaring in agony.

At just that moment, Bayard spun, facing away from the dragon. The great white horse reared, letting out a deafening whinny. Several Timekeepers surrounded them, and Arto raised his arms with them in unison as Bayard came forward onto his front legs. The air around them sucked inward, and the group pushed their palms towards the dirt as Bayard lowered. Bayard's legs landed on the ground with the force of ten giants, and the Timekeepers' power coupled with the blast, causing the earth to shake mightily across the plain under the blow.

The ground under the three-headed beast wavered and shook. Then a large crack formed beneath its legs. The crack fractured, and a great black cavern opened beneath it. Losing its balance, the drake stumbled. Spears and arrows clustered around Ronne's blade that stuck deep in his chest. Then he fell, disappearing in a groaning roar beneath the wall of the dark canyon.

Clouds gathered heavily now over Leyth Castle and the plain. They flickered in and out of focus. Lina gazed over the battlefield, blinking. Her vision was fuzzy around the edges, and the air cloaked her like a thick blanket. Her breath slid into her chest slowly, taking extra effort to push out. She watched as countless foul beasts crawled over the rocks, meeting the warriors on the plain. Lycanths tore flesh and giants hauled stones into great catapults, tossing them to crush warriors beneath. Dark, twisted bodies of centaurs and merrows who had chosen to follow the Court of Orm slashed at the beings who had once been their neighbors and friends.

Lina rubbed at her eyes, attempting to clear her vision as she turned her eyes to the dark castle above. She put her hands onto

Cyrus's back and jumped. It took all her energy to swing herself over against the weight of the air. She paused, breathing heavily. Time was almost up.

To her left, a beautiful woman was walking toward her across the plain. Golden hair hung down her back, and she smiled up at Lina with a familiar face. Her form flickered, and Lina blinked in confusion at her frame. "Mother?" she asked, sliding off Cyrus's back. "I thought you were in the Court of Merrows. What are you doing here?"

Her mother smiled as she raised her arms to embrace Lina, but Lina pulled back at the last moment. She blinked, searching her mother's face. Her form flickered again, and Lina frowned. Something was wrong with her mother's eyes. They were dark around the edges, and the skin was pulled too taut. Lina recoiled at the last moment, just as the woman shifted into a horrifying beast.

The terrible winged creature had no eyes or ears, a gaping mouth full of large teeth taking up her entire face. She screamed, and the foul beast lunged toward her on a woman's legs, knocking her to the ground. Lina held the creature back with her arms, turning her head from its putrid breath. The beast rasped, hissing in her ear. "Evaaangeelinnee. You are nothing. No one. You cannot stop what our Lord Orm has set in motion." She hissed a rasping laugh. "Now, you must die." The horrid creature lunged for her neck, scraping her skin with its sickening teeth. Lina wrestled against it, scratching her fingernails against its wide, membranous wings. The creature howled in pain, reaching her grotesque hands to encircle Lina's throat.

All at once, the horrible beast fell flat on top of her. A long spear protruded from its back. Maria stood over it, her lips curled back over her teeth. She pulled the spear, and the creature crumbled to ash as Lina scrambled from under its weight. She stood, nodding to Maria. The centaur raised her spear, yelling a battle cry, and galloped off in another direction.

To Lina's left, a small dryad was pinned by the great front claw of an enormous scorpion. The foul beast whipped its hooked tail over its head, trying to spear her. The dryad howled as Lina took aim at the beast, firing her arrow. It missed the mark, ricocheting off its large claw. The scorpion turned towards Lina, pausing a moment, then skittered towards her as she frantically grabbed another arrow.

Just then, Bayard descended from the sky, landing on the creature's back. Arto raised his sword over his head, slashing downward through the giant scorpion's midsection. The creature fell to the earth, spilling its innards over the dirt. Its body crumbled to ash as the dryad wiggled free and ran to help two merrows being terrorized by a giant.

The fierce fighting continued, and many in the king's army were fallen. Foul beasts clashed with warriors in numbers too large to count. Bodies littered the plain, and Lina feared that hope was almost lost. Desperately, she turned her eyes to Leyth Castle.

All but her central vision quavered and flickered in and out of darkness. She blinked through the haze toward the doors. She had to reach Orm. And she had to reach him now.

She pulled herself onto Cyrus's back, grunting with exertion against the heavy weight of the air. The griffin flew, beating his great wings with effort, and in moments, he landed on the stone steps. Pelting raindrops fell onto Lina's shoulders as she stepped down onto the stone. She gazed up at the doors. The drops blurred her vision, pausing in front of her face before falling to the earth. She swiped at the air, lifting her heavy legs toward the doors. Taking a deep breath, she pulled them open and stepped inside.

Water from the hem of her dress dripped onto the floor of the main hall. She readied her bow, scanning the dark room. Only the wall lanterns lit the dim passage. Ahead of her, a set of ornate wooden doors marked the entrance to the throne room. She approached them cautiously, swinging her bow at every sound. She paused at the door, examining the wood. She recognized the intricate carvings. They were the same as those on the Great Clock.

Meanwhile, in the Mortal Realm, Jacques bent his feeble white head to the heart of the Great Clock. He held his breath, tapping his crooked finger against the wood. *Tick, tick.* He sat upright, adjusting his glasses, then replaced his head against the clock. He stuck his free hand into the lower door, adjusting the chain mechanism slightly. He sighed. "Come, now, old girl. We must mind the Time," he whispered. He peered up at the Great Clock's face, touching the glass covering gently with his fingers. "Before Time runs out."

Lina paused before the throne room doors, gathering courage. The words from the Book of Blessings recalled in her mind.

> Gerúla Mórloga:
> Bearer of the Great Flame,
> Daughter of the king,
> Thy destiny was, is, and shall remain.
> Strengthen thy heart.
> Steady thy hand,
> For the day grows dark and Time is corrupted.

She pulled open the doors, raising her bow toward the Throne of Mercy. Orm's corrupted serpentine frame sat upon it, his tail slithering over the dais. His milky eyes focused on the sounds of her movement, and he pulled back his pale, thin lips over his horrid teeth. "You've come to me at last, Evangeline Vasily. But you have come too late. What is done cannot be undone, by you or by anyone." He hissed a dark laugh. "Your warriors' blood litters the plain, and my foul beasts kill them for sport." He hissed in glee. "Yes, *all* of creation shall be mine when the Rotha-Am stops its turning and Time is no more." He shook his head slowly back and forth. "Even if you kill me now, the Rotha-Am will not rise. For *I* am the only one who can raise it, and it is only *I* who can restart its turning and create the worlds anew from the coming abyss."

Lina didn't answer him. She narrowed her eyes, pulling her bow tightly against her jaw. Orm grasped the arms of the throne with his clawed fingers. He leaned towards her, raising his voice. "I killed your father, and I'll kill you too!" he shouted. He threw his head back, his hissing laugh rising towards the high ceiling. Lina aimed her arrow, forged from the Great Clock by the Time Minder himself, directly at his chest. The bowstring stretched taut with her pull, and Orm cocked his head to the sound. His eyebrows lifted as he realized what she was doing, and quickly, he lifted his twisted hand towards her. His brow tucked low over his lidless, milky eyes, and he closed his fist, swiftly turning it towards his face as he gripped the open air.

The air around Lina shifted in his grasp. It pressed tightly against her, and she groaned against the heavy weight. The ground began to crumble and shake. She stumbled as a large crack formed beneath her, and as more gave way, she slipped past the side. Her arrow clattered down into darkness, and she narrowly missed falling to meet it as she hung with one hand to the ledge. "You might as well give up, now, my dear," Orm hissed darkly.

Lina eyed the abyss beneath her nervously. Her hand was beginning to slip from the ledge, and she gritted her teeth, gripping with all her might. Rattling chains, like those in the Chasm sounded deep below her, and a groaning hiss slithered out to meet her ears. She tried not to think about the creature that had made the sound, focusing instead on Orm's pale frame still seated on the throne. "There is no hope for you, Evangeline," he spat. "There's no hope for any of you now! *I. Rule. All.*"

Lina took a deep breath. She had come too far to give up now. *Strengthen thy heart.* She swung her hand with the bow up hard, landing it on the ledge. Grunting, arms shaking, she pulled, lifting herself past the opening. Orm was raising his hand again in her peripheral gaze. Before he could twist it, she scrambled to face him, pulling another arrow, aiming at his chest. *Steady thy hand.*

But let the will of the Source now speak.
Let hope rise on the wings of the Four Winds.
Let Time fly true,
And the Rotha-Am be restored.

She fired, watching the arrow push through the weighted air. It pierced the heart of Orm, its tip driving into the back of the Throne of Mercy. Orm's lidless eyelids raised in shock as the arrow made its impact. Then, slowly, he sagged against the throne.

As he released his breath, all the air in the room sucked inward on his twisted body. He pressed flat, sliding from the seat onto the throne room floor. There he crumbled to dark ash, the remnants of him blowing past Lina's body and out the throne room doors.

Arto appeared behind her in the doorway. He moved to place his hand on Lina's shoulder. Silently, she dropped her bow, turning to bury her face in his broad chest.

Meanwhile, on the battlefield below, the foul beasts crumpled to the earth as Orm fell from the Throne of Mercy. The remaining warriors stood, watching them disintegrate on the ground. The ashes blew away in the Winds, and the warriors waited, their eyes on the castle.

Lina turned, moving to the wall of windows behind the throne. Below her lay the Rotha-Am in the Chasm. Its blue light was diffused, and the inscribed wheels were almost at a halt. She turned to Arto, a look of despair on her face. His expression was as hard as stone. "It didn't work," she said softly. "The Rotha-Am didn't rise."

Eyes downcast, she stepped to the Throne of Mercy, where her arrow was still fixed. She reached to pull it free, but just as her hand touched it, a trickle of blood began to flow from throne in the place where the arrow stuck. She pulled the arrow from its spot, drawing back her hand.

Lina watched in amazement as blood gushed from the throne in the spot where the arrow had stuck. It ran down onto the seat and spilled over the dais, the crumbled floor sealing in its wake. Slowly she backed away from it, moving to stand in the middle of the throne room. The dark, red blood ran out over the floor, pooling in a great circle at her feet.

Suddenly a whipping Wind began to blow about the throne room. Lina stepped backward, grasping Arto's hand. As they looked on, the Wind swirled over the pool of blood on the floor. Whispering voices rose out of the Wind as it whirled, and soon, three misty images emerged from the pool in rapid succession.

The first was a great phoenix rising from the ashes. It flapped its flaming wings, rising high into the air. The image of the phoenix involuted and became a great, brown bear who stood on his hind legs. The bear pawed at the sky as it growled ferociously. The bear dissipated, and the image became a lion. He peered at Lina proudly from his great face. Then the lion leaped onto the throne and roared a great and mighty roar.

Lina stared in awe as the Wind collected itself upon the throne. It whipped into a fiery frenzy where the lion sat. Through its haze of flame, Lina could see that the lion had transformed into a man. Then the Wind quieted, and King Ard-Mathan sat before her eyes, real and true. The will of the Source had spoken, and his form had returned, just as Ronne had told her it could. He smiled at her quietly from where he sat, and then he stood, turning regally towards the window. Gazing out upon the Rotha-Am, he lifted his right hand and raised it slowly toward the ceiling.

Outside, the king's soldiers held hands with one another, forming a wide circle. The Wind whipped through the plain, blowing upon the created beings. Inside each chest, each Amloga began to burn brightly, shining an outward light for all to see.

Lina looked down, touching the glowing space on her own left chest. A burning began over the spot as the rocks beside the Chasm began to rumble. The burning spread down her fingers and into her toes as blue light flowed out of her body and toward the Rotha-Am. As she watched, the blue light of the Rotha-Am intensified. Then, all at once, it began to lift out of the Chasm.

The castle walls shook with the whole earth as the Rotha-Am rose, and the ground sealed beneath it. Arto and Lina braced against one another as the rumbling floor quaked beneath them. When the Rotha-Am hovered before the window, King Ard-Mathan turned his palm, and, slowly, its wheels began to spin.

Lina moved to the window, watching the Rotha-Am turn its wheel within a wheel. Faster and faster, it turned, and as she watched, the haze over her vision cleared, the heavy pull of slowing Time lifting as the Rotha-Am's wheels turned steadily around the bright blue orb at its center.

At that exact moment, Jacques balanced the weights of the Great Clock. He put his ear to its chest, listening intently. *Tick, tick, tick, tick.* He drew back, gazing up in disbelief at the Great Clock's face.

The hands ran smoothly, marking Time at the right speed. He laughed, stepping back from the Great Clock and lacing his hands through his white hair. "I can't believe it," he cried. "It works!"

He sat down on the hearth, placing his gnarled hands on his knees. All at once, a warm tingle began at the back of his neck. He frowned, standing as the tingling spread up to his head and down his limbs.

He gasped in surprise as the crook that had plagued his back as he worked straightened, and the strength returned to his knees. He jumped, chuckling brightly as he tested them with his weight. They didn't hurt at all. Quickly, he held his hands out before his face. He frowned down at them in confusion. They were blurred.

Suddenly realizing, he laughed out loud. He pulled off his glasses, blinking down at his hands once more. They were now in focus. The skin was smooth, and the joints were straight, like they had once been. He ran to the mirror, smiling at his reflection. He was young Jacques Thomas again. The Time Minder of the Order of the Flame. And he decided he would remain that way for most of his very long life.

In the West Mountains, a new Tamarisk tree began to grow in the valley of the Timekeeper's Court. Its crown of feathery fronds and light pink flowers spread out before the heavens in Ita's garden. The Four Winds blew through the branches, lifting its tufted seeds up and over the mountainside. The Winds carried the precious cargo over the Southern Sea, laying the seeds gently to rest on a hillside, just south of the Selkie Isles.

EPILOGUE

Evangeline Elikai stood in the throne room while addressing the Court of Ard-Mathan. As usual, Remus was perched near her feet. She grinned down at him, and he peered up at her with his green eyes, his tongue lolling happily out the side of his wolfish mouth.

Her mother, Queen Astrid, and her father, King-Ard Mathan, stood behind her upon the dais. Lina turned her head, smiling at her mother. Each had recently been granted Immortality, and they had changed in the process, stronger and wiser in their new forms.

Lina glanced at her father. He smiled at her proudly, his sparkling blue eyes crinkling at the edges. Lina grinned back at him. She was thankful he was here with them, again.

Ronne stood to the king's left. He looked every bit the

decorated warrior he was. His chest stood broad, and he wore the deep blue sash that designated him as general of her father's court.

Lina's new mate, Arturo Elikai, kneeled before her, his sword balanced in his palms. He grinned up at her from the side of his mouth, his dark eyes shining. It was her wedding day, and the dryads and merrows had crafted her a magnificent gown.

The seafoam dress matched her eyes perfectly, and the silky material hugged her fine curves before falling in rippling folds across the floor. Wildflowers and vines had been woven across the bodice and trailed out over the train. A circlet of blue sea glass rested on her forehead, serving as her crown. Below it lay a long, shimmering veil. Tiny seashells trickled down the delicate fabric and hung as jewelry from her neck and ears.

She gazed down at Arto, her heart bursting with all the love it contained. Opening the Book of Blessings, she recited for all to hear.

> Let all the known worlds rejoice and be very glad,
> For the Source has proven faithful,
> And the king, Ard-Mathan, has risen again.
> Time is restored,
> And the Wheels of the Rotha-Am turn in harmony,
> Once again, with the Great Clock.
> But now, let us grant the redeemed, Arturo Elikai,
> In the name of the Source,
> And for his great strength and bravery,

The position of Master Timekeeper to the king
And Immortality as a sacred member of the Order of the Flame.
Let the Histories record all that has been done,
And all that has come to pass,
Forevermore,
In the Timekeeper's Tale.

Want to read more?
Turn the page for an exclusive first look at the next book in
The Chronicles of Caelium series!

THE SILVER STRAND

CHARLEMAYNE REEVES

THE TREATY OF HIRAETH
BY DECREE OF LORD DOLION

❀ *The selkie clan is hereby banished to the islands. Henceforth, the Selkie Isles shall be their residence.*

❀ *Merrows are forbidden to trespass on selkie lands without expressed permission from the councils and court rulers. Likewise, no selkie shall enter the Court of Merrows without the same expressed permission.*

❀ *It is hereby forbidden for a merrow man to look upon a selkie woman. He will avert his eyes in her presence, lest he risk his own skin.*

❀ *Courtship or intermarriage between clans is hereby forbidden, and likewise, no child borne of such a relationship may stand.*

These rules shall be enforced henceforth,
on penalty of death,
From this day,
Until the end.

CHAPTER 1

The strap of Elysia's shoe was hung in the lattice, again. She glared at it furiously, twisting it left and right. *Why* had she worn these shoes? The gold flats were her favorite, but she made a mental note to burn them as she turned her ankle a little further to the left. The strap slipped free, and she lifted her foot, grinning. But that was when she lost her grip.

Whoosh. She fell from the lattice of climbing vines beneath her high window and smacked the ground hard with her side. She bit her lip, stifling a groan. *Ouch.* She rolled to her belly, silently scanning the palace grounds. She had made a lot of noise with that fall, but luckily, no one was awake. It was just before sunrise, and the grounds were silent.

Quietly, she sat upright. She dusted her palms on her skirt, then held them out to examine them. They were scraped a bit where she had hit the dirt, but the wounds were shallow, and they would heal quickly. She stood slowly to her feet, assessing herself with each movement for further damage. Her side hurt a bit from catching her fall, but otherwise, she was fine.

She took one last look across the grounds, then crept down the left wall of the gardens towards the woods beyond. As she moved to the wall's far edge, she eyed the cluster of sandstone houses marking the edge of the village across the field to her right. The houses were mostly silent, but a candle was lit in the nearest window, and she tucked herself tightly against the wall as a woman passed the frame. She was carrying a large water pot on her hip, and Elysia waited until she stepped out her door and turned away to walk down the lane before she shot from her hiding place.

She only released her breath when she was safe in the cover of the trees. Quietly, she followed the small path she had worn in the soft dirt, and soon, she was deep in the forest. The calming sounds of rushing water tickled her ears and early sunlight streamed between the dense tree branches, creating dancing patterns on the water as Elysia guided her small raft from its hiding place in the river's reeds. Once more, she scanned the wood for watchmen, then she stepped onto her raft and pushed out with her oar. At once, the river swept her into its current, and Elysia crouched flat on her belly, her head safely hidden below the bank as she allowed the river to guide her swiftly around the bend and out of sight.

It wasn't long until she was tugging her raft to shore. She tossed her shoes onto the rocky beach and scaled barefoot up the highest hill, moving to her favorite perch on her secret island. But the spot didn't bring her peace like it normally did.

Elysia sat down heavily, bracing her back against a tree and staring bleakly out over the water. The morning breeze blew in softly from the sea, feathering lightly across her face and stirring the tall grasses and wildflowers on the hillside below. The shimmering rays of the early sun warmed her bare arms, and she watched as they glittered on the surface of the water, creating a kaleidoscope of dancing light. White-breasted gulls flew low above the surf, calling out to one another. She watched as one swooped into the waves, catching a small fish in its beak. Then, the bird took flight, hounded by the group for a bite of his breakfast. She smiled flatly at the display, then lay her head back against the tree and crossed her arms over her chest, grimacing.

It was a beautiful day, but Elysia's heart was anything but light. She hugged her knees to her chest, burying her face. Usually, secreting herself away to the island soothed her spirit, but today, there was nothing that could soothe her. Not one thing.

She sighed heavily, lifting her chin to rest on her knees. Ena would be frantic once she caught wind of her absence. Soon, she would be visiting Elysia's rooms, ready to start the day. Elysia knew she couldn't stay much longer. There was so much to do before tonight. It wouldn't be fair to keep Ena waiting. She turned to glance up at the sun, creeping higher above her with each moment. She had stayed too long, already. As much as she needed the solitude of her secret island, she would have to go, soon.

Elysia had discovered the secret island two cycles ago, and since, it had become her favorite escape. Elysia was adventurous by nature. She loved exploring, and sneaking out of the palace to do so was not a new habit for her. There wasn't a single stone she hadn't uncovered on the Selkie Isles, but the uninhabited island just south of her home had been her greatest discovery of all.

The first time she had gone there, she had thought she was lost forever. The path through the river was twisting and treacherous, and she had been convinced she could never find her way home. Since then, she had visited so many times that she was certain she could find her way to the secret island and back with her eyes closed.

Fifty weaving steps down her worn path in the wood, the wide river flowed to the right, weaving eighteen oar strokes through the forest floor before passing to a fork. The left arm of the fork continued through the forest, spilling into a clear, smooth loch in the glen beyond. To the right, the river flowed beneath a rocky outcropping, its path hidden by the overhang of twisted vines and low tree branches.

It was Elysia's grandmother, Ríona, who had initially led her to the secret island. Ríona was fond of tales of adventure and misfortune, and as a child, Elysia had often listened to these from her place on the threadbare rug beneath her grandmother's cushioned seat. She had listened in rapture as her grandmother told of a wide river behind the palace woods, whose mouth led to a hidden paradise. As with most of her tales, the story came with a warning. She had insisted that Elysia avoid the river, which she called the Brook, for fear that her granddaughter would drown.

Elysia had nodded obediently, but she had struggled to keep her seat, longing to rush from the small sandstone house and find the Brook for herself. It hadn't been easy, but she had forced herself to be still, picking the edge of the rug as she listened with awe. Her grandmother's brown eyes had danced as she told how the Brook passed through the low opening of rock, where it wound through the base of a high cavern. Once hidden in the rock, the wide river collected itself into a slender, winding stream. "The stream appears gentle—shallow, even," her grandmother warned. "But the water beneath churns and swirls in a deadly series of spins, and its depths are immeasurable."

In the Histories Ríona recounted, many selkies had attempted its passage, but most had drowned in the Brook's swirling depths. The Brook was particularly dangerous for land-dwelling sea folk, like Elysia's clan. At one time, the selkies had dwelled beneath the sea, but since the exile, they had been land-locked, and as a result, their sea lungs were shallow and weak. This made survival in the Brook's dark waters almost impossible.

Despite her grandmother's warnings, curiosity got the best of Elysia, and one day, she braved the passage of the Brook on her own. For weeks before, she had fashioned a raft she deemed worthy of the treacherous journey. Excitement swirled in her belly at the thought of passing the Brook, but an equal measure of fear swirled just as strong. She had almost abandoned the idea, but her adventurous nature urged her on.

That first time, she had squeezed her eyes shut and buried her face on the floor of her raft as she passed through the caverns. The dark air inside had pressed heavily against her as she floated onto the narrowing stream. As the rushing waters quieted, she had sat as still as a stone, allowing the churning current to swirl her raft unchecked. It had bounced her left and right, and once, she had thought she would topple overboard, but at last, she made it safely through the cavern to the other side. There, the bright sun shone once again, and the soft sea had carried her the short distance to the secret island's stony shore.

Since that first passage, she had braved the Brook regularly. Often, she visited her secret island several times a week. It had become her place of peace and solitude, a much-needed escape from the pressures of court.

Elysia frowned as she rested her small chin on top of her knees. It was no surprise she needed an escape today. Her mother's expectations, no, the expectations of *everyone*, weighed heavily on her mind. Tonight was the Midsummer Ball. It was usually a favorite of Elysia's, but the schedule of events for this evening were a little different. Tonight, was Elysia's Presentation to the Selkie Court, and with it, came the choice of her suitor. By the end of this evening, she would be betrothed. Elysia wrinkled her nose. Nothing could have displeased her more.

Her mother's words echoed in her mind: *You're overdue for Presentation, Elysia, by at least a full cycle. You simply must pick a suitor. I picked your father at 17 cycles, and every selkie ruler before you has done so on the proper schedule. The council and I have been patient, but now, we expect you to make your decision.* Elysia rolled her eyes. At 18 cycles, picking a suitor could not have been further from her wishes.

For the last two cycles, she had been forced to attend each and every court event and council meeting. All this, on top of her lessons, which taught her the Histories and the ins and outs of becoming the court's next ruler. Though she did her best to please her mother and pay attention to the meetings and her lessons, sitting in a stuffy throne room on the Selkie Isles for the rest of her life was the least of her desires. Especially if she was sitting next to a mate that she had been forced to choose.

Elysia narrowed her eyes, peering out over the water. *No.* That just wouldn't do. She would rather live alone forever on her secret island than endure that.

Silently, she watched the sea lapping against the stony shore. The sun danced across the cresting waves, and secretly, *so secretly,* she longed for adventure beneath its depths. She pressed her lips together, looking away. That would never happen. She was land locked. And soon, her fate would take an even worse turn.

Despite Elysia's best efforts to delay, her mother, Lady Malca, had *insisted* that her Presentation be tonight—at the Midsummer Ball. Traditionally, the Presentation of female selkie rulers and the accompanying selection of their mate occurred on the 17th cycle. By this standard, *and* her mother's, Elysia was already one cycle late. Even so, she didn't understand the rush. What did it matter? So what if it was tradition? Why did it have to happen now?

Elysia frowned. It was probably because the council, or *the Hounds*, as Elysia liked to call them, were biting at Lady Malca's heels for a chance to fling their sons at the next ruler of the selkie throne, thus ensuring their connection to the power the position afforded. And no councilman had been more insistent than Lord Ciar. He had thrust his son Connor before Lady Malca's eyes on more than one occasion, and he'd recounted the benefits his son could afford the court ad nauseum.

Ciar was the wealthy and powerful owner of several of the island's mines, and his son was thus considered the most eligible suitor in the Selkie Islands. Everyone said so, even Ena. Connor was attractive enough with his dark hair and flashing black eyes, but Elysia bristled at the thought of being close to him. She thought of Connor's smug face and cringed. He thought he was so charming, but he couldn't have been more wrong. Charming he was not. If anything, Elysia thought him extremely arrogant.

Unfortunately, Connor appeared to be the forerunner in the game to woo her with his so-called *charms*. After the councils' complaints at the last meeting that Elysia was overdue to pick her suitor, her mother, whom she was certain had been encouraged by Lord Ciar, had made it clear that Connor was to be her choice. Tonight, when the sun dropped below the horizon, she would endure her Presentation, and she would be *forced* to choose Connor as her mate.

Elysia felt like she could vomit every time she thought about it, but her mother and the council were thrilled with the match. They were making a huge fuss. In fact, despite the talk of the islands' lowering resources, this Midsummer Ball was supposed to be the most opulent they'd had in cycles.

Tonight, her life would begin. At least, that's what her mother said. Elysia squeezed her hands into fists. It was more like tonight; her life would be over.

Elysia sighed heavily. Connor certainly wouldn't have been her first choice. He wouldn't have even made the list. In fact, if it were left up to her, there wouldn't *be* a list, and she wouldn't be forced into any of this at all.

Anger singed the back of her neck, and she stood abruptly. She kicked a small stone, watching as it sailed down the hill and skipped through the waves in a satisfying line. At a far distance, it bounced twice, then sank beneath the surface.

She narrowed her eyes at the spot, then marched down the hill, bending to grab another stone from the shoreline. "Grrraahhhh!" she screamed, hurling it into the water. She glared after the stone, imagining it smashing Connor's perfect nose as it dropped into the surf.

Elysia ground her teeth into a grin.

That felt good.

She scrambled to grab two more small rocks and toss them into the dark waves, grinning. Then she scooped up a handful, and then another. Over and over, she sailed fistfuls of stones into the sea, until her face and dress were spattered with silt and a small patch of wet mud remained on the shore at her feet.

The sun was rising higher. It beamed against the back of her dress. Sweat beaded on her back and brow, and she paused, her chest heaving. She glared at the waves, then brought her trembling hands in front of her face, examining her nails. Dirt caked the ends of her fingers, and two nails were broken. She grinned down at them and bent to scrub them into the dirt. Then she wiped them flat against her face, smudging her cheeks. *Ha.* What would Connor think now of his betrothed?

Her joyous display of defiance only lasted for a moment, then Connor's superior expression crept back into her mind. She grimaced at his smug grin and kicked at the lapping waves, sending a spray of water into the air.

Throwing stones was not enough, even if she *had* smushed

Connor's nose in the process. She needed to let off more steam. Shielding her brow with her muddy hand, she peered up at the sun. It was late. Ena was probably already looking for her. She'd have to hurry.

She flicked her eyes to the sea, gazing at the inviting water. Her body was itching for a swim. Quickly, she flung her shoes into a heap and peeled off her stockings. Though she knew no one was there, she still gave the shoreline a furtive scan, then she unbuttoned her cream-colored blouse and dropped her emerald skirt and underthings to the stony shore.

As she dove beneath the waves, the familiar tingle blazed from her toes, and her body transformed. Elysia grinned as she glided through the surf, slicing the water easily with her silvery tail. She angled her arms into a point and pumped her lower body powerfully, diving deep below the surface.

She flipped to her back when she reached the sea floor, pausing to stare up towards the sun. The world looked very different from the bottom of the sea, and for a moment, the problems awaiting her above seemed far away. She wished she could stay, hiding beneath the water, but in a moment, she needed air, and she pushed hard for the surface.

A deep inhale slid into her lungs as she broke above the waves, and a loud *whoop* slid off her tongue as she curved her body into a high arc. For a moment, Elysia felt like she was flying, and she soared through the open air before slicing a perfect dive back into the water. She giggled with pure delight, then gasping, she lay flat on the surface, allowing the smooth waves to lap over her skin. A mixture of heady emotions swirled through her chest, and she closed her eyes, smiling. As always, being in her sea form made her feel free. Joy bubbled in her center, and excitement coursed through her at the possibilities of the strange world beneath the waves. It was one she had never known, but even so, it was one she wished to.

ABOUT THE AUTHOR

Charlemayne Reeves has been writing stories since she can remember. She comes from a family of storytellers, so it's kind of in her blood. Charlemayne is a Christian wife and mom, who enjoys telling epic tales of truth and light. She holds a master's degree from Belmont University and enjoyed a long career in healthcare prior to becoming a writer. Since, she has retreated to the hills of Tennessee with her husband, two children, and their beloved cat, Captain Meow. *The Timekeeper's Tale* is her first novel.

www.ingramcontent.com/pod-product-compliance
Lightning Source LLC
Chambersburg PA
CBHW030117310726
48970CB00004B/1295

www.ingramcontent.com/pod-product-compliance
Lightning Source LLC
Chambersburg PA
CBHW010759310726
48974CB00006B/906